Miles smiled softl[y] [____]
too weird? Like so[_____]
thought couldn't happen between us?
Maybe even *shouldn't* happen?"

Lark raised her hands in a gesture of confusion. "I don't know. Maybe a little too magical. I'm happy when I'm with you."

"Wonder why we so easily went our separate ways years ago?"

She jerked her head back in surprise.

"We were *kids*, Lark," he explained. "I'm not that guy anymore. And yes, my feelings for you have come as a shock. That's why I want more evenings like this."

She squared her shoulders and looked him in the eye. "You're right. When we met so many weeks ago, I never imagined we'd become close again. And about Perrie Lynn—"

"No matter what ultimately happens between us," he said, "from now on, we're united when it comes to our daughter."

Dear Reader,

Welcome to Two Moon Bay, Wisconsin, and thanks for choosing *Girl in the Spotlight*. I'm thrilled that it's my debut book for the Harlequin Heartwarming series.

Several years ago, I told a friend about an adoption story that had been nagging—haunting—me for years. Hardly surprised, my friend teased me with the question "Isn't adoption an important *theme* in your family's history?" Yes, that's true, and as a theme it goes back a couple of generations on both sides of my family. The first article I ever sold was about the joys of becoming a mother in two ways, first through pregnancy and then through adoption. As the years passed and my children grew up, I was privileged to cross paths with several women who wanted nothing more than to one day be reunited with the child who, for complex reasons, they'd placed for adoption.

I hope you enjoy the path Lark and Miles take to learn the identity of their child, and in the process also discover what drives this young girl's life. As someone who yearns for happy endings, it was deeply satisfying to listen to Lark and Miles "tell me" how they rediscovered each other.

Two Moon Bay is a fictional place, but bears close resemblance to many small towns not far from my current home, Green Bay, Wisconsin. I grew up in Chicago, so I completely understand the lure of Lake Michigan and I enjoy characters that fall under its spell.

To happy endings,

Virginia McCullough

HEARTWARMING

Girl in the Spotlight

—

Virginia McCullough

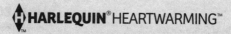

HARLEQUIN® HEARTWARMING™

Recycling programs
for this product may
not exist in your area.

ISBN-13: 978-0-373-36842-6

Girl in the Spotlight

Copyright © 2017 by Virginia McCullough

All rights reserved. Except for use in any review, the reproduction or
utilization of this work in whole or in part in any form by any electronic,
mechanical or other means, now known or hereinafter invented, including
xerography, photocopying and recording, or in any information storage
or retrieval system, is forbidden without the written permission of the
publisher, Harlequin Enterprises Limited, 225 Duncan Mill Road,
Don Mills, Ontario M3B 3K9, Canada.

This is a work of fiction. Names, characters, places and incidents are
either the product of the author's imagination or are used fictitiously,
and any resemblance to actual persons, living or dead, business
establishments, events or locales is entirely coincidental.

This edition published by arrangement with Harlequin Books S.A.

For questions and comments about the quality of this book,
please contact us at CustomerService@Harlequin.com.

® and TM are trademarks of Harlequin Enterprises Limited or its
corporate affiliates. Trademarks indicated with ® are registered in the
United States Patent and Trademark Office, the Canadian Intellectual
Property Office and in other countries.

Printed in U.S.A.

After a childhood spent on Chicago's sandy beaches, **Virginia McCullough** moved to a rocky island in Maine, where she began writing magazine articles. She soon turned to coauthoring and ghostwriting nonfiction books, and eventually began listening to the fictional characters whispering in her ear. Today, when not writing stories, Virginia likes to wander the world.

To contact the author, please visit www.virginiamccullough.com, or find her on Twitter, @vemccullough, and Facebook, www.Facebook.com/virginia.mccullough.7.

This book is for all whose lives have been touched by the heartaches and joys inherent in the adoption experience.

CHAPTER ONE

With his phone next to him on the couch and out of his little girl's sight, Miles Jenkins scrolled through the three new texts. The first was from the meeting planner organizing a management conference in Denver, where Miles was booked to present a seminar in late January. That fell into the category of important, but not urgent. Exactly like the second and third, both sent by a speakers bureau he regularly worked with. Nothing he needed to interrupt his Sunday afternoon to handle.

Brooke tugged on his sleeve. "Daddy, did you see that girl fall down? She won't get a medal now."

"Sure, honey, I saw it." Sort of. Out of the corner of his eye he'd caught a glimpse of the skater on the TV screen. "So, one spill on the ice means she won't get a medal?"

Brooke answered with a solemn nod.

"Well, that's not *always* true, but this time it knocked her right out of the competition."

Miles smiled to himself. From the moment they'd begun watching, his eight-year-old had taken on the role of a professional commentator. Without skipping a beat Brooke predicted who among this group of young women would emerge as medal winners and who'd likely go home empty-handed.

"You know so much about the sport you could be one of those experts on TV."

Brooke responded with an exaggerated roll of her brown eyes. When had she learned to do that?

"I mean it," he said, feigning a defensive tone. "You've taught me more about skating in the last couple of hours than I've learned in my entire life, all thirty-nine years of it." *Or ever cared to know, but that was beside the point.*

Andi had mentioned their daughter's interest in skating had quickly moved from casual to intense, leaving Brooke completely enamored with these real-life princesses performing impossible feats in their glittery costumes. Andi encouraged the interest, too. These self-disciplined girls trained every day and worked hard to compete, she pointed out. They weren't like the out-of-control young celebrities who ended up as headlines on too many glossy magazine covers for all the wrong reasons.

His former wife had also advised against making plans to see a movie with Brooke on Sunday afternoon. "It's the Grand Circuit final," she'd said. "The last event of this year's figure-skating competitive season. Brooke's been looking forward to it all week. It's a big deal, a step on the way to determining who gets on the International Figure Skating Championship team." She'd paused and then laughed. "Listen to me. You'd think I know what I'm talking about. But I don't need to explain the ins and outs. Our skating enthusiast will fill you in. Every last detail."

Andi was right. Brooke had talked about almost nothing else but her favorite figure skaters from the moment he'd picked her up on Saturday morning. It seemed that Mamie, his little girl's babysitter, had created a fan.

"You could take skating lessons yourself," he said. "Would you like that?"

Brooke shook her head. "I already told Mom I want to keep playing soccer. And basketball is fun, too."

"Okay, honey. You let us know if you change your mind."

Photographs on the wall on either side of the TV showed Brooke in her soccer uniform, her auburn hair in two pigtails. He agreed with Andi, who reminded him—often—about research showing that little girls who were involved in sports developed healthy self-esteem. They were less likely to fall in with a bad crowd and do all the risky things that left parents so terrified they could barely breathe.

"I will." Brooke scooped up a handful of popcorn from the bowl on the coffee table. Before putting it in her mouth, she added, "But don't forget about the horse, Daddy. I've already picked out her name."

"Magic," he said, nodding. "I remember."

"Won't be long now."

"I know, less than four years."

"Three years and five months…to be *exact*."

He suppressed a laugh, not wanting her to think he'd ever make light of her longing for a horse. Not long ago, Andi had brought up the horse once again, as if warning him to be prepared. Andi also believed girls who loved horses would be less likely to spend time with boys who'd divert them from their goals. When she'd put it like that, was she subtly reminding him that he'd been a boy— or rather, a young man—who'd once been responsible for interrupting a girl's goals?

As much as he agreed with his ex-wife on almost all their joint parenting issues, Miles thought she was overly concerned about Brooke being a child of divorce. Andi regularly mentioned the emotional risks of divorce and the frightening specter of teenage girls wandering aimlessly through adolescence.

Brooke bounced on the cushion next to him. "Only one more skater to go before Perrie Lynn, Daddy."

"Perrie who? One of your favorites?" He squeezed Brooke's hand to show he was only teasing. Whatever Andi feared might happen in the future, their little girl was 100 percent safe and happy in this moment.

"Her whole name is Perrie Lynn Olson."

He knew that, of course. Brooke had started his education about skating by extolling Perrie Lynn. Still, although he enjoyed these exchanges with his little girl, sometimes he found himself listening with only one ear and much of what she said didn't settle into his memory bank. "And what makes her a special skater?"

Brooke gestured toward the TV with both hands for emphasis. "She's sort of new. She got to go to the Grand Circuit final because she won two big competitions. Mamie said she surprised everyone in the skating world."

Miles grinned at the lingo she'd picked up from Mamie and the commentators. The next skater was a young Canadian woman named Misty, who made a quick trip around the rink in her blue sequined costume. Even her short blond hair sparkled.

No wonder little girls thought these athletes were spinning, jumping princesses. For the next four minutes, the commentators, Katie and Allen, former champions themselves, counted triple jumps and what looked like impossible spins, explaining each move. Allen groaned over two jumps that went awry and caused Misty to, as he put it, lose the landing. Down she went. Misty recovered, though, and flashed a big smile for the audience when she thrust one arm high in the air for her dramatic finish. The smile disappeared almost immediately, replaced with a glum expression as she skated off the ice and into the open arms of her coach.

Miles picked up the remote and muted the sound when the commercials started.

"She was okay," Brooke said, "but not as good as Perrie Lynn's going to be."

Miles hoped Perrie Lynn didn't take a spill and break the spell Brooke had created around the young skater.

The ads over, he got the sound back on in time to listen to Katie and the other commentators discuss Misty's scores, which they all agreed left plenty of room for Perrie Lynn to jump ahead.

"Pay attention, Daddy. Here she comes." Brooke clapped her hands in anticipation.

The dark-haired girl skated onto the ice to rising applause and encouraging cheers. She took her time taking a turn around the periphery of the rink.

"Every detail is attended to," Katie pointed out, "and wow, doesn't she look elegant in her deep red costume?"

"Such a big moment for her," Charlie, the network announcer, added. "It was unexpected, but so welcome."

Katie, Allen and Charlie kept up their patter about the recent changes in Perrie Lynn's life, and why she and her mother had moved from Minnesota to Michigan to train with a new coach.

Brooke lifted her shoulders in a happy shrug. "Look at how pretty she looks, Daddy. Her dress sparkles all over."

"It sure does." Even from the long camera angle, Miles could see the girl was lovely, with olive skin and black hair, much like his own, features he'd inherited from his Italian mother and grandmother.

Miles was impressed as the skater slowed down and glided on one skate to the center of the ice, then stopped abruptly. In one flowing move, she positioned her legs and arms, and finally lifted her chin to signal her readiness to begin. *The girl knows how to work a crowd.*

Bemused, Miles saw in the young skater the qualities of some of his best colleagues in the professional speaking business. They captured the audience before uttering the first word. Perrie Lynn would start her routine with the entire arena and TV audience already focused on her.

Miles glanced at Brooke, who was sitting cross-legged but had leaned forward, as she rested her arms on her knees, her gaze fixed on the screen. When Perrie Lynn began skating backward and picked up speed, Katie described the move and built anticipation for the first jump. The confident young skater's lift off the ice appeared effortless.

"Wow," Allen said, "she opened with a perfect triple flip."

"She got so high in the air, Daddy."

"She sure did," he said, patting Brooke's hand.

Another jump followed, and then another and another.

"A triple-triple combination, Daddy," Brooke said sagely. "Those are hard."

"I bet they are."

More jumps and spins, and a long, graceful glide across the ice followed. To Miles's unschooled eyes it was like watching ballet dancing.

"She has the whole package, all right, athleticism and artistry," Katie remarked. "And now she's finishing with her final set of spins. Fantastic!"

Brooke clapped her hands over her head. "Yay! I think she won a medal, Daddy. She was *that* good."

Miles hoped Brooke wouldn't be disappointed, although he'd heard one of the announcers predict at least a bronze and possibly a silver medal for the girl, who was so new on the international skating scene. In the grand scheme of expectations, a medal for Perrie Lynn would mean an upset and a huge surprise. Others had come to the competition with far more experience.

Perrie Lynn completed what looked like a spectacular spin and came to a sudden stop, then dramatically bent backward, and swept her arms to the side before slowly lowering them and clasping her hands behind her. She held the pose, looking like a statue. Extending her moment, and exploiting the mood, Miles thought. He stared at the screen as the camera zoomed in for a close-up shot of her face.

A brilliant, triumphant smile. His stomach rolled over. *A familiar prominent widow's peak. A heart-shaped face.*

"See, Daddy," Brooke said, bouncing on the couch, "people are clapping and clapping because her skating makes everyone feel happy."

Brooke was right. Perrie Lynn skated off the ice to thunderous applause and was immediately enveloped in her coach's arms. Suddenly, the image disappeared, replaced by a commercial for potato chips. His mouth dry, Miles ran his tongue over his lips and cleared his throat. "So, what happens now, honey?" he asked, his voice barely a croak.

"She has to wait for the scores." Brooke waved her crossed fingers high in the air. "But she was the next-to-the-last skater. Goody, goody, goody. I bet she gets a medal!"

"And I bet you're right." He curled his fingers into a tight fist, then used his knuckle to wipe away beads of sweat above his upper lip. His reaction was ridiculous. Olive skin, a widow's peak. Countless young women would fit that description.

Miles exhaled, forcing himself to focus on Brooke's happy chatter about Perrie Lynn and medals. The commercials over, the commentators picked up their conversation about the surprising turn in the competition.

"So much excitement for such a young woman," Charlie observed, "and on her birthday, no less. She turns eighteen today."

Adrenaline shot through him, putting every cell on alert. *Today.* The minute he'd opened his eyes that morning, he'd remembered this day. The December date sat more or less dormant in his mind the rest of the year, but memories came alive on what was usually a cold, often snowy day. He'd been glad this was his weekend with Brooke, relieved to have something to serve as the distraction he always needed when this day rolled around.

The camera focused on Perrie Lynn's parents seated in the audience. More energy zipped through his body and sent his heart thumping hard. Who were those fair-haired people? They didn't look much like Perrie Lynn.

He swallowed hard as he struggled to focus on Allen's comments about the significance of Perrie Lynn's coaching change. "She also chose a new choreographer," Allen said. "These shifts can make a big difference, but they meant Perrie Lynn and her mother had to leave her dad in Minnesota so she could train with her new coach in Michigan."

"But the decision appears to have paid off," Charlie added.

"Mamie said the coach is really famous," Brooke said.

Miles nodded. "So it seems."

"She's adopted," Brooke said. "Mamie told me."

"Who's adopted, honey?" His voice cracked. "Perrie Lynn?"

Brooke nodded. "Mamie said her parents

got her when she was really tiny. Maybe only a couple of days old."

He swiped his knuckle across his upper lip again. "Really?"

"And it's not like a secret or anything. Maybe 'cuz she doesn't look like her mom and dad."

"I see." He rubbed his chest, as if sending a signal to his heart to slow down.

The camera zoomed closer to Perrie Lynn sitting on the bench next to her coach. He couldn't take his eyes off her. The wide smile that took over her face, her olive skin and the large dark eyes. And the one-of-a-kind widow's peak. *Like Lark.* The birthday. Minnesota. It all added up.

Suddenly the audience roared as the scores came up. Perrie Lynn got to her feet and thrust her arms over her head to wave to the crowd. He heard the commentators talk about her "personal best," and "having a shot at the International Figure Skating Championship." One warned she had to do well at the upcoming North American Figure Skating Competition.

"Did they just say Perrie Lynn could go to the Internationals?" he asked Brooke.

"I guess so. Looks like she won the bronze.

That's a big deal, because no one expected it. Woo-hoo!" Brooke laughed. "Mamie is probably jumping up and down right now."

Wild speculation whirled through his head, spiraled down through his body and left him weak. *Calm down. It's a coincidence. Happenstance.*

Brooke sighed. "I can't wait for the NorAms."

"And when does that happen?" He forced the question through his nearly closed throat.

Brooke frowned. "I'm not sure."

"Want me to look it up?" Not waiting for an answer, he grabbed his phone.

Brooke leaned over his shoulder and watched him search for North American Figure Skating Competition.

"See, it came right up. It's in January. Let's see when the Internationals start."

"Mamie said February," Brooke said.

"Right you are." He focused on the screen, fighting the urge to search for Lark online. He'd wait until he was alone, but once he found her, he'd contact her immediately. She'd either take him seriously or brush off the whole thing. He wouldn't know until he tried. Or maybe this was crazy. These little details could add up to exactly zero.

With the skating program coming to a close, the network had reporters backstage for interviews. When the camera focused on Perrie Lynn, she waved with both hands, her face still showing the thrill of a winner. The curve of her mouth set in a smile sent a pleasant shiver through him. In that moment of happiness, she might have been Lark.

His phone chimed, alerting him to a new text. He glanced at the screen. "It's your mom. She just turned into the complex."

With Brooke following, he got up and crossed the room, then lifted her coat off the hook next to the front door. "Here, put your jacket on and go out to the car. I'll get the rest of your things."

He hurried to Brooke's room and stuffed her clothes into her pack. The hairbrush and pajamas stayed at his house. Only the clothes and her favorite doll-of-the-moment went back and forth, along with the library books he grabbed off the nightstand. With his arms full, he headed down the hall and out the front door to the driveway.

"Sorry," he said to Andi when she buzzed down the passenger window. "We got involved in figure skating." Brooke pulled her backpack through the open window and put it between her knees, then rested the pile of books in her lap.

"No problem," Andi said pleasantly. "We have plenty of time to get to the dinner."

"You give your parents my best."

When he had Brooke for a weekend, which wasn't as often as he'd like because of his work schedule, Miles usually kept her until Monday morning, when he dropped her off at school. But this was a special occasion, a retirement dinner for Andi's dad. Miles was okay with letting Brooke go back to her mother early because he harbored no negativity toward his former in-laws. They'd been nothing but kind, had welcomed him into the family and then expressed sadness when he left it four years later, shortly after Brooke's second birthday.

Six months after that, Andi had impulsively married some guy named Roger, a less than blissful union lasting only a few months. That fiasco caused Miles's stock to rise in his ex-in-laws' eyes. They gave him credit for staying close to Brooke, especially during what turned out to be Andi's tumultuous second divorce.

He squeezed Brooke's arm through the window before giving the roof of the car a quick pat. After Andi raised the window and pulled away, he watched until the car disappeared around the next corner onto the winding road that led out of the complex. When he turned to go back up the walk to his town house, he waved to Edie and Christopher, his elderly neighbors two units down. They were sitting by their patio doors, as they did most days, acting like unpaid security guards as they chronicled the comings and goings of the residents of Bay Trails, the multiunit condo development he'd moved into when he and Andi separated.

As for Edie and Christopher, he'd long harbored the feeling they didn't wholeheartedly approve of him, or maybe they found all single dads suspicious. On the other hand, they assured him they kept an eye on his unit during his frequent absences and were unfailingly pleasant to Brooke. That's all that mattered.

Back inside, he wandered into Brooke's room, straightening up the stuffed animals and making the bed, but all the while images of Perrie Lynn spinning like a magical top raced through his mind. He had a hunch, a strong one. But what to do? Squash it, forget it? Not a chance.

Lark McGee passed through his mind whenever he wondered about the baby— that's what he used to say, *the baby*. But as the years passed, he'd rephrased that. Whoever the baby had become, wherever she lived and whatever she was doing that very minute, she was *their girl, their child*. He always thought about Lark herself on their child's birthday. Today.

Unless she'd moved, Lark likely wasn't far away. He knew a few of the basics. He and Lark had both eventually come home from college and settled in northeast Wisconsin. They'd each married and started their own families. He didn't know the state of her marriage. Maybe she'd had better luck with love than he had. Miles knew she'd married because he'd run into her once about five years back, an awkward encounter consisting of three minutes of superficial small talk. She'd been coming out of a mall in Green Bay as he was heading into it. She'd introduced the boy with her as her son. Miles remembered little about him, other than noting he was older than his Brooke and had inherited Lark's light brown hair. Miles had greeted the boy, who returned a shy smile. He'd then explained he was on the hunt for a present for Brooke's third birthday.

Her eyes had darkened, but just for a second. "How nice," she said, pleasantly. "I'm happy for you."

Miles had almost blurted that he was divorced, but he'd stopped himself in time. Lark wouldn't have taken the slightest interest in his marriage, a sad tale of a mismatch that had revealed itself all too quickly and hadn't changed with Brooke's arrival.

He and Lark had limited their conversation to an exchange of basics, including the fact that she lived with her husband in Two Moon Bay, a lakeside town not too far from his town house in Green Bay. He in turn said he had a condo out near the airport and the botanical garden. When they'd run out of trivial details to exchange, their conversation had come to an excruciating halt. They'd both laughed nervously, wished each other well and gone on about their business.

Miles winced as he remembered that encounter. He wandered into the kitchen, where his laptop sat open on the table. He typed *Lark McGee* into the search box. It was the only name he had for her. If she'd changed it when she married, he'd have to find some other way to reach her.

He breathed deeply to calm the shaky waves of emotion that had been crashing over him from the instant he'd seen a close-up of Perrie Lynn. Her coloring and nearly black hair. *His* skin, *his* hair. Not particularly unique, he reminded himself. But the wide smile, the widow's peak? Lark's distinctive features.

Okay, he'd concede the chances were good the skater's physical resemblance and the fact of her adoption were coincidences. But on national TV he'd heard three commentators wish Perrie Lynn a happy birthday. *Her eighteenth birthday.*

For the first time in his memory, he was glad Brooke wasn't with him on Sunday night. He usually hated to see her leave even one minute early. He especially enjoyed a companionable ride to her school on Monday morning. That was true, even if Brooke's accusations that he wasn't paying attention to some of her meandering conversations were justified. He had to watch it. His little girl was getting old enough to notice that in these days of texting and emails, he was at least half-distracted more often than he cared to admit.

His search yielded pages of citations for Lark, including her website as the first item. She used her own name, professionally, anyway. He clicked on the link and a second later, there she was. He grinned at the small photo on her home page. He'd always thought of her as pretty in a distinctive way, defined by the prominent widow's peak at the top of a heart-shaped face. Her smile appealed, too, maybe because it looked like the prelude to a hearty laugh. Lark's hair hadn't changed and, of course, neither had her clear blue eyes.

Miles drew in a breath. Wow. If Perrie Lynn really was their daughter, the mix of their features had made her an unusual beauty, like Lark.

The website filled in a few impressive facts about what Lark had done with her life. Like him, she worked for herself. He hadn't known Lark for very long, but she'd talked of becoming a writer, and she'd accomplished that goal. She was a health and parenting journalist, and an impressive list of her latest published articles appeared on the right side of the screen.

The short bio told him she still lived in

Two Moon Bay. He knew that town, if only because it was usually noted as one of northeast Wisconsin's most charming among the collection of quaint small towns on Lake Michigan. It was about an hour away from where he lived on the far west side of Green Bay. But that was enough distance to explain why he and Lark hadn't crossed paths more than once in all these years. Since Brooke spent so much time with Andi's family at their cottage on a small lake up in northern Wisconsin, Miles rarely took his daughter to the Lake Michigan shore.

Miles clicked on the "About" page, quickly scanning the longer bio that reinforced his first impression that Lark had done herself proud. She'd even coauthored three books with doctors. He'd fulfilled his dream when he'd found his niche as a consultant and speaker specializing in collaboration and team building, and now he took satisfaction in knowing Lark had also made her dream come true. She deserved her success. He was certain of that.

He mulled over his options. He could forget the whole thing and simply write off the afternoon as a string of coincidences. He scoffed out loud. Out of the question. Not when he couldn't get his mind off the dazzling girl who had turned eighteen that very day. Was there any possibility Lark would have forgotten their daughter's birthday? Somehow, he didn't think so.

He scanned the bio again. It said nothing about a husband, but he'd need to tread carefully. She could be married and have chosen not to put that detail in her bio. He noted she'd written many articles about kids' health issues and tied them to parenting, so mentioning a son in her bio made sense.

Deciding to keep it simple, Miles used the email address on the website and typed in his cell number and a message: Need to talk, please call tonight.

CHAPTER TWO

LARK SIPPED HER decaf coffee, hoping the waiter would come by to top off her cup. Pretending to reach into her handbag that sat on the floor, she checked her wristwatch. Only 7:45 p.m. This dinner was crawling by. She'd give it another thirty minutes, and then she could politely make her exit.

Why had she said yes to this fix-up in the first place? To distract herself? She'd never forgotten the significance of the date, so what made her think this year would be different? But she'd behaved as if packing her schedule would allow the day to pass unnoticed. Lark had started the morning with brunch with half a dozen women friends from her book club, followed by Christmas shopping in a nearby town. That should have been sufficient to keep her distracted. Of course, it could have been fifty women wandering the streets of Paris and her mind still would have drifted into the past. But she'd known one thing for sure—this could well be the year she'd finally disclose what she'd kept hidden in her heart for so long.

Lark had always thought it curious that no one could look at her and detect the slightest clue about her secrets or regrets or her deepest hopes. In every external way she'd lived out the adoption cliché. She'd gone on with her life. But every year, as November faded into the flurry of December and the holidays, the memory of the tiny newborn baby she'd held in her arms, oh, so briefly, rippled beneath the rhythm of each day, strengthening and intensifying as the date came closer. The rest of the year, Lark managed to tuck that period of her life away. Instead of dominating her days, it was more like a low hum in the background, not intrusive or disruptive, but never completely vanishing, either.

"*Lark* is a big movie fan," Dawn said, casting a pointed look her way.

Hearing her name gave her a jolt and forced her to refocus. She shifted in her chair and said, "I sure am."

"But I bet you and Dawn only like chick flicks." Bruce, Lark's blind date, mocked a reproachful tone.

"I plead guilty." Lark grinned. "Bring on a screen filled with women talking about life."

The loudest groan came from Dawn's boyfriend, Chip, whose youthful looks matched his nickname. Real name, Henry. Lark found it odd, even a little off-putting, that he'd never outgrown being called Chip.

"I guess that means you'll pass on the latest zombie takeover movie," Bruce teased.

"We'll both take a pass, thank you," Dawn said, rolling her eyes.

Lark could find nothing wrong with Bruce, an affable fortyish bachelor looking to settle down. At long last, Dawn claimed. Too bad he wasn't romantically appealing—to Lark, anyway.

Guilt alone forced her back into the conversation. Filled with optimism about introducing Lark to Bruce, Dawn had done everything a best friend could to make this evening a success.

Lark sent Dawn a reassuring smile. It wasn't her friend's fault that on this particular evening she couldn't quiet her inner turmoil and be 100 percent present at the table. She vowed to be pleasant, even enthusiastic, until she could duck out. Thankfully, she had her own car, so there'd be no awkward moments at the door to contend with.

"How long have you two been friends?" Bruce asked, pointing back and forth between Dawn and Lark.

"Not all that long, really," Dawn responded. "Three years or so. We bonded over the snack committee for our sons' basketball team."

"Dawn and I noted that it was left to the mothers to figure out the snacks on game days." Lark knew she sounded resentful, but so what? Way too many of these school sports rituals fell to the moms to handle, as if the dads couldn't manage to pick up boxes of granola bars on their way to the games.

Dawn playfully bumped her shoulder against Chip's. "We actually solidified our friendship over the plan we hatched to get the kids' dads more involved."

"Did it work?" Bruce asked.

"Not really," Lark said, chuckling, "but we planted a seed, or so we like to think."

This small talk was getting old. As close as Lark was to Dawn, she'd never for one minute considered confiding details about certain parts of her past. Lark could talk freely and without embarrassment about her ill-fated marriage and, paradoxically, her confidence-building divorce. She had no trouble bragging about her son, or grousing about her sometimes troublesome parents, but she'd become completely resigned to silence about one of the most significant—and wrenching—events of her life.

Lark was content to listen as Dawn switched topics. "Lark and I have our best times during our weekly coffee dates, where we brainstorm about our businesses. We've both worked for ourselves for years, but it can be isolating, too, especially for Lark. She spends so much time hunched over her laptop."

"Ah, yes," Lark said, putting the back of her hand on her forehead, "the loneliness of the writer in her garret. Seriously, though, I do have my nose buried in research much of the time. My regular trips to the Bean Grinder with Dawn provide the best breaks."

"It sounds interesting, what you do," Chip said. "Were you a science major in school?"

"No. Typical English major, specifically creative writing and literature. Not the most practical degree, but rewarding in other ways."

"Seems so," Bruce said, smiling in a genuinely admiring way.

By the time they'd finished their coffee, Lark's spirits had lifted. They'd passed a pleasant hour chatting about Dawn's latest PR client, a new fitness center and Lark's recent series of articles about learning disabilities for a parenting magazine. Chip and Bruce contributed stories about office politics in the accounting department of the energy consortium they worked for.

The stilted conversation that defined the atmosphere over dinner had subtly given way to an amicable camaraderie as they topped off the evening with blueberry pie and coffee. By the time they said good-night in front of the restaurant, Lark was sincere in telling Bruce she'd enjoy seeing him again. Perhaps for dinner one night soon.

And for almost one whole hour, she'd pushed the memories into the storage box in her mind. She arrived home and let herself into her house, grateful that Evan was with his dad for the weekend. After shedding her coat and boots, she filled the kettle to make herb tea. Then she sat at her table to check her phone, starting with the texts. Nothing urgent. Mom seeing if they could meet for lunch at the Half Moon Café soon, maybe on her day off from the gift shop in town, where she'd recently been promoted to assistant manager. Lark mentally pictured her day planner. She could probably manage time for lunch with her mother. She hadn't seen her in quite a while.

A text from Dawn. A thumbs-up on their dinner with Chip and Bruce. Lark grinned. It had taken her friend less than half an hour to send a message about their double date.

She thumbed quickly through unimportant emails, mostly from journals and health newsletters. The kettle began its boiling-point hum at the instant the familiar name popped up on her screen. She quickly turned off the burner to stop the rising volume. A strong buzz traveled through her chest and down her arms to the tips of her fingers. *Miles Jenkins.* Not letting go of her phone, she used her other hand to go through the motion of pouring water over a bag of ginger tea. She let it sit on the counter to steep and went back to the table and stared at her phone.

Miles had never tried to contact her before. Why now? On this day. Could it be he wanted to talk to her for no other reason than to acknowledge this landmark eighteenth birthday? This was the day their daughter would leave childhood behind. Legally, anyway.

Years ago, Lark had been clear about not wanting to be in touch with Miles. But that was way in the past. Now he'd left his phone number. Same area code as hers, so he wasn't far away, and he wanted to talk that very night.

Jittery nerves expanded inside her. Before she could take the next deep breath she sat at the table and held her head in her hands, conscious of the rapid beating of her heart as panic moved up from her solar plexus and filled her chest. This birthday meant so much to her, but Miles hadn't figured into her thoughts. Not at all. He'd played no part in the hopes she harbored over what could—would—happen in the years to come, now that their little girl had turned eighteen. She'd seen Miles only once since their final meeting after giving up their baby, and their stilted conversation was painful to recall.

Odd, though, as much as she'd tried to suppress them, her memories of Miles weren't all bad. When her thoughts drifted back to that cold December day in a hospital in Minnesota, Miles's soft dark eyes appeared in her mind. In reality, he'd been her only comfort. But she'd been so wrapped up in herself, she hadn't given much thought to his emotions. Whatever he'd been feeling he kept to himself and, instead, concentrated on her.

She and Miles had shared an important— and irreversible—decision. They'd given up their baby. Since neither had told anyone about her pregnancy, they'd acted entirely in secret. She didn't know whom he'd confided in over the subsequent years, but she'd never spoken one word about the infant who'd come into the world already sporting thick dark hair and perfect hands. She'd counted the fingers and toes, a distraction, she later realized, from the moment she'd allowed the nurse to carry her baby away.

Her arms empty, Lark had gone limp, dead weight falling back against Miles. He'd half carried her to a chair, holding her until she'd pulled away.

His support in the moment aside, Lark also cynically assumed what Miles felt was relief—deep, profound relief. He'd been free and unencumbered as he headed back to Stevens Point to finish his senior year at the University of Wisconsin. Determined to keep her secret from the start, Lark had already transferred to a small private college in Minnesota early that fall. She'd known no one when she arrived and deliberately had made few connections.

She'd never blamed Miles for what happened, not for a minute. He had offered to help her with the baby if she decided to keep her. Sure, he'd said the right words, but Lark knew that's all they were. No emotion, no conviction, propped them up and gave them a spine. He'd made gestures, but hadn't tried to persuade her to make a different choice.

"Why don't you go home, Lark?" he'd asked many times, genuinely confused about her refusal to confide in her mother.

"Impossible," she'd insisted. "My parents will be fighting each other in court for months to come." On the day she was with Miles in that hospital room in Minnesota, her parents were in Wisconsin locked in a struggle over custody of her younger brother, who was constantly acting out. Her dad had wanted to ship off Dennis to military school, but her mother refused, so the fight went on and on. Simply making it through Christmas at home would be a miracle.

She and Miles had covered that ground before. Lark preferred to keep this chapter of her life completely private, even from her mother. She *would* put it behind her.

When the hospital released Lark, she and Miles had gone to the shoe box of a studio apartment she'd rented near the campus. She'd spent the previous months studying, working in the library and pretty much keeping to herself as she slogged through the days.

Still weak, she'd settled into bed and watched Miles heat tomato soup on her two-burner stove and crush crackers on top.

"This is the champion of comfort food," she'd said, feeling her mouth turning up in a smile for the first time since they'd left the hospital.

"Yeah, it is," he agreed. But he hadn't met her eyes and his mouth was set in a grim slash.

"You should go back to school right away," she said. "I've got to study for my last two finals, anyway."

He shook his head. "I can't believe you're really going to take finals."

"You are, aren't you?" she shot back, her voice sharp.

"I didn't just go through what you… I didn't have a baby. And I'm not driving back to Stevens Point today, or tomorrow. I'm staying here." He pointed with his chin to the tiny stove. "I'm going to keep heating up soup and when you're ready I'll go out for pizza or Chinese food."

"You're welcome to stay as long as you don't nag me about resting." She felt surprisingly okay, physically, anyway. She'd been terrified of childbirth, but bringing their baby into the world hadn't been all that grueling. Lark had prepared herself to face much worse. Even one of the nurses said she'd sailed through it. If she had anything to be grateful for, and at that time it was difficult to count her blessings, she'd been thankful for her strong body.

Over the next day and a half, Miles had kept his word and had seen to it that she ate regularly. He'd made a couple of trips down the street to the Hot Wok, the second time bringing enough egg-drop soup, vegetable shrimp and chicken-fried rice to last through her finals.

Most of the time they avoided talking about what they'd done. When he tried to express regret, she waved him off. They'd been careful, responsible. But they'd realized too late that nothing was completely safe.

"I'm sorry," she'd finally said, hoping to end the conversation once and for all, "because we never should have let things go that far between us. It's not like we were in love or anything." She'd exhaled with a soft groan. "It was all supposed to be casual... you know, fun and games."

Now, so many years later, Lark ran that conversation through her head. It had ended when she'd convinced him to head back to his apartment in Stevens Point. Then she'd carried out her plans to the letter. She took her finals and passed her classes, and dutifully went home for Christmas, where no one had any inkling that she'd had a baby a couple of weeks earlier. On New Year's Day, she'd boarded a plane in Green Bay for the first leg of her trip to Dublin, where she'd spent her next semester.

Sitting at her kitchen table on a cold, clear night eighteen years later, she concluded that Miles must be going through some kind of flashback and for some reason wanted to acknowledge the years that had passed. But she wasn't ready to talk to him. Monday was soon enough to return the call. She rubbed her forehead. She was accustomed to these solo trips into the past and unsure if she could handle a companion walking the same path.

She turned off her kitchen light and carried her mug of tea into the living room, where she stared out the window at the expanse of Lake Michigan visible from her picture window. The sliver of a moon vaguely illuminated the whitecaps dancing erratically across the water's surface in the strong wind. The scene mirrored her unsettled mood. She couldn't shake off Miles's call. Maybe something important had happened. What if he had information about their child? Or, what if he wanted to find their daughter? She let her mind drift to another place. Impossible as it seemed, could their daughter have found him?

She'd never sleep until she talked to him. She went back to the kitchen to retrieve her phone.

HE WAS GETTING way ahead of himself. Like an observer of his own thoughts, Miles had watched his mind take so many twists and turns he hardly knew how to go back to the starting point. He stared at his phone, desperate to hear it ring. All evening the house had seemed painfully empty. Pushing away from the table—with his phone in his pocket—he wandered to the doorway of Brooke's room and studied the shelves overflowing with stuffed animals. She had yet to outgrow the desire for them—a dopey-looking whale, a couple of grinning giraffes, a kangaroo with a baby in her pouch and a white horse with a red-and-white-striped ribbon braided in her tail. His little girl had named the horse Magic, the same name Brooke reserved for the real one she longed for.

Brooke's collection of knickknacks, mostly ceramic and wooden horses, lived in her room at her mother's house, which she called home. She talked about going to Daddy's house, as if visiting, but then said she was going home when it was time to leave. That stung a little. But he consoled himself with the knowledge of how lucky he was to be deeply involved in Brooke's life.

What was Perrie Lynn's room filled with? Medals? Were those sparkly skating costumes hanging in her closet? What had she been like ten years ago when she was Brooke's age?

Slow down. You can't be sure Perrie Lynn is that baby, your little girl. Young woman, really. Odd that the possibility the young skater *wasn't* his child sat heavy with him now. Before he'd seen Perrie Lynn earlier that afternoon, thoughts of the child he'd given up had receded more and more over the years as being a good dad to Brooke became priority number one. It was as if he'd put the past behind him once and for all. Now, another voice in his head nagged that he'd betrayed this first child, a stranger.

His phone chimed. Finally. The screen ID confirmed it was Lark.

"Hello," he said, "thanks for getting back to me."

"What is it, Miles? Is something wrong?"

Detecting an edge of apprehension in her voice, he said, "Oh, Lark, it's nothing bad. No need to worry." He put his hand on his chest, hoping to slow the pounding of his heart. "It's just that I believe it's possible, not a certainty, but *possible*, our—our child, our daughter…is a figure skater. Sort of a rising star."

A sharp intake of air. Then silence.

"Lark?"

"I'm—I'm here, Miles." A loud exhale followed. "I don't know what to say—or what to ask first."

As he walked away from Brooke's room

and back to the living room, he heard her gulp, or choke, he wasn't sure which.

"Are you okay? I can tell you—"

"Yes, yes, tell me how—" her voice quavered "—how this came about. Your speculation."

He cleared his throat. "Again, nothing is certain. But something happened earlier today. Brooke, my eight-year-old, is a skating fan."

From there, the words flowed more easily. He described the afternoon and the shock he'd experienced when he saw the skater up close and was struck by the shape of her face. "She has dark hair and skin like mine, common enough, but her smile, and especially the shape of her face, are all you. Or *could* be."

"But that's probably coincidence, isn't it?" she asked, sighing. "I mean, more likely than not, it's a chance resemblance. Right?"

"Of course." He deliberately lowered his voice to mask the jumble of emotions swirling in his gut. "But I'm not done." He paused, almost afraid to say the words. "Today's her birthday."

"Today? That skater turned *eighteen* today?"

From the strength of her voice alone,

Miles knew he'd planted the conversation on firmer ground. "That's what the announcers discussed—this competition was a big deal so they went on at length about what a great present the medal was on such an important birthday."

"Wow. I don't follow skating," Lark said, rushing the words. "You know, except when the Internationals are on TV. Then I tune in like everyone else. I would have missed this entirely."

He was almost afraid to go on, but it was the detail that made the others fit like puzzle pieces. "There's more. One other thing—something big."

"What?"

"Perrie Lynn is adopted."

He waited out the seconds of silence.

"How do you know that?" she whispered.

"The announcers said so, Lark."

"They discussed something so private? On TV?"

Miles chuckled. "Well, according to Brooke, this is not a secret. You see, her parents, the Olsons, are classic blond, blue-eyed Scandinavians. Apparently, she's always known she was adopted." He paused, calling up his grandmother's face. "I can't even describe how much she resembles the early photos of my mother, but especially my grandmother."

"Oh, Miles, it's still so hard to believe. I'm afraid to hope it's true."

He heard the longing in her soft voice. An eighteen-year-old memory of her fighting off tears—and failing—slipped into his mind. "I know. But to tell you the truth, Lark, it really was the widow's peak and her pretty smile that made me think of you."

Silence.

"But it still might not be true."

Her skepticism sounded forced. "You sound like me. Like you're putting the brakes on your thoughts. You don't want to let hope run away with you."

"Yes," she said, "not that I know what to do with the information. I mean, I've been thinking about her all day, and I filled up time with Christmas shopping. Just now I was out on a…well, out for dinner with friends, but for a couple of hours before I left the house I picked up the phone half a dozen times wanting to beg off, make some excuse not to leave the house."

"I understand. It was on my mind, too. I was listening to Brooke talk with half my attention. Until the camera zoomed in on Perrie Lynn's face and the commentators bantered about all these details of her life."

"It seems so unlikely."

He held back, not wanting to reveal exactly how convinced he was that Perrie Lynn was their child. He also suspected this birthday was more complicated for Lark than it was for him. "All that aside, I want to find out for sure, even though I don't have a plan in place. Obviously, we'll act in a way that won't intrude on this girl's life. If it's all a big coincidence, then that will be that."

"Yes. I understand."

"Can you meet me for breakfast, maybe tomorrow morning?" he asked. "I leave for Richmond on a late afternoon flight, but I'd like to see you first. We should talk about what to do next."

"Yes, talk. We need to…take the next step, whatever…" She let out a frustrated groan. "Listen to me. I'm a writer, but I can't string words together in a complete sentence. Tomorrow morning? Let me check."

The line went quiet. The seconds ticked by.

"Yes, yes, that's good. I was double-checking my calendar. I have a phone interview scheduled in the afternoon. I write articles about health. I'm talking to a doctor about a new drug for..." She sighed. "Now I'm babbling. None of that matters. Tomorrow morning is fine."

What a relief. He hadn't wanted to leave town without seeing her face-to-face. He suggested meeting at eight o'clock at Hugo's, a café just east of Green Bay, not too far for either of them.

"Hugo's it is," she said.

Silence.

He cleared his throat. "Well, then, I'll see you tomorrow."

"Wait! One more thing, Miles."

"What is it?"

"You have a strong hunch about this, don't you?"

The unexpected question threw him, but not for long. "Yes, I do."

"Me, too." She ended the call.

He stared at the phone, amused by the abrupt end to their conversation. At least it saved them from an awkward goodbye. He closed his eyes and rested his forehead on his folded arms. The oak table felt cold under his hands, but he welcomed it. He needed to cool the heat of the moment. *Lark had your child.*

Yet a simple matter of setting up a meeting was stiff and strange.

Would it have been easier to talk with her if they'd been in love back then, or at least infatuated? Maybe they were awkward with each other because they'd shared so little. Back in college, they'd spent a few carefree nights listening to bands at a local pub. Their handful of dates had been more like hanging out. They'd spent a couple of chilly spring Sundays in his room in an apartment he shared with a couple of guys. Studying. Obviously doing more than that.

With all he'd said, he'd failed to mention another clue. Perrie Lynn had grown up in Minnesota. Where he and Lark had given up their baby. And, at the time, without even one other person in their lives aware of what they'd done.

So awkward. She hadn't helped by more or less hanging up on him to end the call. But what was the protocol in situations like this? The etiquette? Silly question. She snickered to herself. Had she really used the words *protocol* and *etiquette*, as if this was a case of choosing the correct way to interact with Miles? The facts spoke for themselves. When they'd left the hospital, Miles had driven her back to her studio apartment in St. Paul and looked after her for a couple of days. Since then she'd seen him exactly twice, the first time two weeks after they'd given up their baby.

Miles had come home for the holiday break, too, and asked her to have dinner with him. She'd agreed to meet him at a local pub. He was just checking in, he'd said, concerned by the way he'd left her in her apartment after they'd turned over their baby girl.

She remembered their evening well, but not happily. They'd struggled to make conversation. She'd held back her tears, tried to be strong, but failed. As much as he'd shown concern for her, his relief bled through. He was free and clear. When they'd left the pub and walked to their cars, she'd told him her plan was to try her best to put what happened between them behind her. First, she didn't want him worrying about her, but second, she didn't want him to contact her ever again. Miles had started to respond, but apparently had nothing meaningful to say. He'd nodded tersely and they parted ways.

Sitting at her desk, Lark took a deep breath, hoping to chase away gathering hope mixed with fear. Yet she wanted—needed—to savor this moment, just in case it all turned out to be true. She opened her laptop and within seconds was staring at an image of Perrie Lynn Olson in a red sequined skating costume. She was exactly as Miles had described, right down to the same pronounced widow's peak Lark saw in the mirror every day. The girl's warm skin tone and her rich brown eyes reminded her of Miles—the Miles of years ago when he was twenty and she was nineteen. Not much older than their daughter was now.

Their daughter? "Get hold of yourself," she said aloud. These similarities didn't prove anything. She read on, following the highlights of Perrie Lynn's skating life, including a newly added banner announcing the medal she'd just won. As a skater she was fresh and new, having spent the previous year on the senior circuit before bursting out of the pack during this, her second season, and surprising skating experts and fans alike.

"You look happy," she whispered as she lightly brushed her fingertips across Perrie Lynn's image on the screen. "That's all I ever wanted." It was the hope that overrode all the heartbreak in the walled-off part of Lark that remained isolated from the outside world. She'd longed—sometimes desperately—for her little girl to grow up loved and happy.

One photo on a website confirmed nothing. Still, Lark couldn't help but think this beautiful young woman would go to sleep that night basking in her big win and happy with her life. "I hope it's true," Lark said, "and that one day soon you'll tell me yourself."

Reluctantly, she shut down the computer and left her desk to get ready for bed.

CHAPTER THREE

MILES ARRIVED FIRST, and after scanning the customers in the café, he waited for Lark inside near the front window. He studied the faces of women coming in to order to-go coffee or claim a table. He couldn't be positive he'd immediately recognize her, even though he'd seen her pretty face on her website photo. And most coffee seekers entering Hugo's were camouflaged in heavy coats and thick scarves, their hats pulled down over their ears as protection against the frigid December air.

He'd suggested Hugo's because he'd been there before, the last time on a forgettable late-afternoon coffee date with a woman he'd met on a flight from Detroit to Green Bay. Pleasant enough conversation, but as so often happened in the past few years, nothing about the date compelled him to follow up. She hadn't shown any enthusiasm for a second meeting, either. No matter. He'd lost nothing but a couple of hours.

Through the front window he spotted Lark walking toward the entrance. His whole body warmed at the sight of her. She appeared so young in a bright red jacket, jeans and knee-high black boots. A large leather bag hung from one shoulder. She gingerly stepped around patches of ice on the sidewalk, but then glanced up and caught him watching her. Her mouth turned up in a shy smile.

He walked closer to the door to greet her, wanting to lean over and kiss her cheek, maybe give her a quick hug. But she'd turned her face away to check out the café.

"How about that table in the corner?" She spoke in a businesslike tone, pointing to a small table for two.

"Fine," he said, following her quick steps. Still not looking at him, she shrugged out of her jacket and draped it over the back of her chair before she sat down. Then she pulled out a menu card from behind the napkin holder.

He also shed his coat and sat across from her. "Lark?"

She lifted her head, her expression quiz-zical.

"Hello."

She snorted a laugh. "Don't mind me, Miles. I'm nervous as can be."

"Believe me, I understand." He paused, but decided to acknowledge what they both knew to be true. "This is awkward."

"No kidding." She lifted her eyes to the ceiling and gave her head a quick shake. "But not as awful as bumping into you at the mall a few years ago."

Oh, boy, she didn't mince words. Neither would he. "True. That was *excruciating*."

She swiped her hand across her forehead. "Whew. We got that out of the way." She went back to studying the menu. "Let's order right away. I'm starving. I usually eat much earlier than this."

Right on cue, the waitress stopped at their table and took their identical orders of coffee and omelet platters with the cranberry-walnut muffin of the day. As if the intervening years had been wiped away, he recalled her big appetite, even the image of her shaking peanuts from a can into her palm. She'd snacked nonstop while they sat on his bed with open textbooks in front of them and unapologetically polished off huge plates of burgers and fries at the pub where they'd hung out.

"You're grinning," she said. "Are you shocked at my hearty breakfast order?"

"Not exactly," he said with a snicker. "I was remembering how you ate me out of house and home."

"And I haven't slowed down a bit." She peered into his face, as if really seeing him for the first time. "You haven't changed at all."

"Neither have you," he said. "Not on the outside, anyway."

"Yes, the inside is another thing." She leaned across the table, folding her hands in front of her. "Tell me about your daughter— and your wife, assuming you're married."

Since they hadn't exchanged many details on the phone, he filled in the facts of his brief marriage to Andi. "Brooke is the light of my life, though, and her mother and I have managed to raise her together without too much conflict."

"I'm divorced, too." She spoke matter-of-factly. "And my son is by far the best thing to come from my misbegotten marriage. Evan is almost thirteen now, and pretty close to his dad, which is good."

Miles nodded, happy to have this exchange out of the way. For reasons he didn't understand, he was relieved that no husband was in the picture. Maybe because a spouse was more likely to interfere with plans Miles wanted to share only with Lark.

They were quiet when the waitress brought a carafe of coffee to the table and filled their white diner-style mugs. He watched Lark add cream from the pitcher drop by drop, until the color suited her. He remembered she was precise about her coffee.

"It's odd how I recall little things about you," he said, nodding at the cup in front of her.

"Is that so?"

"The way you drip cream into your coffee, for one thing."

"My coffee habits and my huge appetite. That seems especially odd because we never knew each other well."

"I know," he said, suddenly filled with regret, "and I'm sorry."

She frowned. "For what?"

He responded with a one-shoulder shrug. "I'm not sure. Maybe I'm sorry we weren't closer, or I regret that you went through so much." He hesitated to find the right words. "I didn't do as much as I could've."

She averted her eyes and took a few sips of her coffee. His words seemed hollow, even to him. He could only imagine how ridiculous they must have sounded to her ears.

"I shouldn't have jumped into the past like that," he said. "Not when there's something so immediate to talk about."

"It's natural, I suppose. I shuffled through some memories myself last night." She smiled. "I'll admit to spending a restless night. I guess I managed a couple of hours sleep. Evan was at his father's house all weekend, so I was alone. He'll come home after school today."

Home was Lark's house, just like Andi's house was Brooke's real home. He wondered if Lark's ex was as resigned to that as he was.

After their omelets and muffins arrived, Lark squared her shoulders. "I'm calling this meeting to order."

"No more small talk, huh?"

"Another time. I'd really like to find out more about your life, but my stomach is flip-flopping—and growling." She tensed her shoulders and then released them. "I'm nervous. I'll be okay when we get on with whatever we need to do." She turned her head and glanced at the table for four behind her.

"Are you checking the place for someone you know?" he asked.

"Am I that obvious? But I've been silent for eighteen years and will stay that way, at least for now."

"No explanation needed." Lowering his voice, he asked, "I assume you went to Perrie Lynn's website?"

She nodded vigorously. "I saw exactly what you were talking about." She stared out into the crowded café. "She's simply breathtaking. There's no other word for her. And she definitely reminded me of you, and not just the hair and skin. There was something else. An expression, maybe an attitude. Even in the photo she exuded an air of confidence."

He chose not to probe further into what she'd just said. Yes, he'd been a fairly confident twenty-year-old back when he and Lark were seeing each other. He was considered a good-looking guy, and he'd made his way through college without a lot of drama, at least until what happened with Lark. Up to that point he'd been carefree, with his eyes on the future, specifically his career plans.

"I think we could make a good case for exploring this further based solely on her resemblance to us," Miles offered, "but the other details line up perfectly, almost too perfectly. If there is such a thing."

"It's premature to start thinking of this precious girl as our daughter, Miles, but we have a place to start. From the beginning, I've always known I'd do what I could to prepare for her eighteenth birthday, a landmark year in adoption terms. So I'm ready."

"What do you mean by 'prepare'?"

She frowned. "I've registered with the adoption agency and it's cross-referenced on a state list. If our child decides she wants to look for me now that she's old enough to make her own decisions, I made sure I could be found."

That felt like a blow. Irrationally, he was hurt. "You mean, you've already begun a process to find her."

"Well, yes, in a way. But it's not a matter of me finding her," she explained. "As I said, if she looks, she'll be able to find me—easily."

Still nursing an open wound, he asked, "Would you have told me if she'd found you?"

"Of course, if that's what she wanted." She dropped her fork, letting it clatter on the plate. "I can see from your pained expression that I've upset you. But I think you're getting the wrong impression."

"Then fill me in." His voice had turned cold, but he couldn't help it.

"Statistically, adopted kids tend to think of searching for their birth mothers first."

Good point. "I suppose that's true."

"It makes sense when you think about it." She spoke in a low voice. "Adopted kids, girls and boys, tend to think about the woman who actually gave birth to them more than they think about their father."

She leaned forward, her tone earnest. "Many people search, especially as young adults, because if they don't, they always wonder. The first step was providing my information to the adoption agency, and with their cooperation, to the state office that responds to inquiries. But I'd *never* have disrupted this young woman's life by popping up unannounced."

She picked up her fork and jabbed the air for emphasis. "I've always hoped she'd look for me. For all we know, now that she's turned eighteen…"

She didn't need to finish the sentence, and he nodded to acknowledge he understood. The image of the graceful skater, so triumphant in her medal win, flashed in his mind. He couldn't see that focused girl taking a detour to search for biological parents, not while she stood in the very spotlight her adoptive parents undoubtedly had worked hard to help her reach.

"We can't assume she'd search right now," Miles said, giving voice to his doubts. "From what I understand, which is based on what the TV commentators said, she trains every day to prepare for the next event." He paused. "I won't do anything on my own, by the way. Whatever we do to locate our child, I want us to do it together."

She raised her eyebrows. "In contrast to what I've already done, you mean?"

"I don't want to be petty about it, but it's just that I thought of you first when this possibility became clear. I wouldn't have checked it out without talking to you."

"I see."

"And it's apparent you would have plunged in alone."

"Yes, to be honest, I would—I did." She

bit the corner of her lower lip. "But, Miles, I haven't ever told *anyone* about our daughter."

"I'm not anyone. I always thought that having the baby was something we went through together. If you were talking to that agency we worked with, you should have called me to see if I wanted to be included."

Her eyes opened wide in surprise. It was clear she didn't share his stance on that. She pushed a slice of bacon to the side of her plate and focused on buttering a chunk of the muffin.

"Your silence speaks volumes, Lark." He'd never expected this wave of reproach, even anger, that was coming over him now.

Raising her head, she stared boldly into his eyes. "Okay, to be perfectly honest, until now I've felt entirely alone with my secret. But starting today, we're together in this."

He forced a smile. "Okay. I guess that will have to be good enough."

"Oh, tell the truth, Miles," she said, her voice low but impatient. "How much did you think about me over the years? Did you ever wonder if I thought about the baby we gave up? You know, like *every day of my life*."

Uncertain where to begin, he said nothing.

But she wadded up her napkin and tossed it on her plate.

"Are you finished picking at that mountain of food?" he asked.

She nodded.

"Then let's take a walk." He signaled the waitress and took cash from his wallet to pay the bill. The chair legs scraped on the wooden floor when Lark stood. With her face pinched in emotional pain, she struggled to pull on her jacket. He grabbed it and held it so she could shove her arm through the sleeve. Last night when he pictured this reunion of sorts, he'd imagined it would be all about strategies and plans. Dispassionate and businesslike. What a fool he could be sometimes. He might have known resentments, old and new, would be dredged up.

Once outside, they stood on the sidewalk in front of the café.

"I didn't want to start an argument, Miles."

He shook his head. "Me, neither, but it seems we need to clear the air. Let's do it where we're certain no one will overhear us."

The coffee had left him jittery, or maybe he'd have been anxious, anyway. Especially now, knowing he'd put Lark even more on edge.

"Do you have time for a drive?" she asked. "We still haven't made any decisions. That's what this morning was supposed to be about."

He nodded. "I didn't expect to be so stirred up inside. Where do you want to go?"

"Follow me. I'm right next to the south end of the waterfront park in Two Moon Bay. I'll pull into the lot in the park. We can walk on the beach and jetty and talk this through. Then we can warm up inside my cottage."

He nodded. "Let's go."

TWENTY MINUTES AFTER leaving Hugo's, Lark pulled into the lot adjacent to the beach and waited for Miles to park next to her. She watched him get out of his car and walk toward her while pulling a knit hat over his ears. Staring at the whitecaps forming on the water, he looked grim, his forehead wrinkled in thought, or perhaps consternation.

Unfortunately, Lark didn't know him well enough to draw conclusions. Back in college he'd been an easygoing guy, out for a fun time. Now he was divorced and a responsible dad.

Regardless of what he was feeling at the moment, she'd bet money their baby had barely produced a ripple in the pond of his life. Not like the boulder that had crashed into hers.

"Let's walk down to the end of the jetty." She pointed to the left, where the concrete pier looked clear of ice.

"Lead the way."

They headed down the beach, one of two jewels along Two Moon Bay's waterfront. The other stretch was a stony beach and marina closer to downtown. Both offered grassy areas with picnic tables under the trees to provide shade in the summer. The concrete jetty, about a block long, appeared abandoned, even lonely on the cold, overcast day. The rising wind stirred up the water, sending spray flying over the far end of the jetty. In a couple of weeks the shallow water in this part of the bay would likely freeze over.

"No one else is crazy enough to be out here today," she said, glancing at his glum face. She stopped abruptly. "Look, I didn't mean to rile you."

"I know." He stared out at the lake. "It's completely irrational, but yesterday I immediately thought of you as a partner when I suspected Perrie Lynn was our daughter. You weren't the first person I thought to call. You were the *only* person."

She closed the gap between them by lightly touching his arm. "Let me finish my whole thought. Then you can judge." She repeated her reasoning for listing herself on the registry with the state of Minnesota. She'd assumed their daughter would look for her first. That pattern was well documented by decades of research. "But I would never have gone beyond the first contact—if I were blessed enough to have a contact at all— without making it clear to her that I could, and would, get in touch with her father."

His features relaxed and a faint smile appeared. "Thanks for that."

"Here's the other reason for acting alone. I didn't know how you turned out, or what kind of life you have. Or whom you'd confided in." She lifted her open hands high in the air to emphasize her point. "After I saw you at the mall I assumed you were married. I could have tried to reach you, but I imagined that would have disrupted your life— in a big way."

"Funny you should say that," he said, nodding. "My ex-wife is the *only* person who knows about what happened. No one else."

"Ha! That's one more person than I told."

"What? You must have told your ex-husband."

She lowered her gaze and studied her boots. "Not on your life."

His voice turned from puzzled to concerned. "I don't understand."

She waved him off. "Oh, it was very calculating on my part. I decided that if I'd, you know, confessed, then he'd have had a big fat issue as an arrow in his quiver. Sooner or later, he would have pulled it out and sent it flying toward me to wound me in some way."

"*Wound* you?"

His shock surprised her, although it shouldn't have. She'd already sized up Miles as a far more decent man than Lyle. The irony of that thought threatened to sink her into a bout of harsh self-doubt about her choices. "Lyle would have made me pay. One way or another."

"Wow."

She smiled wryly. "My ex is not a particularly nice guy."

"Okay, I admit it. I'm stunned that you were afraid to talk with the man you married about such a significant part of your life."

It was time to change the subject. "Tell me how your ex-wife reacted when you told her."

"She was a little shocked." Once again he stared off into the distance. "But I told her before we decided to get married. And I never believed she'd use it as a weapon against me—and she never did." He turned to Lark. "We divorced for other reasons, and they had nothing to do with the past. It never came up."

Lark met his eyes directly. "My ex didn't fight fair. That's what I'm saying. He looked for advantages, a little edge here and a point to score there. He still enjoys the sense of power any weakness on my part provides."

Miles's eyes had softened with sadness. "It can't have been easy."

"I didn't mean to draw you into what's old news." She hesitated. "Or, more or less old news. Lyle and I still have our struggles."

"I understand that."

"Did your wife wonder why we didn't keep the baby?"

Miles stared at the ground. "At first. But I told her we weren't…"

She watched his face change as he seemed to struggle for words. "*Serious* about each other. Is that the word you're looking for?"

"It will do. But I explained that we weren't *ready*. Either of us." He sighed. "Probably mostly me."

She nodded, but didn't like seeming to agree with him. Or maybe she didn't want to let him off the hook, or be let off the hook herself. They could have done better, couldn't they? Was adoption really their only choice? Why had it felt that way, so much so that she hadn't seriously entertained the notion of keeping the child and raising her alone? At least she hadn't considered that choice for long and never to the point of forming a plan. Why? Back then she'd blamed the emotional chaos of her parents' split. She shook off that train of thought. Her parents and their troubles were issues to address another day.

"I know you're leaving town, so let's get on with it." She pointed down the beach. "My house is just past the edge of the park. You can pull into the drive behind me."

"We say we're going to make our plans, but we take these side trips instead." He stared at the lake. "And I want to know what's happened with you over the years. Now I wish we'd kept in touch. Ever since I saw you walking toward Hugo's with your hair flying in the breeze, the past has come rushing back for me."

Feeling her face warm, she pointed to their cars and started walking toward them. "We'll be at my place in two minutes."

CHAPTER FOUR

"DID YOUR FAMILY own this place before you moved in?" he asked, scanning the room.

She smiled. "Nope. *I* chose it after Lyle bought me out of my share of our house. I could have found a larger home for the same money, but I traded all those possibilities for this cottage with a view of the lake and empty space on each side of me."

She beckoned him farther inside and pointed to the cushioned window seat as an invitation to sit. "The location meant much more to me than the size of the rooms."

A sleek wooden desk sat angled so her office chair looked out the window at the lake. High bookcases lined the wall next to it and three tall file cabinets provided a boundary where the living room and dining area ended and the office began.

The main room housed a short couch and a couple of reading chairs and lamps, but left no space available for more shelves or even a TV.

As if reading his mind, she said, "We have three tiny bedrooms, and the smallest is our TV and game room, more or less. Evan regularly grumbles about being cramped in there. His father's place—our old house—is about four times the size. We have joint custody, so Evan spends a lot of time there, too. But this place is big enough for him to bring friends around, especially in the summer, when we grill on the patio at the side of the house."

Miles stared at the whitecaps rippling over the gray water. "Don't worry, one day Evan will tell stories about the great little cottage he grew up in."

"Promise?" she said with a laugh. "Somehow, we do manage to make it work. His room has a good view, and he has his space, small as it is, fixed up exactly the way he wants it—and it's that way at his dad's, too."

He recognized something in her voice. The same wistfulness that came over him from time to time. Lark, too, had been forced to accept a family arrangement that bore no resemblance to the one she'd imagined on the day she'd married this Lyle guy. Miles well understood the back-and-forth shuffle common for divorced parents—if they were lucky and managed to work out an arrangement with their ex.

"Brooke's life is like your son's. She has a set of things in her room in my house, more stuff at her mother's and a few belongings she carries from one place to the other in her backpack."

Wanting to change the subject, he pointed to piles of files, clippings and a laptop. "So, what are you working on now?"

"A series on various types of migraines." She tapped three file folders in turn. "Plus, I'm a contributing editor for an online monthly for parents of kids with disabilities." She picked up a file from another stack. "Research abstracts. Seems like almost everything I do these days circles back to autism."

Her expression darkened.

"What is it?"

"I see—or rather hear and read about—so much pain," she said, wincing. "Parents hurting because their kids struggle. They're constantly hoping for an autism breakthrough. Something that gives their kids a chance at a so-called normal life. I've been so lucky with Evan. It makes all the hard times as a parent pale in comparison to what other people go through."

She tapped her temple. "It just occurred to me that if Perrie Lynn is the one, then we truly are among the luckiest people I know."

"Because we're pretty sure she's okay? Is that what you're saying?" He extended his hands toward her. "Well, better than okay— she has dreams, a passion."

Nodding, she added, "And she's pursuing those dreams and making them come true. I've so hoped she was happy and healthy." She cast a pointed look his way. "I imagine you've had the same thought."

No, he hadn't. He'd *assumed* everything was fine. He didn't know how to explain that detachment or his lack of worry. Sometimes, what he and Lark had been through barely seemed real. But he wasn't going to admit to that now. Instead, he smiled and nodded.

He turned to the window. "Not much separates you from the park. Some maples and birches, and a few rows of cedars."

She moved to his side. "I love those trees. They frame my view. And for about eight months of the year I walk the beach almost every day. I head over to the stony beach way beyond the downtown park. Even when tourist season peaks in the summer few people venture that far. Fall is the best season of all."

"The water is a little rough today. And it looks cold."

She grinned. "But you should see it when the moon is out on a still, clear night. No wonder someone thought to name this town Two Moon Bay. The moon is reflected so perfectly it's easy to believe you could swim out and lift it right out of the water."

"And take a bite out of it, too, I imagine."

"Right you are. And it's not cheese. I like to think of it as a big sugar cookie."

Miles grinned. He was having a difficult time keeping his eyes off her. When Lark had come to mind these past few years, he'd thought of her as taller. But the top of her head reached just above his shoulder. Her hair matched his memory, though. Thick and wavy, it brushed her shoulders. His mother used the word *extravagant* to describe hair like Lark's. Her delicate features were a stark contrast to his sharply angled face.

"This is what I propose," Lark said, backing away from the window and resting her hip on the corner of her desk. "Let's start by investigating the adoption and disclosure laws in Michigan. I can check back with the adoption agency in Minnesota to see how this works across state agencies."

"According to what Brooke told me, and that came by way of her babysitter, Mamie, Perrie Lynn and her mother are in Ann Arbor only to work with a specific coach," Miles explained. "Her father stayed in Minneapolis, where he runs a business. Their home is still there."

"Are you sure about that? The website mentioned Michigan."

"I know, but apparently, uprooting part of the family isn't unusual for these skaters. They accept that they'll be living in two places for a time. The commentators talked about it yesterday. Perrie Lynn and her mother made the move by themselves and her dad visits and goes to the competitions."

"I get it. That happens in gymnastics, as well." Lark laughed. "Your little Brooke is becoming a walking encyclopedia of figure skating. Mamie must be quite a babysitter."

"She is, and Brooke likes her a lot. By the way, from what the commentators said, Perrie Lynn's new coach is the main reason for her fast rise in the standings." Miles paused and searched his memory. "I caught his name. I think, no, I'm sure it's Declan

Rivers. He's coached a few International medalists and world champions."

"You picked up a lot of information in one afternoon," Lark said, grinning.

"Hey, I'm on a first-name basis with Katie and Allen, the commentators. They fed me all kinds of random facts."

"Okay, then," she said, "let's start with what we know and see if we can figure out a way to reach her."

"No, at the most, we could reach her parents," he said, enunciating each word. He needed confirmation they were of one mind on this.

Lark's hand flew up in a defensive gesture. "Yes, of course. I meant to say her parents."

He chose to believe her.

"Perrie Lynn's father is Eric and her mother is Maxine," he said. "The website provided that information."

"I can only imagine how many Eric Olsons are listed in the Minneapolis phone book," she said, "but maybe not so many Maxines. And we could see if she has a Facebook page and send her a message."

He held up his hand. "Wait. You're suggesting we get in touch through a Facebook page?"

"Well, she's more likely to be active on Facebook than Eric, and we can't message Perrie Lynn on her page—and she has one. I checked. Besides, Maxine and Eric might restrict Perrie Lynn's access. She's a public person now, and I'd be surprised if the Olsons let her manage it by herself."

Miles shook his head, amazed he was even having this conversation. "Listen to us talking about Maxine and Eric, as if we know them."

"You're right." She clasped her hands in front of her chest.

"And you're nervous. Are you afraid?"

"Of course I'm afraid," she snapped. "What if we send a message and Maxine doesn't reply? What if they message back and tell us they aren't the right people in the first place? That they aren't even her adoptive parents."

"Her *parents*," Miles warned. "Once people adopt children, they're parents, no qualifiers."

She waved him off. "I know, I know. You don't need to lecture me."

"Okay, but it seems as if you're thinking of yourself as Perrie Lynn's mother, I mean, now that she's turned eighteen." He'd raised his voice, startling Lark, but he had to make the point. "Even if we find her, we'll always be on the edges of her life."

He drew back slightly in response to the flicker of anger in her eyes.

"What makes you so sure of that?"

Forcing himself to lower his voice, he said, "C'mon. You're jumping way ahead of yourself."

She hunched her shoulders defensively. "I've been jumping ahead of myself for eighteen years. This is the first time I can take a step, a real step, other than listing myself with the agency. Besides, like you said, her parents don't call every shot now that she's of age."

She stalked away, disappearing through the small dining room and into the kitchen. Out of his sight.

There it was again, her expectations. He and Lark weren't on the same page. Maybe they weren't reading from the same book.

Not knowing if he should go after her or leave her alone, he stared out the window, allowing indecision to take over.

"I'm sorry," she said, coming back into the room a few minutes later.

"Are you okay?"

"As okay as I'm going to be." She flopped down on her desk chair and turned it sideways so she wasn't facing him. "You're right. I know perfectly well that she'll never be my daughter in the same way Evan is my son. *Never*. That train left the station the minute I let that nurse, the one with the bright red hair and freckles all over her face and arms, carry my baby out the door."

"What? Freckles? Red hair? What do you mean?"

She swiveled the chair, facing him. "I remember the moment like it was yesterday." She tapped her forehead. "It's all like a photograph stored up here. Every detail sharp and distinct." She splayed her fingers across her heart. "And the feelings, too."

Her face reddened as she spoke.

"Of course I remember the nurse's hair and her freckles. And our baby's scent, her tiny hands and the shape of her face—*my* face, a miniature heart."

He looked away. A memory formed for him, too. Young and stupid, with no idea the moment would be imprinted on him with such power, he'd stood behind her, hands squeezing her shoulders. He remembered, but Lark was right, the frozen moment in time was different for him.

"And you, Miles? You gripped my shoulders harder when the nurse left with our baby and closed the door behind her. You kept me standing when my knees buckled. I fell back and covered my eyes and sobbed. It was only minutes, but it felt like hours."

"I remember." His mental image lacked something, though. Intensity. Reality. Something. "But it feels distant, as if it happened in another life," he admitted. He'd never given a thought to the nurse. No trace of her remained in his memory. Even the baby who carried another generation of his genes had become more of an abstraction as the years passed, reawakened only with Brooke's birth. Then, when he was home alone after holding his new baby girl for the first time, memories of Lark and the hospital came back, but in an unwelcome flashback that taunted him until he managed to push away the images.

Making no attempt to fill the silence, he turned to the window, watching the gray water, chaotic with spray scattering every which way in the wind. Suddenly, he had an idea for moving out of the past and going forward. A safe, nonthreatening way to reach the Olsons. Facebook messages were out of the question, almost certain to alarm Eric and Maxine.

"So, should we try to contact Maxine?" Lark's voice was calm again, if not pleasant. "You know, through Facebook."

He shook his head. "No. Definitely not. Something tells me that would scare the Olsons. Make them uneasy, as if we're threatening to them in some way. Put yourself in their position. Imagine Maxine seeing a message out of the blue from strangers claiming to be their daughter's birth parents."

Lark shrugged. "No matter what we do, it will seem like it's out of the blue."

"True. But hear me out. What if we were to contact the coach? We could explain the situation, assure him we have no intention of disrupting anyone's life, least of all Perrie Lynn's." The idea grew in appeal, mainly because it was so safe. "Reaching out to the coach first is a way to demonstrate that we're responsible people. We only want to find out if we're Perrie Lynn's birth parents. If we are, we can go from there. If not, we'll disappear, no harm done."

Lark turned away and propped her elbows on her desk, holding her head in her hands.

His heart raced. Apparently, she hated his idea, but even worse, he'd upset her—again.

"Lark? It's okay. We'll come up—"

"No, no." She lifted her head, facing him with tears welling in her eyes. "It's a great idea. Reasonable and sensible."

"Then why are you angry?"

She cupped her cheeks in her palms. "I'm just furious with myself for not considering the ramifications. Reaching out through Facebook with something this important? I'm a mother. I should know better. Of course we'd scare Maxine and Eric."

"So, you're okay with the coach idea?"

She nodded, smiling now. "I was so careful and systematic years ago when I contacted the adoption agency. I saw it as a long-term quest and knew it could take years to make contact after our baby's eighteenth birthday. I made myself accept that it might never happen. But now I can't seem to think straight."

He took a tentative step toward her, wanting to reach out, touch her shoulder, but he held back. "It's okay. I understand. Whatever we do, I don't want to upset you, that's all."

"Don't worry about me. These are difficult decisions." She held out her hand, letting him see it tremble. "My feelings are simmering on the surface, ready to boil over. Talking about all these details—past, present and even future—skewed my thinking."

"Well, how about this? I'll call Declan Rivers and explain the situation. I'll provide our phone numbers and websites and all that, so he can start checking us out." He grew calmer as he thought out the next steps. "If it's okay with you, I'll give him the name of my attorney, the one I used for my divorce and still use for some business issues. I'll fill in the basic facts. We can let Declan Rivers contact Eric and Maxine—or at least advise us the best way to go about it."

"What if Declan doesn't return your call? What then?"

"We'll cross that bridge, you know, later. But I think he'll respond."

"Okay," she said with a slow nod, "go ahead and make the call."

"One thing, though. If they take us seriously, we shouldn't be surprised if we hear from their attorney," Miles added. "Be prepared for a DNA test and background checks."

Another nod. "I'm fine with whatever they want."

He glanced at his watch. "I need to go. Pack for my trip and all that."

She stood and shooed him toward the door. "Go, go. I've got an interview to prepare for, anyway. First, though, I'll research the coach. I'll text you his phone number or email address, or whatever I can find."

Miles retrieved his coat from the couch. "We have a plan, huh?"

"We do," she said, frowning. "But in spite of the way I'm talking, be prepared. Coincidences and resemblances aside, it's quite possible Perrie Lynn isn't our child after all."

"I'm trying to stay reasonable," he said slipping into his coat, "but if she isn't, that only means our daughter is out there somewhere."

"Oh, Miles. Then you'll contact the adoption agency, so we can both be found? If she looks for us, that is?"

"Yes. What's happened in these last twenty-four hours has changed everything for me."

Lark moved in front of him and opened the door. "Safe travels and all that."

He said a quick goodbye. One way or another, they'd talk again soon.

CHAPTER FIVE

A WOMAN ANSWERED Declan Rivers's phone and in a girlish voice identified herself as Tricia. No last name. But in a stiff, formal tone, she responded to Miles's request to speak to the coach by informing him that *Mr.* Rivers was unavailable at this time. She, however, was *Mr.* Rivers's assistant, and would be glad to help. "And what's the nature of your call?" she asked.

"It's a personal matter," Miles said.

"I see," Tricia said. "Could you be more specific?"

"Uh, well, it concerns one of his skaters, Perrie Lynn Olson."

"And whom do you represent?"

Represent? She had the wrong impression. "I'm not with a media organization, if that's what you mean."

Was that a sigh he heard on the other end of the phone?

"As I said, this is a personal matter." Miles

suggested that he could call later at a time convenient for the coach.

"No need," she said in a flat, almost dry tone. "How can Declan reach you? He'll get back to you."

And so he had, late that night when Miles was sitting in a reading chair with his feet propped up on the hotel desk. For the better part of an hour he'd been pretending to focus on pages of the *Richmond Times-Dispatch*. Mostly, though, he stared at his phone and willed it to ring. He'd already responded to two texts from Lark, in which she admitted feeling restless and impatient.

He jumped when his phone buzzed, the adrenaline rush swift and strong.

"Declan Rivers here, returning your call," the deep male voice said abruptly, "but I must warn you I've returned a few calls today already."

"I understand," Miles replied with a quick laugh, although he didn't feel all that good-humored. "I'll keep this brief. I'm calling to discuss a matter related to Perrie Lynn Olson."

"Yes, yes," Declan said brusquely, "I see that in the notes."

Miles ate up a couple of seconds considering his next move, but finally got to the point. "I won't waste your time. I believe there's a good chance I'm Perrie Lynn's biological father. And I'm in touch with the woman who would be her birth mother." Without pausing, Miles added, "Please understand, we have no desire to alarm Perrie Lynn or disrupt her or her parents in any way. We mean that. We only want to learn the truth."

"Okay, then, why do you think you're her parents? You and quite a few other people, by the way." Declan's tone wasn't exactly rude, but it fell short of friendly. "And did this sudden *realization* come after you saw her skate this weekend?"

Mild sarcasm had seeped into the coach's tone, but Miles didn't let it divert him from briefly explaining how he became aware of Perrie Lynn. He recounted his conversations with Lark, and her earlier contact with the adoption agency and the Minnesota registry. "In other words, if our child, whoever she is, wants to find her birth parents now that she's eighteen, the information is available."

"So why did you call me?"

Miles took a deep breath. "Ms. McGee— Lark—and I agreed it was best not to approach the family. We want to be discreet, and we'd never intrude. It could all be a case of mistaken assumptions. Frankly, we're parents, too, and social media seemed way too risky."

"Funny you should say that." Declan scoffed. "Just today, Mrs. Olson has received more than a couple of dozen legitimate Facebook messages. And then there are all the random ones that regularly come around, like the person last week who claimed Perrie Lynn is an alien from the Pleiades on a mission to save humanity. You see, theoretically, it's Perrie Lynn's page, but Maxine—Mrs. Olson—monitors it and deletes anything that's not legit."

"I understand the problems with kids and social media. And it starts so young." Miles rubbed his forehead. He already worried about keeping Brooke safe from internet trolls and predators. He could only imagine what having a teenager newly in the public eye must be like.

"Maxine would be happy to shut the page down," Declan said. "Naturally, given recent press coverage of Perrie Lynn, Eric and Maxine are worried about stalkers—internet and otherwise. That's a factor for all athletes in the spotlight."

"No parent should have to worry about that, Mr. Rivers. For what it's worth, Lark and I will follow the family's lead. Whatever they want. Under no circumstances would we do anything to harm Perrie Lynn or the Olsons. That's the last thing on our minds."

As if to fortify his words, he filled in some information about Lark and her work and then his own. "I'm a professional speaker with a consulting practice. When I called earlier, I was home in Green Bay, Wisconsin, but now I'm on a consulting job in Richmond, Virginia. And by the way, we'd be happy to channel all communications through an attorney if that's what you prefer."

"Are you and Ms. McGee married?"

Miles had to quickly switch gears. He didn't welcome the need to explain. "No, we married other people, but we're both divorced now. Lark has a son and I have a daughter. We haven't been in touch for eighteen years. At this point, all we want is to make ourselves easy to find if our child wants to locate us, even if it's just to satisfy her curiosity. Believe me, we understand that physical resemblance and the birthday could be a coincidence."

"I see." Declan's tone had softened. "We

immediately ruled out some of the people who sent messages. I think a few of them were attracted to the idea that their long-lost baby could have grown up to be a rising star." He paused. "Kind of sad, really."

"I assume the Olsons have an attorney," Miles said, making an effort to hide his frustration. It wasn't rational, but he was insulted the coach put Lark and him in the same category as all the other people claiming to be Perrie Lynn's birth parents. But that was unfair. Declan Rivers had no idea who he and Lark were. "We'll be happy to speak with whoever represents the family. Screen us, test us, investigate. We understand the need for scrutiny."

"The Olsons' attorney is involved," Declan said. "These inquiries began coming in earlier in the year when Perrie Lynn was invited to perform with the Magic on Ice tour. Then she did well at Skate America. But the pace really picked up after yesterday's competition." Declan huffed, his frustration coming through the phone.

"I can only imagine," Miles said, trying hard to maintain his professional tone.

"Many more people are aware of Perrie Lynn now. And we've had to take the problems along with the spotlight," Declan said. "So, I'll pass on your information and the Olsons' attorney will get back to you." He paused. "For, uh, some reason, Eric and Maxine are okay with…let's just say they're okay having the issue resolved."

Miles frowned, wondering exactly what that meant. But he had a hunch more questions would not be welcomed, so he provided contact information, including his attorney. Just to be thorough, he also recited their website addresses. He hoped the Olsons' attorney would take the time to thoroughly check them out. He couldn't stop himself from again bristling at the notion that he and Lark would ever be considered frauds.

By the time Miles was off the phone and had checked the time, he wondered if eight thirty in the evening was a bad time to call Lark. Her son would likely be around. She probably couldn't talk, anyway. He settled on sending a brief text. Declan returned call. Talk positive. Next steps underway.

Two minutes later, his phone buzzed. His eagerness to hear her voice surprised him.

"Why didn't you just call?" she asked with a light laugh.

"I thought your boy might be around and you couldn't talk freely."

"Ah, I see. But I'm alone in my bedroom. Evan is in his room contemplating chess plays for a big match he has tomorrow. So, give me the details," she said, excitement in her voice.

"It turns out the Olsons have been receiving all kinds of messages in the last twenty-four hours." He repeated what Declan had told him.

"I suppose that's not surprising, especially since you said it was never a secret that Perrie Lynn is adopted. Aren't the Olsons used to this kind of attention?"

"It's different now. Perrie Lynn has never been the object of so much media focus before. But millions of people have been watching her during this skating season," Miles explained. "Maybe those TV commentators didn't realize where their casual talk would lead."

"Seems kind of risky to be so open about private information," Lark added. "No wonder the Olsons are concerned. On the other hand, I know what it's like to chase a story."

An image of her came to mind. A handbag slung over her shoulder and hands tucked into the pockets of her red jacket as she pursued an interview. "I'll bet you do. And it occurred to me the Olsons have probably done their best to navigate the skating world. It has an aura of glamour. But I assured Declan over and over that we were responsible people. Anyway, their attorney will check us out." He chuckled. "Even on our websites, we appear like such upstanding citizens and all that."

"I've got nothing to hide, except this one thing," Lark said, lowering her voice. "In the Olsons' shoes, I'd be calling in the troops to make sure we aren't stalkers or unbalanced. Whatever."

"Declan sounded a little gruff," Miles admitted, "and impatient with all the messages coming in just today. But, no surprise there."

"What's next, then?"

"A preliminary look at any legitimate inquiries, I gather. No telling how long that will take."

"Life goes on for now, huh?" she said with an ironic laugh. "As if that's possible."

"It's an hour later here in Richmond," Miles said. "And now that I'm not waiting for Declan's call, at least I'll be able to sleep. I think. I'm still kind of wound up."

"Me, too," Lark said. "I've been sitting on the edge of my chair since we spoke last night. I just wish we knew when we'd hear from the coach again."

Miles chose his words carefully. "I believe Declan took me seriously. And caution makes sense. In a way, it's kind of surprising that they're open to inquiries at all."

"You're right, not to mention sensible and understanding. You're a nicer person than I am, Miles," she teased. "I want to wave my arms in front of their faces and demand a DNA test and all that. I want to *know* she's my daughter!" She paused. "*Our* daughter."

She has to practice bringing me in. Irrationally, her possessiveness got under his skin. He tried to maintain his even tone as he said, "I know you want this resolved in the next few minutes. One way or another. The thing is, I can't shake the feeling that this…" He hesitated, searching for the right words. "Let's just say I'd be shocked to learn she isn't our daughter."

"Keep saying that, please keep saying that," she whispered. "I'm all over the place. Maybe I'm trying to protect myself from disappointment."

"Totally understandable."

Lark sighed. "I better go. I have a couple of calls to return. I often end up talking to west coast editors in the evening."

"Okay. Let me know if anyone contacts you. Declan has your phone number as well as mine."

"Believe me, you'll hear me shouting way out east in Richmond."

"You sleep well," he said, quickly ending the call.

Did she really have calls to return? Maybe it was a way to get off the phone. Hellos and goodbyes had proved so clumsy between them. He couldn't say why. True, they'd been okay after their first awkward moments at the café, but leaving her cottage earlier had been difficult. He'd again had a strong urge to kiss her cheek or wrap his arms around her, but he kept a good couple of feet between them. He'd walked to his car with the sense that something was left undone. Just now on the phone, he'd wanted to keep talking, unsure where the conversation would lead them. But he knew he'd struggle to find a graceful way to end the call. Maybe she felt the same way.

He pulled back the covers of the hotel bed, unable to get his mind off her. The pretty girl had turned into an even more attractive, complex woman. Her variable moods got to him, along with the pain in her eyes when she'd recounted her detailed memories of giving up their baby.

As he drifted off to sleep, he thought about how upset she'd been not to recognize how cautious the Olsons needed to be to protect their daughter. It had hurt to see her in turmoil, her intelligent blue eyes filled with self-reproach, not to mention tears.

Sleep well, Lark.

THE NEXT MORNING, a mug of freshly brewed coffee in hand, Miles sat at the desk in the suite and pulled up the file with a list of travel dates for January and February meetings at all three locations of Home Comforts, Inc. Far from being a household name, the company sold home-accent products to various companies who marketed them through mail-order catalogs. The rapid growth of online shopping had been the best thing that ever happened to Home Comforts.

As for his work today, Miles had scheduled a face-to-face workshop-style meeting designed to help key players cope with the inevitable growing pains of a company that had poorly managed its own rapid expansion. The worst of it involved three top-tier managers who had poisoned employee morale with a combination of their own panic and an iron hand. Now it was his job to unravel the damage and move the staff in the direction of a collaborative workplace.

As Miles had discovered, business owners and corporate execs rarely wanted to accept the simple fact that no disgruntled-employee story went untold. That had always been true, but in the age of texting and social media, companies couldn't ignore complaints about rude behavior among their service reps and sales staff. They couldn't be blind and ignore internal breakdowns in communication, either. Fortunately, these were exactly the kinds of challenges that kept his consulting practice and speaking calendar booked.

Satisfied that he was as prepared for the day's work as he'd ever be, he pulled up Lark's website. Not for any particular reason. He just wanted to look at her photo and her warm, inviting expression. Whoever designed her site knew that approachability mattered. It continued to surprise him that she was even prettier than he remembered.

Was it only last night that he'd quickly

scanned her impressive list of recent publications? He took his time now. Her work had been published in every health and fitness magazine he'd ever heard of, plus a bunch he hadn't. She also had dozens of credits in household-name women's magazines and big-city dailies.

She'd made good, all right. That pleased him. He could have spent the day just following links to all her publications. An interview with a brash but innovative cancer scientist had appeared only a few days ago in the *Wall Street Journal*. Another piece in a journal for chiropractors focused on nutritional remedies for ten common conditions. He smiled to himself. She appeared to be a walking encyclopedia of nutritional supplements and herbs, and that was just a start. Based on her publications, she was equally conversant with subjects as varied as brain injuries and superbugs. She'd even written a handful of columns to calm parents' fears about Ebola.

He clicked back to her home page and stared at the photo, knowing that behind those sparkling eyes and radiant smile lived a woman who'd made one of the toughest decisions anyone could imagine. He flopped back in the chair and ran his fingers through his hair. Over the years he'd never wavered in *his* conviction that they—or rather, Lark—had made the right choice eighteen years ago. That decision had allowed him to move forward with his life without ever needing to talk about Lark and their baby. He'd always known he'd paid a very small price.

On the other hand, although Lark also had gone on with her life, she'd obviously never stopped questioning her choice. Maybe that was why she'd married the wrong man. That ex of hers sure sounded like a jerk. Mean-spirited and spiteful. She deserved better than armoring herself against a man she feared would throw her past in her face.

Shaking off dark thoughts about Lark's ex-husband, Miles forced himself to refocus on Home Comforts. He grabbed his computer and headed to the hotel conference room. It was probably already filled with the company's executives and managers milling about and chatting over coffee. Concentrating on his work was usually so easy. Not today. He could picture Lark struggling to keep her mind on migraine headaches or learning disabilities or whatever she had on her plate.

There she was again. For eighteen years, Lark had rarely crossed his mind. Now she'd taken a front row seat.

CHAPTER SIX

EXPECTING A CALL from an editor at *Wellness Plus*, Lark answered the phone on the first buzz and didn't bother glancing at the caller ID. "Lark McGee."

"Oh, hello," a woman's startled voice said. "Uh, I guess I reached you."

"Yes, this is Lark. And how can I help you?" She straightened in her desk chair, suddenly on guard.

The woman laughed softly. "I'd prepared one of those twenty-second voice-mail messages. Anyway, I'm, uh…this is Maxine. Maxine Olson."

Lark lurched forward in her chair, light-headed, her vision blurry. She grabbed the side of the desk to steady herself. She closed her eyes, and spluttered, "I'm sorry. I can barely speak."

"I can imagine," Maxine said, her voice low. "I didn't know any other good way to reach out. Somehow, an email wouldn't do."

Such a pleasant tone. Gentle, even sweet.

Lark took a calming breath. "Can I assume Mr. Rivers called you? About—"

"Yes, yes," Maxine said impatiently, "but let me explain why I'm calling *you* directly."

Lark swallowed hard. "Please…go ahead."

"I want to get some things out of the way. It's true, Declan gave us your names—you and Miles, I mean."

Lark tightened her grip on her desk.

"And I'm not going to keep you in the dark. I always intended to make this easy—when the time came, that is. We're just a little thrown by how and when this unfolded." She paused. "You see, I'm quite certain that you *are* Perrie Lynn's biological mother."

A gasp lodged in Lark's throat. She struggled to breathe.

"Hearing the words must come as a shock."

"Yes and no." Lark cleared her throat. "I mean, I wanted it…longed to hear those words at some point in my life."

"After Declan made us aware of Miles's call," Maxine said, "things started happening fast. You did the right thing."

Naturally, Perrie Lynn's mother would say that. "Yes, I know," she whispered.

Silence.

"I mean that contacting Declan was the right thing," Maxine explained.

Of course. "Uh, that's what we hoped. We didn't want to…scare you."

The tangled mix of thoughts racing around in Lark's mind began slowing down, but the past and the present fused as questions now piled up, one after the other. And all the while, rising elation traveled up her body, intensifying, gathering strength. She yearned to sing out her news, dance through the cottage waving her arms in the air. Sob in relief. But she needed to hold herself steady because she wanted—needed—every detail.

"I'll make a long story short," Maxine continued. "First, I must tell you our attorney wasn't thrilled about my decision to make this call."

"No, I suppose not." For the first time, fear crept in. Why *would* Maxine reach out herself, rather than leave that job to the attorney? What piece was missing?

"You'll be hearing from our lawyer soon. Her name is Lisa Mandel."

"I understand," Lark said, finding her voice, "but you have to know I wouldn't do anything to hurt you or Perrie Lynn. Nor would Miles."

"That's the thing. I know it sounds improbable, but I trust you. There are other considerations, though." Maxine exaggerated a sigh. "Let me start at the beginning. The real beginning."

Lark winced against her own painful memories of the beginning.

"This is all sensitive information, difficult to talk about, but I want it on the table," Maxine said. "I know who you are because I saw your name on the papers you signed. It happened on the day we finalized Perrie Lynn's adoption."

"My *name*? But…how?"

"Believe me, I'm aware I wasn't supposed to see those papers. The fact they were open and spread out on a conference table was our original attorney's oversight. A big mistake." Maxine's voice rose in frustration. "Frankly, he was incompetent, and even the original birth certificate was there in plain sight, along with the new one with our names on it."

True enough, someone messed up. But Lark didn't care. "So, all these years you've known my name."

Maxine cleared her throat. "To be perfectly honest, I tried to forget it. I *willed* myself to wipe it out of my memory. But you have such an unusual first name and easily remembered last name that I couldn't wipe it away. It wasn't like erasing words on a blackboard. No matter what I did, the name Lark McGee was branded on my brain."

"I find myself without words," Lark said. It was almost too much to think about. This woman, a stranger, had known her name all along. But did Perrie Lynn?

Now it was Maxine's turn to clear her throat. "I'm going to make a promise, right now. You *will* meet Perrie Lynn one day. I can say with confidence that Eric and I will arrange it. You see, a few years ago we assured Perrie Lynn that when she was old enough—and ready—we'd help her find her birth parents."

"But does she know—"

"Who you are? No, *no*, absolutely not!"

A definitive answer. But Maxine could reveal the information to Perrie Lynn at any time. The facts were there. They only needed to shine a light on them. Then secrets wouldn't be secrets for long. Just thinking about that birth certificate and her name there for Maxine to see had transformed her elation into wonderment.

Maxine exhaled loud enough for Lark to hear. "Frankly, I had a more orderly conversation in mind. I realize now you have a million questions. I'll answer them, but I need something from you first."

"Of course. What is it?"

"We have terms, Eric and I, which is why our attorney didn't want me to contact you. She preferred we keep you at arm's length at all times. And I'll go along with that from now on. But for some reason, I wanted—needed—this initial conversation with you."

"Thank you," Lark whispered, the tension in her body melting away, replaced with even more wonderment and overwhelming gratitude.

"I'm not sure how much you know about figure skating, but Perrie Lynn is on her way to the NorAms in only a few weeks," Maxine said, her voice low but earnest. "It's a *critical* competition for skaters. Winning a medal is one of the biggest dreams for all skaters, and it starts forming the minute these young kids wobble their way onto the ice and begin to have a special feeling about skating."

Lark closed her eyes, imagining a tiny dark-haired girl in skates, joyfully finding her footing on the ice.

"At first it's the sense of freedom they feel on the ice," Maxine said. "Many kids fall in love with that, but the hard reality of daily training and skating through pain comes a little later."

Just as Miles had said.

"Perrie Lynn has been working toward this goal since she was seven years old. If she does well at the NorAms she could earn a place on the US team going to the Internationals in February."

Tears stung Lark's eyes. How easy it was to slip into Maxine's shoes. "You must be so proud."

"Yes." A long sigh followed. "I can't even describe my thrill over what she's accomplished. This kind of commitment is bigger than anything I've ever experienced."

For the next few minutes, Lark listened while Maxine supplied the answers to so many questions that had run through her mind. The information tracked what Miles had said, right up to Perrie Lynn leaving Minnesota to train with Declan.

"So, you understand why Eric and I will do whatever it takes to withhold this information from Perrie Lynn for a while longer."

"It's about focus, isn't it?" Lark asked,

grateful her normal voice had returned. "I've watched so many online clips of Perrie Lynn performing. They're not hard to find, and Miles and his little girl had watched Perrie Lynn's performance at the Grand Circuit. He repeated everything those TV commentators said about focus. And there's no room in Perrie Lynn's life now for anything but training. That's what you're saying? No distractions?"

"Yes. I'm glad you understand why meeting her biological parents is the last thing on her mind right now."

Tears rolled down Lark's cheeks. Why did Maxine trust her? She gulped back a sob before she spoke. "Miles and I agreed together that we'd never interfere."

Lark both meant and didn't mean what she'd just said. A little voice, irrational and demanding, urged her to beg Maxine to let her see Perrie Lynn now. *Stupid, stupid.* So ironic, too, since Lark was acutely aware Maxine was being nothing more than a wise mother. Lark would have drawn these same lines herself.

"Thank you," Maxine said. "It means a lot to me that you aren't asking for something we can't give."

"I should be thanking you." Lark felt the

strength return to her muscles, along with a normal heartbeat. She chuckled softly. "I *am* thanking you. It's such a relief, you see, not only to have our hunch be right, but knowing that our... *She* is okay. Better than okay. Her life, I mean, has been good."

"Hmm...yes, I can imagine that's a relief."

"Miles feels that way, too," Lark said, quickly adding, "and really, all this is his doing."

"His little girl's doing, according to Declan," Maxine said, her tone amused.

"That's true. His eight-year-old is Perrie Lynn's biggest fan."

"So I hear. She's not alone, I can tell you that for sure. Once the kids start following the skaters they eat up information for breakfast." She hesitated. "Uh, that's why I manage the social media. We keep Perrie Lynn away from it, although now that she's eighteen that won't last much longer."

"Good choice," Lark said, suddenly realizing that she was speaking in a mom-to-mom voice. "I mean, I have a son, but he's not in the public eye. Even so, we keep close watch on his computer and phone."

"Yes, Declan mentioned your son." She

cleared her throat again. "Before I go, I need to set some conditions."

Lark touched her chest in the vain hope she could remain calm. "I'm listening. Whatever you need."

"This will be the last time you'll hear from me for quite a while. Speaking of focus, all of mine is on Perrie Lynn now, and so is her father's. As I mentioned, if she does exceptionally well at the NorAms, she'll be on the International team, with all the intensity that goes with it. The world championships follow that." Maxine took in a breath. "At some point when the competitive season is over, Eric and I will approach her and tell her what we've learned about you and Miles. What happens after that is up to her."

"I see," Lark said, closing her eyes to hold back tears.

"So, I won't contact you until the time is right. If things go well, we're talking about several months."

Months...not what I want to hear. She considered her words carefully, because based on Maxine's actions thus far, she was Lark's ally. *And I need to keep it that way.*

"I've been thinking about Perrie Lynn for all these years, Maxine." Her voice broke, but she didn't care. "Knowing where she is and what she's become is…*miraculous* is the only word strong enough for this. Relieved, ecstatic, grateful. Those words all fit, but are still inadequate."

"I suspected that would be the case."

"Miles and I will watch Perrie Lynn from a distance." Lark let out a quick, happy laugh. "But we'll be cheering her on, you can bet on that."

"You better." Maxine's tone was light, almost teasing. "Okay, so that's it for now. Our attorney will call you. She'll take it from there. All communication will go through her."

Lark grimaced. Lawyers and agreements aside, she couldn't get her mind off how many months would pass before she could see Perrie Lynn in person. Christmas and Valentine's Day would come and go and the daffodils would bloom in the spring before she spoke with Maxine again. Assuming the best happened and Perrie Lynn continued winning medals.

"Whatever you want, we'll do," Lark said, simply, taking on a businesslike tone to end a conversation she wished would last and last. She yearned to learn so much more.

And with that, Maxine said goodbye and ended the call.

Alone at her desk, Lark bent over and buried her face in her hands and wept. Relief and joy fueled her tears in equal measure. She made no attempt to hold them back. Minutes passed, until at last she caught her breath and smoothed her palms over her cheeks to clear the tears. She straightened up, but immediately flopped back in her office chair. Eighteen years of emotion, regret, loss, hope and longing had jumbled together inside and become a living being. And now it caught up with her, larger than life, and transformed into overwhelming relief—and release. At least in that moment, it had left her weak. As her breathing eased, a sense of peace gently seeped into her cells and soon filled her body, energizing her. At last, healing peace.

As much as she longed to see Perrie Lynn that very minute, Maxine's reassuring voice had acted as a balm, soothing Lark's deepest wound. For the moment, that would have to be enough.

MILES SAT IN the airline's lounge in Richmond, working on the text of a luncheon speech he was giving at a small corporate training session in Milwaukee the next day. Concentration wasn't coming easily. He caught himself watching icy rain batter the floor-to-ceiling glass wall, his mind nowhere close to training topics. No telling how long his flight would be delayed.

When the phone buzzed, he quickly looked at the screen, hoping it was Lark. Instead, the name stunned him. "Miles Jenkins here," he said.

"And Eric Olson here."

Miles jolted at the clipped tone. "Hello. I'm kind of shocked. I mean, I wasn't expecting—"

"My wife spoke to Ms. McGee a little earlier," Eric said, "but I thought I should be the one to talk to you."

What? Maxine contacted Lark? Blindsided, he searched for words and couldn't find them, other than wondering why Lark hadn't left a message.

"Uh, I haven't spoken to Lark today. So, I didn't know they talked."

"I see. Well, then, she will tell you all about it, I'm sure," Eric said, his tone matter-of-fact. "Look. I'll be brief. We—my wife and I—know that Ms. McGee is Perrie Lynn's biological mother."

Another jolt of energy shot through him. "You do? But how?"

"It involved a mistake—papers left out where they shouldn't have been. Ms. McGee can fill you in."

Mistake? What did that mean?

"But that's not why I called you." Eric spoke as if in a rush, leaving the impression he couldn't wait to get off the phone.

"At this time, we're assuming you're Perrie Lynn's biological father. But we'll need to verify it. You know, make it official. That's easily done—when the time is right."

"Whew…this has come out of left field."

"Ha! Tell me about it," Eric said with a huff. "It's not exactly the way we'd have chosen to handle it. Especially me."

"I'm not sure what you mean."

"Maxine and I are a team," Eric said, "and years ago, Perrie Lynn started asking about her birth parents, you know, typical stuff. At that point, we assured her we'd help her locate them when she turned eighteen—if that's what she wanted. That satisfied her at the time. But we wanted to do it on our terms." He paused. "And speaking of terms, Maxine and I have some."

"Yes, I understand that you would. Tell

me what you want," Miles blurted, running his hand down his cheek. "Lark and I have no intention of causing trouble. And we've told no one that we've reached out to you. *No one.*"

Without responding to Miles's words, Eric described the bubble the skaters lived in.

Miles resisted the urge to interrupt. He already knew this part, and he desperately wanted to get on with more important things—these so-called terms.

By the time Eric finished, Miles had been put in his place, more or less. But, oddly, even the chilly tone hadn't put him off Eric. In fact, Miles realized, he respected him more for it. Overnight, the Olsons' world had been rocked, just as his and Lark's lives had been changed. As for the way forward, the only thing Miles knew for sure was that Perrie Lynn would be told nothing about Lark or Miles for at least a couple of months.

Eric stopped to take a breath. "You'll be hearing from Lisa Mandel, our attorney."

"That's fine," Miles said. "I—we—expected you would protect your daughter any way you can. And believe me when I say I never anticipated casually being invited into Perrie Lynn's life. I hope you get that."

Eric sighed. "When it comes to Perrie Lynn there's no such thing as being too careful. That's why I needed to have a talk with you." His voice softer, he added, "One dad to another. I was told you have your own little girl now."

The spinning sensation lessened with the turn of the conversation. "Yes, I do, Eric. That's why I understand your terms."

"Let's get something straight," Eric said, chuckling softly. "I'm not just Perrie Lynn's father, if you know what I mean. I'm her dad. I was Daddy until she was almost sixteen."

Miles knew well the indescribable pleasure of a little girl calling him Daddy. "If I'm lucky like you, Eric, I'll be Daddy for a few more years. By the way, I'm still in shock, like you and Maxine. You see, Lark and I have only been in touch for a couple of days. Right after the baby...uh, Perrie Lynn...was born, we went our separate ways." *She asked me not to ever contact her again. But Eric wouldn't care about that part of the story.*

"Hmm... I see. Well, I suppose I've come across as a little harsh here," Eric said, a hint of regret in his voice. "Maxine and I still talk about the day we brought Perrie Lynn home. The happiest day of our lives. Our families were thrilled. Her three grandparents were in the house waiting for us. My mother was already gone, but my dad was about as happy as I'd ever seen him. He's been watching Perrie Lynn from his place down in Santa Fe— never misses a performance on TV."

Miles felt a catch in his throat. The image of a grandpa loving his little granddaughter nearly did him in. Something in the conversation made every muscle in his body ache. From regret? Maybe. Miles had to finally face the fact that he hadn't been all that young when Perrie Lynn was born—plenty of twenty-year-olds became good dads. How immature he'd been.

"We made a promise," Eric said softly, "that we'd help her find her roots—"

"But not now," Miles interrupted, enunciating the words. "I get it…*we* get it. We really do. We'll be like your father, watching from a distance."

A couple of seconds passed in silence.

"Are you certain Ms. McGee is with you on this?"

"Yes, absolutely," Miles replied, exuding confidence, although doubts insisted on breaking through. He'd already witnessed Lark's resolve melt and then harden again in a matter of minutes.

"I had to ask. It's my job to make sure Perrie Lynn and her mom have whatever they need to get that girl to the NorAms for the big show and then on to the Internationals for the even bigger one."

"Brooke, my little eight-year-old, told me all about it," Miles said, deliberately lightening his tone. "It sounds like I'm pandering somehow, but she's a big Perrie Lynn fan. The other day, Brooke explained that going to the Internationals is the pot of gold at the end of the rainbow."

Eric laughed. "Hey—correction. It's the rainbow, but don't go talking about gold yet. She only graduated from high school last June. The girl's got time—and getting a medal at all is astounding."

"Okay, it's a deal," replied Miles.

"So, you won't hear from us for months," Eric said. "It's all about Perrie Lynn now."

With that, the call was done. And the weather had broken. The boarding call for Miles's flight came over the loudspeaker. Not wanting to grill Lark in a crowded plane, he decided his call to her would have to wait.

"COULDN'T YOU HAVE found a minute to even send a text?" Miles asked. "When Eric called I had no idea that all the steps had more or less been bypassed."

"A text was too remote, even cold." How was she to know Eric would reach out to Miles? And so soon? "I had to handle a couple things. I was just about to call."

"Well, maybe so, but I was blindsided."

"I'm sorry, Miles. Really, I am."

"It would have helped if you'd left me a message, even if it said you couldn't talk. Don't you get that?"

"I do, but—but…you won't understand."

"Understand what, Lark?"

When his tone softened, she let her guard down. "I *couldn't* call, because I couldn't talk. I could barely move at first. When I got off the phone, it was…I mean, the relief was overwhelming. I can't describe it."

Silence.

"Please, Lark, try."

"Okay. The truth is, I couldn't stop sobbing. After eighteen years of worrying, and now suddenly the joy of knowing what happened to… Maxine's empathy, her kindness, it all just overwhelmed me. So I cried.

I couldn't stop. And then I had to move. I started to pace. I can't even—"

"Oh, Lark, I'm so sorry."

"Don't take this the wrong way," she said, rising from the chair and going into the kitchen, "but I don't think you understand, as much as you might want to."

"When you blurt out things like that, you box me in as a less involved father." Miles's tone was edgy.

"Neither of us was *involved*," Lark snapped. She picked up the kettle and filled it with water for tea. "That's the point."

"Are you deliberately misunderstanding me?"

Sighing, she said, "No. But at the moment, I'm frustrated. We should be, oh, I don't know, celebrating. That's not exactly the right word, but it's the best I can do."

"Right." He laughed. "Trust the wordsmith to rack her brain for the perfect word that expresses exactly what this is about."

"It's all happened so fast. I don't even know how to think about it."

"We can start by exchanging some information. Eric said you'd tell me why they called quickly after we contacted Declan."

"Ah, no wonder you're impatient."

While the water heated for tea, Lark recounted her conversation with Maxine. "For eighteen years, she had my name in the back of her mind."

"I'm really glad," Miles said, relief permeating his voice. "Ha! Look at all the trouble your beautiful name saved us."

Suddenly self-conscious, Lark said, "I know, and that's part of what washed over me, Miles. I didn't intend *not* to call. I just couldn't make my brain connect with my mouth."

"It's okay. I get it now. Sort of, anyway. It's all so unbelievable."

"Yep. We're sitting here in near shock because their lawyer made a mistake eighteen years ago." She moved away from the counter as the sound of the water heating in the kettle grew louder. "But we're in for a long wait."

"Hmm...not really, if you consider what Perrie Lynn is doing."

She scoffed at that. "Quit being so reasonable, would you?"

"It's my job," Miles quipped. "I have a business—clients—because I'm the voice of reason."

"Speaking of that, where are you?"

"Milwaukee. I'm speaking at a manufacturing conference and then I'll be home for a few days."

Lark smiled. It didn't take much imagination to see Miles standing tall in front of audiences, handsome in a suit and tie. The appealing kid had grown into a worldly and self-assured man. "I bet you're good at what you do."

"I like to think so," he said. "It can be a travel grind, though."

They hadn't talked in detail about their work before, but she wanted to engage, defuse the earlier anger and get right with Miles. "No jitters or nerves when the introduction is over?"

"Always," he said with a chuckle, "but in a good way. I get the kind of butterflies that raise my game."

"Stage excitement, not stage fright?"

"Something like that."

Dead end. It was so often like that. Lark had the sense there was more to say, but she didn't know what.

"Well," she said, "I should get back to work."

"Um, yeah, I need to get down to a conference reception and mingle."

"And I bet you're good at that, too. Let's stay in touch. Christmas is coming up fast."

"And the North American Figure Skating Competition follows close behind," he said. "So, yes, I'll text, call, whatever. And if you hear from anyone…well, you get the picture."

"Yes, of course. I'll let you know. 'Bye, then."

The call ended. Awkwardly. When would she see him again? Odd how much he was on her mind now that she was mulling over the past. And the future. The events of the last couple of days even had her second-guessing their decision to get in touch with Declan. She stopped that train of thought. *Who am I kidding? They* hadn't decided anything. She had made the choice and Miles hadn't argued.

CHAPTER SEVEN

LARK CLOSED HER eyes and rested her head on the back of the couch in the TV room. It had been a half-hearted kind of day, she thought, playing with words to describe her divided attention. That included feigning disappointment when her mother called to beg off their tentative lunch date. With the increase of holiday shoppers and one salesperson out sick, her mom's days off vanished. That was fine with Lark, convinced as she was that it was best to keep news of Perrie Lynn to herself a while longer. She wasn't ready to delve into the past with her mother and spill her big secret.

Meanwhile, Lark managed to finish the first article in her series on migraine headaches. Now she was giving half her attention to the political commentators on TV. It was after 10:00 p.m., but she wasn't ready to climb into bed just yet. She was both tired and wired, living on two levels, trying to

patiently wait while carrying on and working as usual.

She lifted her head when she heard Evan's
footsteps in the tiny hall separating the two
bedrooms, bathroom and linen closet on this
side of the cottage. Her bedroom and her
postage-stamp-size bath were on the other
side of the kitchen and living room.

"You okay?" he asked, sticking his head
in the room.

"Fine, honey." She grinned. "I'm trying
to decide if I should get up and go to bed or
keep watching news."

"I was talking to Dad. He was going over
the Christmas plans."

She muted the TV. "Oh? Anything different. I thought it was all settled."

Since their divorce, she and Lyle split
their holiday time with Evan—their son
spent Christmas Eve with Lyle and his family, Christmas Day with her parents and her
brother Dennis's family.

"He wants me to go shopping with him
this weekend to help him pick out stuff on
his list."

Lark bit her tongue to keep from blurt-
ing some sarcastic remark. Typical of Lyle
to wait until nearly the last minute. Smugly,

she patted herself on the back for having already done her shopping. But she wouldn't comment on the small stuff. As long as Lyle didn't mess with the Christmas Day arrangement, she was happy.

"Who does he need to shop for?" she asked, pretending to be interested.

"I dunno. Probably everybody."

Evan spoke in as few words as possible, his aloof attitude typical for his age. But he didn't yet carry that cynical edge to his voice that so often characterized Lyle.

"Well, you'll have a good time. Enjoy the big festive crowds at the mall and all that."

"I'd rather ski."

"You'll be doing that, too, soon enough."

Lyle had planned a three-day ski trip during Christmas break, something she couldn't afford to give their son. At first she resented the goodies Lyle provided, and with such a casual attitude, too. But on the other hand, things like skiing up in central Wisconsin and camping during the summer made Evan feel as if his life wasn't so different from his friends' whose parents were still together.

"Do you ever think about ice-skating?" she blurted. "Do you remember when I took you out on the pond? You had brand-new skates."

He responded with a quick shrug. "Sort of."

"Okay, you didn't enjoy it very much," she admitted. "Maybe you were too young."

"Seems like a waste of time unless you're going to play hockey. We don't have hockey at school." He grinned and brushed his hair out of his eyes. "I don't like it, anyway."

"But skating itself is fun, Evan. There's nothing like building up speed on a stretch of ice."

He scrunched his face. "If you say so."

"Message received." She cast a sheepish grin Evan's way, aware it was time to back off. "But anytime you want to give it another try, you can rent skates at the pond."

"Okay."

That's as far as she was going to get. Not that it mattered. Opening up the topic was her substitute for sitting him down to tell him something big. Really big. A sister. What would he think of that? Probably not much, she admitted, at least at first.

As Lark's mind drifted to the future conversation she'd have with Evan, he said goodnight and gave her a quick wave, then went back into his room and shut the door. How *would* she announce the news that he had a half sister? She expected shock, maybe anger in response. He'd no doubt be embarrassed. Feel left out, displaced somehow? Maybe.

Before she talked to her son, though, the painful and risky conversation with Lyle loomed. Each time she started down that road in her mind, she shifted into Reverse and backed her way out of it. The exchange with Miles about their ex-spouses came back to her, especially his troubled expression when she explained why she'd kept that part of her past from Lyle. It was as if Miles had never considered using someone's vulnerabilities to his advantage.

Her buzzing phone yanked her back to the present. She smiled when she saw his name on the screen.

"It's not too late to call, I hope," Miles said.

"Not at all. I'm here with my feet up in the TV room watching a cable news show. Not concentrating too well, though." She pressed the power button and both the picture and the sound disappeared. "There, that's better."

"Can you talk?" he asked.

She got to her feet and walked through the

house to her bedroom. "I can now. I'm in my room, just shutting the door." Suddenly uneasy, she asked, "Do you have news?"

"No, no. Nothing like that. It's just that we haven't spoken in a couple of days, not since the lawyers and all that."

His voice was smooth, a radio voice. No wonder he was such a good professional speaker.

"Let me guess," she said. "You're mentally going over and over your conversation with Eric."

"Sort of. I understand him, so even though he was abrupt, I get it."

"I understood Maxine, maybe because she could identify with me, just as I could with her. But when Lisa-the-lawyer called a couple of days ago and was so terse on the phone, I resented her. Plain and simple." Knowing exactly how she'd sound, Lark plowed ahead, anyway. "And I wanted to tell her exactly what I thought about her so-called *conditions*."

"Whoa! But you do understand we have to stay away. Right?"

She heard apprehension in his voice. "Oh, don't take me so literally, Miles. You know a part of me wants to throw caution to the wind and all that."

"Lark—"

"Don't worry, I would do no such thing. I have a knee-jerk response to being lectured about anything, so I was a little irked by the attorney. She was so different from Maxine." She paused. "But she's just doing her job."

"Okay, then. You've convinced me." A muffled sound came through the phone.

"Did you just snicker?" she teased.

"More like a snort. A *little* irked, huh? I'll be sure not to bring up Lisa-the-lawyer again. I promise."

She hesitated, almost embarrassed to ask. "Look, you're the only person I can talk to about Perrie Lynn. Aren't you almost bursting, you know, wanting to shout the news to the world?"

"One step at a time, Lark."

"You really *are* logical," she said, laughing.

"So I'm told—and not always in such a nice tone."

Another awkward moment, Lark thought, because she had no light response to keep the banter going.

"I actually called to run something by

you," Miles said. "But it's probably too late. I mean, because you've already got Christmas plans."

"For Christmas Day," she said. "I take Evan to my brother's house."

"But Christmas Eve?"

"He goes to Lyle's family. Then he drives Evan to my brother's house in the morning."

"Oh, well, then, maybe we could have dinner together on Christmas Eve. What would you think of that?"

Lark grinned. Was she really excited at the prospect of seeing him again? She tried to moderate her tone a little when she said, "Sounds good. Did you have a place in mind?"

"Something close to you. Do you have a favorite restaurant in Two Moon Bay?"

She knew exactly where she wanted to go. "Since you asked, the Half Moon Café runs a Christmas Eve special buffet—roast beef to grilled salmon and everything to go with it. I could make a reservation. You wouldn't believe how many people—even big families—have dinner there on Christmas Eve."

"Sounds like a great idea," he said in an energized, upbeat voice. "Make the reservation. I think I know exactly where it is."

"Great. I'll send them a text as soon as we get off the phone," Lark said. "Meanwhile, I suppose I should get some rest."

"Yes, see you in a few days, then. Shall I pick you up?"

"No need, Miles. It's practically walking distance for me. I'll meet you there. So, 'bye for now."

Lark felt unreasonably happy. Their dinner, she wouldn't call it a date, was only four days away. She hadn't made a really fun plan for Christmas Eve in a long time. Virtually all her friends had family plans that packed the two days. Lark hunched her shoulders and clasped her hands in front of her chest. In a million years, she'd never have imagined having plans with Miles.

As she finished getting ready for bed and turned off both her phone and the light, she realized that when he'd suggested getting together for Christmas Eve, Perrie Lynn hadn't immediately come to mind. She looked forward to seeing Miles just for himself.

LARK HAD BEEN avoiding Dawn ever since the night of their double date. First, she'd begged off their regular coffee meeting, and then had answered a couple of texts with rapid-fire responses promising "more later." But when she saw Dawn's name appear on her phone, she knew she couldn't dodge her friend any longer.

"Hey…how are you? Sorry it's—"

"Save it, Lark. You're going to tell me it's been crazy and you're scheduled to the minute."

"Well, it's true," she said defensively.

"Do you have a minute now?" Dawn asked, exasperation coming through.

Lark checked her watch. Needlessly. She had no phone interviews that afternoon. "Sure."

"Good. Then tell me what's going on?"

"Uh, what do you mean?"

"Oh, please… I just talked to Chip, and he'd spoken with Bruce. What's this about a family issue that's suddenly come up? The reason you gave for not going out with him again."

"I can explain." She might have known something as simple as cutting things off with Bruce—before they even started—would get back to Dawn.

"But I thought you liked Bruce. What gives?"

"I did… I do. But something really has

come up and I can't get involved with anyone just now."

Silence on the other end.

She drummed her fingers on the desk, then
crossed and uncrossed her ankles. This was
no way to treat Dawn, who'd been a good
friend to her. "Uh, it's something kind of private." Maybe that would buy her some time.

"I don't mean to pry, Lark, but since when
do we keep secrets? Are you sick? Is there
some kind of diagnosis that you're not telling me about?"

"Uh…" The nerves in her gut tingled. Was
it fear? Apprehension? She didn't know, but
words wouldn't form.

"Well, okay. I get the message."

"No, no. Wait, Dawn. I *do* need to tell you
about this. But not on the phone. Can you
meet me this afternoon?"

"When and where?"

"Now. At the Bean Grinder." She tried to
keep a casual tone in her voice. "That will
give us time to talk before we have to pick
up the boys after practice."

"Okay. Like I said, I didn't want to pry, but
you've been putting me off for days."

"You're right. I *am* keeping secrets. One
secret. A big one. But it's not a bad diagno-

sis or anything like that. I'll tell you what's going on. But only you."

They agreed to meet in thirty minutes, which left little time for second-guessing herself. Just as well, because the instant Lark ended the call, she wanted to back out. She'd been silent so long it was difficult to come up with the right words to tell the story.

She ran a brush through her hair and gave her lips a quick once-over with fresh gloss. Looking in the mirror, she noted her pink cheeks. Probably flushed from stress, she mused. She'd been on high alert for a few days now.

When Lark arrived at the Bean Grinder, Dawn had already found a table for two and was absorbed in jotting notes in her thick day planner. Lark smiled at the reading glasses perched on the end of her nose. Their color, bright teal, was a perfect contrast to her strawberry blond hair.

Lark navigated her way around tables and chairs to join her, but didn't sit. After a quick glance around the crowded café, she knew they couldn't stay there.

"Let's take a walk first. Then we can come back and get coffee," Lark said, still standing next to the table. She nodded at the crowded room, silently communicating the lack of privacy.

At first, Dawn looked mildly miffed, but her expression instantly changed to concern. She packed her shoulder-bag-style attaché case and put on her coat.

"You were madly writing notes for something," Lark said, leading the way out the door and onto the sidewalk. "Is it urgent?"

"New client. The Party Perfect women want to start a major PR program after the first of the year. They're booked for the holidays, but they have holes in the schedule after Valentine's Day." Dawn leaned forward and whispered, "They offered a six-month retainer. With any luck they'll get so much coverage, they'll sign up for the rest of the year."

"Without question," Lark said, grinning. "You'll dazzle them with creative ideas, as usual." She pointed down the side street away from the waterfront park, where the Bean Grinder occupied an old but refurbished octagonal wooden building "Let's head that way, toward the winery. At least it will get us out of the wind."

"If you say so," Dawn said, pulling up the

collar of her coat. "It's such a perfect day for a stroll through town."

"I'm sorry," Lark said, meaning it, "but I should have thought about the café being crowded. It's critical that no one overhear what I have to tell you."

Dawn shook her head. "This must be some secret."

Lark closed her eyes and tilted her head back. "It is. Trust me. And I wasn't planning to talk about it. Yet."

Once they reached the Silver Moon Winery, Lark led them across the street to a small playground. On such a cold afternoon, no kids or parents were around. "We probably can't get much more isolated than this," she said.

Dawn frowned at the benches. "If the weather were different, I'd say we should sit, but not today."

Lark put her hand on Dawn's arm. "I don't know what I'm waiting for. And it's nothing you should worry about."

"That's reassuring," Dawn said, shifting her weight from one foot to another.

"It's about a baby, a girl. A girl who just had her eighteenth birthday." Tears pooled in her eyes but she blinked them back. "My baby."

Dawn slowly drew her into a hug. "You had a baby before Evan? That's what you're telling me?"

Lark nodded. "Before I met Lyle." She quickly filled in the background, including a quick sketch of Miles. "He's the one who alerted me about the possibility this girl is ours."

"And you know for certain she's the baby?" Dawn asked, lowering her arms and peering into Lark's face.

Lark smiled. It took less than thirty seconds to explain how she came to talk with Maxine on the phone. "Little coincidences piled up and here we are."

"You referred to her as 'this girl.' Are you afraid to tell me her name?"

She nodded. "I suppose I am. But since I've revealed this much, I'll tell you. As long as you promise—"

Dawn groaned. "Of course, I promise."

"Do you follow figure skating?"

With her forehead wrinkled in a frown, Dawn stared off in the distance as if considering her answer. "Not really, but I saw something about a young American skater who's rising really fast. It was on one of the news sites." Her eyes opened wide. "Is *she…?*"

Lark drew in a breath. "Yes. Perrie Lynn Olson. She's the rising star they're talking about. And her celebrity is precisely why Miles and I can't talk about her. We can't meet her now, either."

This time, when Dawn hugged her she added an extra squeeze. "Wow, wow, wow. That's all I can say."

Lark crossed her hands and pressed them against her chest. "But I'm so impatient. Miles keeps reminding me that we have no say about anything that happens next. The Olsons are in control."

Dawn tilted her head from side to side, considering the situation. "I guess that's true enough, and the way it should be, frankly. But I can understand why you're jumping out of your skin."

Lark laughed. "Thanks for understanding. Miles is being so calm, at least compared to me. But I feel better now that I've revealed my secret. Helps lessen the burden. You can understand why I can't think about Bruce and dating and all that. Even though I won't have a chance to meet Perrie Lynn for a long time—several months, if all goes well for her. She's a girl—a young woman—with a goal. With a steel spine, too, from the looks of it."

Lark grabbed Dawn's sleeve and turned around. "Back to the Bean Grinder. I'm ready for our latte, my friend. My treat. You've been so patient with my evasiveness."

"Good, I'm freezing out here," Dawn said, but with a happy lilt in her voice. "And by the way, you never mentioned Miles before. Was he important?"

Lark shrugged. "No, that's the thing. He was a good guy. Like me, he had some ambitions and was pretty serious about school. But he was fun, the type who liked to go out to see the bands that came to town. He was a great dancer, and so many other guys I dated weren't. But we both understood it was just fun and games. Casual college stuff." Lark stopped walking and stared into space. "That all went wrong, obviously."

"But what about now? Do you trust him? Do you *like* him?"

Lark smiled at the question. "It never occurred to me not to trust him." She explained what steps she'd taken with the adoption agency, all on her own. "My challenge was getting Miles to trust me. It was complicated. I figured he had a wife and a family."

"So he's married?" Dawn asked.

"He was, but it didn't last long—his little girl was only two when they separated. He spends a lot of time with her, though, which is how they happened to be watching the figure-skating competition on Sunday afternoon." She paused and took a few steps in silence. "To think, eighteen years ago, Miles and I were, for a brief hour or so, in the same building as the Olsons. And now, next year, I'll meet them."

"Have you thought much about Miles over the years?"

Good question, and with bigger implications than the simple words would imply. Did she think of him, or regret not working something out with him in order to keep their baby? "No, to tell you the truth I've barely thought about him all this time. I was focused entirely on the baby, Perrie Lynn." And asking herself why she hadn't kept her, why she hadn't made a plan.

"Perrie Lynn," Dawn repeated slowly. "Such a lovely name." She paused. "Did the Olsons choose it?"

Lark nodded. "I always wondered what

they'd decided to call her. Perrie Lynn could be a family name, I suppose. The Olsons took her home when she was only two days old. When the hospital released me, they released her." She smiled wistfully. "Miles and I agree that somehow, it's a perfect name for a skater."

"Hey, didn't you once tell me you skated as a kid?"

Lark chuckled and shook her head. "I did, briefly, and I loved it. But it wasn't figure skating. My mom used to drive me and a bunch of my friends to the outdoor rink. Sometimes we'd skate on the river for the eight or ten weeks a year when it was frozen solid." A wave of nostalgia hit hard. She hadn't thought about those days for years. "I used to win a few impromptu races. I'd hoped Evan would show some interest, maybe in speed skating or even hockey. But no, basketball is it—and chess. And now skiing."

When they got to the Bean Grinder, Lark put her hand on Dawn's arm before going inside. "When you asked about Miles, I didn't know exactly what to say. I can't really describe him, other than to say he's a really decent man." She stared down the street. "Back in college, we weren't in love or anything like that. But now that we're adults with kids and professional lives, he's made me wonder why I settled for Lyle."

Dawn let out a soft groan. "That's rough. And complicated."

"And kind of useless to dwell on." Lark playfully tugged on Dawn's sleeve. "So, now you'll tell me all about Party Perfect and your plans for them. Okay? You'll shush me up if I say one more word about me and my life."

"Hey, there's some work for you, too, my friend," Dawn said, moving toward the door. "These women are serious about expanding and hiring more staff. So, they want a party-planning handbook and some tip sheets for their clients. I told them I had a writer in mind."

"You're such a good friend," Lark said. "Even more reason the lattes are on me today."

When they'd placed their order and claimed a table, Dawn leaned forward in her seat. "One last question," she whispered. "When will you tell your parents and brother? What about Evan?"

Lark instinctively put her hand across her middle, as if trying to settle the powerful ripples of anxiety there. "I haven't decided how to approach any of my family, including Evan. Much less when. But for sure it won't be until I'm closer to actually meeting Perrie Lynn."

Dawn showed her skepticism with raised eyebrows. "Don't you think you should prepare everybody for this? Especially Evan."

"I will, but it has to be on my own timetable. And to tell you the truth, I don't care much about my parents' reaction. Dealing with Evan is much more important. Back when Miles and I were hanging out, my parents were fighting over everything, including custody of my brother. That's why I never seriously considered telling them I was pregnant, and I never mentioned Miles, either." She shrugged. "Besides, it's almost Christmas. I wouldn't drop something like this on any of them. Besides, it's risky to tell too many people—one slip and it could end up a media story."

"I get it," Dawn said with a supportive nod. "Who to tell, and when, is your call."

Lark stared out into the crowded café. "It's kind of odd how much I'm looking forward to seeing Miles on Christmas Eve."

"What?"

Lark chuckled. "I guess that sounded like

an afterthought. He called the other night and suggested it. We're going to the Half Moon for their special buffet."

Dawn leaned across the table and patted Lark's hand. "Well, well, well."

Lark put up her palm. "Stop. It's dinner. I'm sure we'll spend all our time talking about…" She glanced around the room. "You know."

Dawn rolled her eyes. "For once in your single life, *keep your heart open*."

Her impulse was to laugh dismissively, but her friend's earnest expression stopped her. Instead, Lark squared her shoulders and said, "Back to the party planners."

For the next half hour she gratefully detoured away from Perrie Lynn and Miles. By the time she and Dawn hurried to their cars to pick up their sons, the late-afternoon light was fading fast.

Lark maneuvered her car down the streets to the middle school and mentally prepared herself to deal with her son, who was becoming more temperamental as he neared his official teenage years. With arms and legs out of proportion to the rest of him, Evan was, Lark hoped, nearing the end of his awkward stage. Ah, probably wishful thinking.

Evan's turned-down mouth and frown warned her about his mood. He yanked open the car door in back and tossed his backpack inside. Then he settled into the passenger seat and grabbed the seat belt as easily as anybody in a puffy down jacket and heavy gloves could. He was hatless. She decided against mentioning it.

"What's up?" Lark asked, disheartened by his glum expression.

"Nothing. I'm just hungry." Evan jerked his head back and to the side, his futile attempt to get the hair out of his eyes.

"Grab a package of peanut-butter crackers out of the glove box." Lark clamped her lips together to avoid adding a comment about Evan's bangs. If Lyle hadn't insisted on being in charge of their son's haircuts, she'd have detoured to the quick-cut shop and solved the problem in ten minutes. *Not my concern.* She'd sworn off getting in the middle of the father-and-son battles over hair length. One day soon, none of it would matter and Evan would make his own decisions about the full head of light brown hair he'd inherited from her.

"What's for dinner?"

The perennial question.

Lark abruptly flipped the turn signal and maneuvered into the left lane. "Pizza. At Lou's."

"Really? How come?"

"No reason. I'm in the mood for a treat." She glanced at her son's face, a little more pleasant now. "You got a problem with that?"

At last, Evan laughed at her tough-guy tone. It was a real laugh, too, the kind that made her heart hum a little melody.

"No, as long as it has extra cheese and extra sausage, at least on *my* half."

"You're pushing it, I see."

Evan snickered. "I guess."

Lark pulled into the parking lot of Lou's, her favorite place for pizza since she was Evan's age. Walking inside, she studied his easy, loose-limbed gait. A couple of years ago, they'd stood shoulder-to-shoulder. Now he towered over her, and he wasn't yet thirteen.

A sense of excitement began to build. By the time they finished this ordinary event, ordering their large pizza with extra everything, Lark was nearly euphoric, ready to explode with a kind of joy she'd never experienced before. For the first time in eighteen years, she knew for certain that *both* her children were taken care of, safe and deeply loved.

CHAPTER EIGHT

MILES HADN'T PREDICTED Andi's response.

"You must be kidding." She let her weight fall back against her kitchen counter and—with conviction—swept her long dark hair off her shoulder so it hung straight down her back. "It was *that* easy to find her?"

Odd, Miles thought, observing her behavior. She seemed impatient with the news, not at all curious. "Of course I'm not kidding, but for the time being, you're the only person I've told about this new, well, I'll call it a new development."

Her guttural sound of frustration filled the kitchen. "You picked a great time to throw this at me. It's almost Christmas, you know."

What did Christmas have to do with anything? "First, I didn't plan it, and I'm not throwing anything at you," he said, annoyed that his news was greeted as an inconvenience. "You still are the only person in my life who knows about Lark and the baby."

"And the last time that subject came up was over ten years ago," Andi said dismissively.

"I didn't plan this. Lark and I just learned who and where she is."

"Lark? You refused to tell me her name way back when." With her arms folded tightly across her chest, Andi's stance had escalated to frank resentment.

"Yes, I did. It was a privacy thing—it still is." He didn't like having to defend that decision, especially when it didn't matter anymore. "She's Lark McGee, a writer who lives with her twelve-year-old son in Two Moon Bay."

Earlier that day, he'd assumed this would be a good time to see Andi and talk through any issues that might come up. Brooke was in school and Andi had half a day off. He'd told the story right up to his conversations with Eric and, later, the lawyer, Lisa. Andi's attitude was the opposite of what he'd expected.

"What is it that's bothering you so much about this?" he asked. "Are you worried about Brooke? I can assure you—"

"You can assure me of nothing," she interrupted. "Of course I'm concerned about Brooke. How are you going to explain it?

She's eight! And she's already superaware of the girl. That skater is practically a celebrity."

As if he hadn't considered all that himself. He'd thought of little else. Well, except for Lark. And their upcoming Christmas Eve dinner. She'd been a presence in his head, filling his days—and his nights.

"I'm not saying it will be easy, Andi."

"You have to admit that this girl's fame is going to complicate things." Andi pulled out a stool at the breakfast bar across from Miles. "Won't Brooke think you're going to favor Perrie Lynn? She's not like other girls. She's a princess who floats on ice in sparkly little dresses."

"You're traveling way ahead on this." He extended his arm in front of him to indicate distance. "We have no idea that she's going to actually want to meet us. We won't even have a chance to meet her for months."

"*We? Us?* What's that supposed to mean? You and Brooke?"

"No, Andi, I'm referring to Lark and me." Her terse tone had thrown him completely. "Tell me what's going on? This isn't like you. No matter what happened between us in the past, we've always talked things out. You seem genuinely angry with me."

Miles didn't want to bring up mistakes of the past, but her impulsive marriage to Roger hadn't been a cakewalk for Brooke. Somehow, though, they'd even survived that with their goodwill intact. Eventually, the dust settled and they'd put it behind them.

"Yes and no," she said, finally offering an exasperated smile. "It's just that two days ago, I learned that I'll be laid off within the next year—no one can tell me exactly when. A major health-care consortium bought the practice. They're bringing in their own people." She shrugged. "So that's that. I hate the idea of looking for another job. I'm going to start cutting expenses now, and prepare for a long job search."

"I'm really sorry to hear that." He meant it. "You've always liked your job, and you never mentioned something like this on the horizon." Andi had spent years managing health-care practices, starting at a small chiropractic group and then moving into bigger settings. She'd been the practice manager of a regional women's health center. It had to be a blow and he'd try to soften it. "It may be small comfort, Andi, but I'm doing okay right now. I can pick up some expenses. I'll start by covering all of Mamie's hours. You tell me what else you need."

She nodded, and offered a faint smile—at last.

"Is there anything about Perrie Lynn and Brooke we need to address now, you know, right before Christmas?" she asked.

"No, no." He waved off her concern. "If Perrie Lynn makes the International team and then goes on to the world championships, it will be spring before the Olsons will even talk with her about Lark and me."

Andi plunked her elbow on the counter and rested her chin in her palm "I can't believe you've actually spoken with them. And they aren't trying to keep you away—like maybe forever?"

The old Andi was coming back. He saw it in her relaxed posture and an almost light tone. "Years ago, they promised to help find her birth parents when she turned eighteen. Knowing Lark's name just hastened the process. But I don't want you to worry about this at all, especially now."

Andi dragged her hand down her cheek. "Get real—anything that affects Brooke is bound to worry me. But thanks for the shoulder to lean on over my job." She stared into the room, suddenly lost in thought.

"What is it?" he asked.

"Nothing important. But it seems so long ago that you told me about what happened with Lark. Remember? We were having a drink before going to a Packer game." Andi flashed a playful smirk. "You were so nervous you could barely get the words out. But over the years I more or less forgot about it."

Miles nodded. "It didn't dominate my life, either. I ran into Lark at the mall once when Brooke was turning three. She had her young son with her." He snickered. "Even Lark agrees it wins a prize for awkward conversations."

"That was such a chaotic time in *our* lives," Andi said, shaking her head. "I don't look back at those days often."

Miles knew she was embarrassed not only by her quick demand for a divorce, but also by her superfast remarriage. Ironic, too, because she'd claimed that she didn't like being married, end of story. That was the reason for their breakup, or so she'd insisted. It had nothing to do with him. She simply *needed* to be single again.

"How has Lark fared over these years?" Andi asked.

"She's managed her life pretty well. Went on and became a writer, which was her dream back in college. But she kept her secret. Never told even one person."

"Except her husband, I assume."

Miles supplied an abbreviated version of what Lark had told him about Lyle. "She didn't feel safe enough with him to reveal that part of her past," he said, sad all over again when he imagined Lark so fearful.

"She was smart." Andi narrowed her eyes, as if considering her words carefully. "A guy like that? Oh, yeah, he would have found a way to hurt her with it."

"That's what she said." Miles slipped off the stool and put on his jacket. The last thing he wanted to do was get into a back-and-forth about Lyle's bad qualities, although it was tempting. But Miles was still stinging from his own failures—specifically, that he'd let Lark down eighteen years ago.

"Do you still like her?"

He jerked his head back. He hadn't expected that question, especially delivered in such a soft tone. "Of course. She's a terrific person. She's worked hard to raise her son and put a good life together, despite her marriage falling apart."

Andi laughed. "Oh, Miles, you always were a little dense."

Getting her meaning, albeit late, he felt the rising heat on his face. At least his olive skin didn't easily turn pink.

"Ah, I get it. You *do* like her. Oh, brother. And here I thought it was only your grown-up daughter that complicated things."

"There's nothing between Lark and me," he insisted, although his mind flashed on the airline tickets to Boston he'd booked online, along with the hotel reservations he'd made only hours ago. His surprise for Lark. If it didn't backfire. "The possibility Perrie Lynn is our daughter is the only reason we saw each other."

"It's okay to like her, Miles." Once again, Andi spoke in a low voice.

She means it…take it for what it is.

He grinned and opened the door. "Let me know if you need anything." He paused. "And don't worry about Brooke."

She responded with a familiar mock groan. "Oh, sure, and maybe I won't breathe, either."

When no quick comeback popped into his head, he let himself out. After pulling away from Andi's house he headed to the YMCA to keep his commitment to put in an hour on the treadmill. He could work out at home, but he was jumpy and needed the distraction of people. Christmas Eve was only two days away.

CHAPTER NINE

MILES PICKED UP the wine list, grinning as he pointed to the cover. The bright half moon stood out against a star-flecked midnight blue background. "This town never misses a chance to play on its name, does it?"

"Two Moon Bay is a great address for my business," Lark remarked. "I get dozens of questions about the town, especially since I live on Night Beach Road. It's like the magic of the place never quits."

Another round of small talk, Lark mused, not unlike the day at Hugo's. They'd talked on the phone nearly every day, almost as if checking in had become routine. But this was only the second time they'd been together. And, of all times, on Christmas Eve.

"I can't stop mulling over how easily we found Perrie Lynn," Miles said, putting the wine list aside. "In a way, Maxine and Eric found us."

"Not all adoptive parents are so at ease

with their children's search for their birth parents." Lark had understood that reality from the start. "When I began building my freelance business, I placed a couple of parenting pieces with the *Milwaukee Journal*, and then the editor called one day to see if I'd accept an assignment for a three-part series on adoption in Wisconsin." She closed her eyes and sighed. "Objectively, it was the kind of call I'd been hoping for. I can't recall what excuse I used to refuse, but the anxiety gripping me sent me a clear message. I could never be a just-the-facts journalist or even a detached analyst on adoption. No way."

Miles nodded, but his features pinched as if he were surprised by a puzzling thought. "From what I've read, some parents are like the Olsons and discuss their kids' need to search. It's an open topic. But some parents are devastated—deeply hurt—by their children's desire to find birth parents."

"And you can bet I had all those angles in mind when I formed my own plan to search." She heard the note of irony in her laugh.

Miles's troubled expression made her want to swallow back her words. It was true she harbored resentment at the casual way he seemed to have moved on. But it was unfair to keep getting in digs at him.

"Forget I said that," she said, reaching over to touch his hand. It was meant to be a quick conciliatory gesture, but Miles immediately covered her fingers with his.

"I let you down before," he said, "so I understand why you didn't include me in your plans."

"It's not fair to say you did something wrong."

"Doesn't matter whether it's fair or not. This unspoken thing between us makes me hold back. I find myself overthinking everything I say."

The waitress appeared at the table to take their drink order and Lark was grateful for the interruption. But no matter the sensitive subject, she couldn't deny that she'd enjoyed the sensation of Miles's warm palm on her hand.

They quickly agreed to share a bottle of the featured merlot. "I think you'll like the buffet," Lark said, keeping the mood light, "but save room for dessert."

Miles chuckled. "So, no heavy topics during dinner. But Lark, really, we need to talk about what this next year will bring, but we can't do that until we resolve this barrier between us."

Lark groaned. "Why can't you be like the typical guy who runs for the hills when anything even remotely involving feelings comes up."

"Well, Ms. McGee, like it or not, communication is my business." He grinned. "We're actually in the same field, you and I."

"Okay, okay… I get it." But she wasn't ready to delve into her own feelings right now, so she changed the subject. "There is something I wanted to talk to you about. For quite a long time now, I've been doing research on young athletes—particularly how many of them overtrain."

"Are you suggesting that Perrie Lynn—"

"No, no, not at all," she interrupted. "Most of the data come from boys who are encouraged to bulk up for sports like football and wrestling. But their bodies aren't ready for the weight training. According to my research, skaters, especially the boys, tend to start training for the triple and quadruple jumps too early. I guess I'm also interested because Evan plays basketball."

"I think there's a potential for overtraining in any sport. Andi worries about Brooke and her soccer, but she figures the benefits outweigh the risks."

Lark nodded. "That's the consensus among pediatricians. Since most kids won't become elite athletes, overtraining isn't a risk. But it got me thinking about Perrie Lynn."

Miles cast an amused smile her way. "You're also a concerned mom, just like Andi. She keeps up with any research related to raising kids. I'll bet she's come across some of your articles—you've done a lot of writing for the major dailies."

"I've done a few articles."

"More than a few," he teased. "Quit being modest." The waitress came back with the merlot and filled their glasses, and when she walked away Miles held up his wine. "First, a toast."

"To the New Year," she said, touching her glass to his.

"And to a very *long* competitive season for Perrie Lynn," Miles added.

Rather than breaking the toast, he kept his glass pressed against hers, a gesture so intimate she couldn't speak.

"Do I dare toast the Internationals?" he asked.

"Go ahead, live dangerously," she said.

"To the Internationals, then."

She smiled and nodded. "To Perrie Lynn and the Internationals."

Only then did they separate their glasses and each take a sip.

"I think of her more as a dancer than an athlete," Miles said, "even though I know better."

Lark closed her eyes, suddenly overtaken with the image of Perrie Lynn crossing the rink with her leg extended in a dazzling arabesque. "I get a little thrill when commentators and bloggers use the word *artistry* to describe Perrie Lynn's strengths. I realize her technical skills come from years of practice and determination, but I know deep inside me that Perrie Lynn's grace comes from within."

"I couldn't have said it better myself." Miles's voice shook and his eyes moistened.

The air buzzed around Lark's head in that shared moment.

Still light-headed, Lark looked away and took another sip of wine. Finally, she said, "I'm hungry, and it's time you got a taste of this spectacular food."

Miles silently followed her to the elegant buffet, where they filled their plates with grilled salmon and slices of rare roast beef and roasted vegetables shaped and arranged by someone with a flair for presentation.

"Good choice, Lark," Miles said. "The hotel food I get on the road doesn't measure up."

"Neither does the food I throw together at home," Lark said with a hoot. "Evan thinks pizza from Lou's here in town is the pinnacle. I score Mom points whenever we go there."

Halfway through dinner, Lark was struck by how much she enjoyed hearing about Miles's work with companies, and his belief in collaboration and team building. The way he talked about his work showed her how much the young man had grown into the career he'd dreamed of. His genuine interest in her work hadn't waned over the past week, either. The contrast with her ex-husband was stark.

At first, Lyle had considered her writing a harmless pastime. He'd joke about it, oblivious to the insult. Writing kept her out of the malls, so her little hobby didn't cost him. Then, when money started coming in regularly, he claimed her writing business was a lazy way out of finding a real job. After their divorce, he'd joked with Evan about having a "starving artist" mother. It was outrageous, but she'd forced herself not to overreact and create an opening for Lyle to play with their finances or custody arrangements.

Lark pushed away those thoughts and focused on what Miles was saying about their work sometimes overlapping. He gave presentations about morale and burnout, and she'd written articles about the ways stress at work caused trouble in marriages and families.

They talked shop all the way through dinner and generous squares of raspberry torte. Finally, Miles refilled their coffee cups from the carafe the waitress had left on the table. He wore both a faint smile and a faint frown as he settled back against the cushioned booth seat.

"You look serious. Pensive." Lark knew what was coming, or thought she did.

"I have a lot on my mind," he said, leaning forward again. "I realized that although we weren't close back in college, you never questioned my ambition about becoming a professional speaker. Most everyone else did. Especially my family. They didn't see how I could take a major in psychology and a minor in business and eventually earn a living presenting seminars or giving speeches. It seemed much too risky to my parents. But I remember thinking that being a writer was something you *could* achieve. And all these years later we're both doing what we love."

Lark shrugged. "I never doubted your ability to get what you wanted. For me, though, wandering around Dublin gave me some healing space away from my family drama. I came back believing I had a future as a writer. My lowly job as an assistant in the newspaper office up in Sturgeon Bay was a start."

Miles rested his forearms on the table. "I'm glad to hear that. But speaking of family drama, it won't be long before we have to talk to our families about what's going on. Andi knows, but no one else."

She let her shoulders slump. "Oh, boy, another happy thought. I'm really not that worried about my parents or my brother, mainly because I don't much care what they think. I've gone my own way most of my life. It's Evan, and to a lesser extent Lyle, who give me anxious thoughts."

Miles nodded. "Speaking of anxious, I've been thinking about the way I felt years ago after I left you in Minnesota, took my finals in Stevens Point, and then drove home. Every minute I was in my parents' house over Christmas break, my hands shook, my stomach churned. I even lost weight."

Puzzled, Lark said, "I don't understand."

"Let's just say I was pretending all the time." He moved one hand in a rolling motion as he spoke. "'Miles took his finals, Miles opened a gift box holding a silk necktie, Miles hugged Aunt Rosa and shook hands with Uncle Art.' Inside, I was jumpy, fearful that I'd be found out. It was irrational, but it wasn't until I was back for my last semester that I stopped looking over my shoulder."

"And I was safely tucked away in Ireland. Safe from myself, anyway."

Miles frowned at her and tilted his head, as if expecting her to elaborate.

Rejecting the option to say nothing, she rushed her words. "Having an ocean between Minnesota and me kept me from acting on the urge to go bang on the door of the agency and shout that I'd changed my mind. I wanted my baby back."

A flicker of pain crossed Miles's eyes. This was the emotional point where they truly had gone their separate ways.

Lark reached out and put her hand on his forearm. "It was a beautiful dinner, Miles. But let's leave now." An idea came to her. Something to lighten the mood. It would give them privacy if the big talk was coming. "If you're up for a walk, I know a lovely place we can go. We can come back for our cars later. But I don't want to finish this conversation here."

Miles swallowed hard, but didn't look away. "You're right. Let's go."

"I'M EAGER TO know where this walk is going to take us," Miles said, buttoning his coat. He smiled down at Lark, whose hair was tamed in some kind of twist. But she seemed vulnerable, even deceptively delicate in her high-heel boots. As he followed her out the door, he was struck that she looked so different from that morning they'd met at Hugo's, but equally pretty and appealing.

Lark tilted her head back and pointed to the sky. "It's actually a beautiful night. Not too cold and a nearly full moon. And you'll like where we're going." She led the way down a side street, where houses were decked out with elaborate holiday lights. "By the way, just to be clear, going off to Ireland was one of the best decisions I've ever made. It kept me from making some big mistakes. In a way it saved my life."

"Wow." The pressure in his chest spoke of the intensity of emotion behind Lark's words. "That's a strong statement."

She stepped around a not-quite-frozen puddle on the sidewalk. He offered his hand in case she wanted support, but she ignored it, apparently preferring to navigate the sidewalk in her spiky, heeled boots on her own. Like she'd done everything else. She was good at taking care of herself. But then again, so was he.

"What I said is one-hundred-percent true," Lark responded in a low voice. "Most of the time the urge to get our baby back lived inside me on a low-level frequency. But every now and again I thought I'd burst out of my skin with regret." She let out a long sigh. "That's why being so far away allowed me to gradually get used to the idea that I *could* move ahead. At least I pretended to tuck thoughts of the baby away in some category of my brain labeled 'safely handled.'"

They strolled past a large brick house all but obscured by white lights. A Christmas tree also decorated with only white lights stood in the center of the bay window. A man and a woman were moving around in the living room. Presumably content? Maybe. Miles knew that unhappiness, even misery, could be hidden behind the perfect facade. He and Andi had played that game.

"Are you saying you didn't worry about her being well taken care of by her new parents?" Miles asked.

"I wouldn't go that far. For all the angst I had about the whole experience, I've always had faith in the agency, I guess. Why do you ask? Were you worried about her well-being?"

Stopping to stare at the brightly lit house, Miles grunted. "No. It's embarrassing to admit how little I thought about her. The whole experience, really, start to finish. Once I got through Christmas break, that is."

"You mean you were relieved, right?"

"It always comes back to that. You believe my dominant feeling was *relief*. Not regret or sadness."

"Okay, Miles, if that's not true, then convince me otherwise."

The strength of her voice startled him. He swallowed past a heavy lump in his throat. "I can't. Because you're right. I felt profound relief over escaping something that would have completely changed the course of my life. Even worse, I didn't want to lose my parents' respect. That's why I didn't tell them, and why I was so jittery over the holiday break when I couldn't avoid spending time with them."

He stared at a cluster of small spruce trees in the next front yard. No lights, no holiday transformation. "And I always knew I could keep it secret. At least in those early years I didn't regret or even second-guess our decision."

There it is, Lark...it's the best I can do.

"Thank you for being honest," she said, starting off down the street.

If she wanted silence for the moment, then he'd give it to her. They passed one house and then another and another.

"Winter in Ireland was a lot like the weather we've had lately," she said. "Damp, chilly, but not so very cold. I walked a lot and fell in with a crowd of students in the various arts programs. It was the first time I didn't have the voices of Mom and Dad reminding me about the practical stuff, you know, like making a living."

With a soft laugh, she pointed to the turret of a house across the street. "Mom used to warn me about having my head in the clouds, and being satisfied with living in an attic somewhere and filling journals and notebooks with my golden words." She shook her head. "Both my parents think my little cottage is equivalent to that attic—charming, but impractical."

Ridiculous. "For what it's worth, *I* think your cottage is wonderful. It reflects who you are and what you value most. Evan will see that one day."

She laughed. "You promise?"

"I wish I could make that promise." He hesitated. "I wish a lot of things."

Now it was her turn to stop. "What do you mean?"

He wasn't sure if what he was about to say was a true regret, but it had been on his mind for a while. It was right that he finally voiced it. "I wish I had *seriously* considered a plan to keep the baby."

"And why didn't you?"

He exhaled. "Because I wanted the problem to go away."

"Well, that's the point, isn't it? If not, I would have found a way to keep her, instead of just fantasizing about doing it. I'd have done it whether you wanted her or not." Her voice was hoarse when she added, "That's why when it was way too late I wanted to pound on the agency's door and demand her back. I never felt totally right with my decision."

She began walking again, obviously eager to get to wherever she'd chosen as their destination.

"Every once in a while I imagine what might have happened if I had done that," Lark said. "But now, this last week, I think of the great life Perrie Lynn has had. Who am I to believe I'd have done as well?"

"But you would have found a way to do a great job," Miles said, surprised by his emphatic insistence. "With or without me."

"I appreciate the vote of confidence, but at some point I had to at least try to make peace with myself. But I never forgot her."

"And you think I did. That's the crux of it. Right? The critical point."

She waved her hand across the street toward a row of lights. "Where we're headed is up ahead. You can see the lights."

Hmm…she hadn't answered the question. But then, he'd hedged his own response. It would be wrong to say that he'd forgotten their child, but neither was she at the front of his mind every day.

As they approached the lights, their formation made sense. He laughed out loud. "It's a skating rink. That's where you've brought me."

"I used to skate here as a kid." She pointed across the fence. "The warming shed is over there next to a concession stand, but both buildings are probably closed tonight."

He nodded to a couple skating hand-in-hand. "That didn't keep those skaters away."

A white wooden fence surrounded the rink, along with trees spiraled with fairy lights. "We can watch from here," she said, resting her elbows on the top of the fence. "Once Evan made it clear skating wasn't his thing, I never gave this rink much thought. And now, here I am, going to the internet to watch clips of skating competitions. I can even tell you all about the origin of the Biellmann spin."

"You can, huh?" Miles was getting eager to pop his surprise, but it was too early. They still had ground to cover.

"Tell me one more thing. If you weren't thinking about our baby every day, I get that. But where did she fit into your life and memories as the years passed?"

He let the question hang in the air until he slowly exhaled, ready to answer. "She receded into a kind of hazy background, at least until Brooke was born. As her birth approached, I became increasingly nervous. I was terrified something would go wrong."

She laid her hand on his arm. "Was it a superstitious feeling that you'd be punished?"

"Probably. I tried not to analyze it. But once Brooke arrived, I was overwhelmed. Our baby receded from my mind again. Then, less than two years later, Andi wanted—demanded—a divorce." Miles shook his head thinking back on those chaotic days. "Mere months after it was final, she remarried a really unreliable guy, and divorced him less than a year later. Meanwhile, I got the opportunity to be Daddy. Perrie Lynn's birthdays were always *odd* days. But I have to admit that she stopped being real to me much of the time."

"Ah, a sense that it never happened?"

"More or less. Did that ever happen—"

"No, if that's what you're asking. It never happened for me. She was all too real."

"All the more reason you could have reached out to me," Miles insisted, "like maybe on her birthday. Why didn't you?"

"Oh, please, Miles. Be honest. Would you

have welcomed such a call?" She mimed putting a phone to her ear. "'Hi, Miles, just wanted to talk about the baby we gave away. Hope I'm not bothering you in your new life.'"

He raised his hands in a defensive motion. "Okay. Enough. I get the message."

"You know I'm right. We had to go our separate ways."

But he didn't believe that was completely true. "Let's just say, I wouldn't have ignored you if you'd tried to reach out. We could have found a time and place to talk in private."

He glanced down and watched Lark's gaze following the couple taking yet another turn around the rink. The two glided with easy grace on the ice, their movements smooth, synchronized. She couldn't take her eyes off them.

"To contact you would also have forced me to admit I hadn't moved on. I was full of bitterness and angry with myself. Why hadn't I made a different decision? Maybe if my parents hadn't been in such a horrible crisis, I would have told them, gone home, kept the baby. Maybe I should have asked you to help me."

"But I didn't step up." He hated thinking

about the obligatory things he'd said to let her know he'd manage to adjust if she kept the baby. But looking back he judged himself a coward. "*This* is what needs to be said, Lark. You couldn't lean on me or even involve me much in your decision. I didn't give you that option."

"You're right," she said, not looking at him. "From the minute I confirmed I was pregnant, I knew I was more or less on my own. Sure, you did all the *decent* things. Helped with the bills, were with me during labor and all that. But you didn't want her. But then, neither did I—at the time."

She didn't fill in the blank, leaving him to speculate what had changed as time passed.

"I'm sorry I didn't reassure you that I'd help you raise her. I'll regret that until I take my last breath."

Lark nodded slowly, her gaze cast down. "I don't mean to hand off all the blame to you. Like any major decision, the consequences are complicated. Whenever regret threatens to overwhelm me, I remind myself that if I'd made a different choice, I might not have married Lyle and had Evan. Regardless of the mismatch with Lyle, I can't imagine life without my son."

"Yes," Miles said, nodding, "I get that."

"I also consoled myself with the notion that whoever adopted her had been longing for a child, likely not able to have their own baby." Lark sighed as she shook her head. "I'll never forget how horrified I was, not just scared, but *horrified* to learn I was pregnant."

"You seemed resigned by the time you told me," Miles said, recalling the sick feeling that had come over him. Initially he'd been pleased to see her at his door, but as soon as she'd blurted out "I'm pregnant," he'd had no idea what to say. The first words out of his mouth had been "What do you plan to do?"

But he and Lark had already been over that ground. He didn't want to cover it again.

The damp wind picked up. Lark tightened her scarf around her neck. They'd need to walk back to their cars soon, but he still had his so-called surprise.

Staring at the skaters on the ice, she said, "In the end, Miles, I've tormented myself with what-ifs and might-have-beens, but I usually quickly circle back to the notion that I—we—did the right thing. The Olsons wanted a child. All these years, that's what got me through and lifted some of the pain."

He touched her shoulder. "I'm sorry you've been haunted by this—and I will always regret not stepping up at the time. You have to believe me."

She lightly tugged at the fabric of his coat with her gloved fingers. "I do." She dropped her hand. "There's more we could hash through, but I don't see the point now. I'm just glad, really glad, both of us had a chance to have a family."

"Me, too." In a dry tone he added, "Even if the marriage part didn't work out so well."

"You can say that again."

Her smile was back. It was time. "Uh, I know you're getting cold, but before we call it a night, there's something I want to ask you. Nothing bad." He laughed. "I'm nervous like a kid. Actually, it's something good."

She cocked her head. "Well, then, out with it."

He reached into the inside pocket of his coat. "Being an optimist at heart, I went ahead and did this without asking you first. I'm hoping you can make it work with your schedule." He opened a folded paper and handed it to her. "It's dark, I know, but the paper is the email confirmation for two tickets to the North American Figure Skating

Competition next month. It involves four days in Boston."

She studied the paper and then pressed it to her chest. "You mean we'd get to see Perrie Lynn skate? Live?"

"That's right. And I've booked our flights and two hotel rooms. But if you can't go—"

"Oh, I can go," she interrupted. "I'll find a way. Lyle can keep Evan for an extra day or two or we'll switch weekends or something." She glanced at the paper again. "But, Miles, would being there at the event violate our agreement with the Olsons?"

He shook his head. "No, no. I thought of that. I booked seats that are about as high in the arena as you can get. We're staying in a hotel more than a block down the street." He explained that the tickets covered all the major events, so they'd see the pairs' competition and the ice dancers, too.

"This is fantastic!" She laughed and threw her arms around him for a quick hug. "I can't believe it. We'll be hidden from view, but we'll be there to see her compete. Ha!"

Not knowing Lark's financial situation, he wanted to clarify that he was paying for the whole trip. "I took a chance because I wanted it to be a surprise, but the tickets are refundable if it turned out you couldn't go. I wouldn't have gone to the competition without you."

"Are you sure, Miles? I can pay my way. Really."

"Absolutely not. As it happens, I have to be in Boston for work right after the event. Your flight home leaves on Monday, but I don't come back for another couple of days."

"Well, well. Merry Christmas, Miles!" She tilted her head back and laughed with joy.

One-hundred-percent satisfied he'd made a good choice, Miles exhaled the breath he'd been holding and laughed along with her.

CHAPTER TEN

WHEN LARK LET herself in the unlocked door of her brother Dennis's house on Christmas morning, Evan was already explaining the rules of the board game Candy Land to his five-year-old twin cousins, Jillie and Jerry. Actual names, Jillian and Jeremiah. Wanting to capture the adorable moment, Lark pulled out her phone from her jacket pocket and took a shot of the scene. One of the qualities she most cherished in Evan was his kindness to kids younger than himself, at school and in the family. No one had ever accused him of being a bully or mean. Knock wood.

Before joining the rest of the family in the kitchen, she couldn't resist checking her phone. Another text from Miles. She'd expected it, though. She'd sent him a thank-you text last night after she'd come home and settled at the window in her office to watch the moon's wavy reflection on the water. Mostly she contemplated her own Christmas miracle, a chance to see, if not meet, her grown-up child. He'd texted right back. She'd sent another before she left the house that morning and now he'd replied. Fun, she thought, this communication. But it was odd, too, in a way. Texting, going off to Boston. More shared secrets.

On the other hand, Christmas Day or not, by dawn she'd been at her desk composing a pitch for a piece on overtraining child athletes for one of the online parenting sites she wrote for. Later, she'd set up phone interviews with a couple of skating coaches on the junior circuit to legitimize her trip, and she'd already compiled a list of pediatricians known to be outspoken on concussion risks in youth sports.

"How did it go last night, Evan?" she asked as she unloaded her tote bag and tucked the gifts under the tree. She and Evan had exchanged their presents yesterday before she'd dropped him off at Lyle's house. She and her son preferred a private time with just the two of them. His gift list had been easy, the main item an obscure video game based on chess strategy. He'd also asked for a book of photographs showing the art of chess sets through the ages. Evan had given her a red-and-black hand-dyed scarf from a local international boutique. He'd learned a few years back that anything from that store was a winning gift.

Evan looked up from the game to answer her question. "Fine, good. Grandma Sharon said to say hello."

She wasn't surprised her former mother-in-law, Sharon, would pass on greetings. Only her father-in-law, Lyle Senior, blamed her for the demise of the marriage to his son. Lyle's dad would have liked Lark much better if she'd been an ornament in the corner, content to be seen and most definitely not heard. Because she had no such inclination, he'd eyed her suspiciously from the beginning.

Lark wandered into the kitchen, where the adults were hanging out, enjoying coffee and her sister-in-law's homemade Swedish coffee bread spread thick with butter. Donna, one of Lark's favorite family members, had brought her Scandinavian traditions into a family eager to accept them.

"I followed my nose," Lark said to Donna as she cut off a chunk of the coffee bread. "I arrived just in time, Dennis. You've already eaten half of your wife's mouthwatering creation."

"What do you expect?" her brother said, grinning.

After adding a layer of softened butter and taking a quick bite, Lark moved a few feet to stand alongside her mother, who was dressed, as usual, in clothes she could have bought from the teen shops at the mall—in the 1990s. The too-tight jeans had rhinestone-studded pockets, and her off-the-shoulder fluffy pink sweater was embellished with half a dozen cats made of silver sequins. Lark had inherited her light brown hair, but Cora had long ago decided blondes really did have more fun, and her now yellowish hair was fixed in her signature beehive.

Lark called a halt to her inventory of her mom's fashion transgressions, except to wonder how she managed to walk in five-inch pink heels. *Give it a rest, Lark.* She knew perfectly well she ought to be used to these quirks, and besides, her mother was an endlessly fun grandma to the kids.

"So sorry we couldn't have lunch, darling," Cora said, "but we were busier than we ever imagined and short-staffed, too."

"Maybe this coming week we can schedule something." For Lark, the days between Christmas and the first week or two of January usually meant organizing her office and preparing for what she hoped would be a wave of new work. "The pace won't get too crazy again for a little while."

"No business problems, I hope," Dennis said.

"Not at all." Lark wasn't bothered by her brother's remark. Like everyone else in her family, he'd been skeptical of her ability to make a go of a full-time writing business. At first he and her parents seemed to study her from a distance, as if waiting for her to fail. Given the years of ugly battles in their family, the irony that her brother became a family therapist wasn't lost on Lark. Currently on the counseling staff at the largest health-care group in the region, Dennis hoped to soon go into private practice and had recently told Lark she was his role model for establishing a business.

The adults took their coffee into the living room, where the twins were still under Evan's spell. The game set aside, Evan was now helping the kids assemble a pretend town in a corner of the living room, starting with Jerry's wooden schoolhouse and Jillie's zoo, complete with brightly painted animals and habitats.

Dennis clapped his hands to get everyone's attention before announcing that it was time for another round of presents. Lark reached under the tree and pulled out Evan's wrapped gifts for his cousins—matching sets of colored pencils, crayons, coloring books and plain drawing pads. "Okay, kids, let the fun and games begin!"

As the twins tore the paper off their collection of art supplies, Lark scanned the room and looked at the adult faces, all fixed on the little kids. Her stomach tightened in mild anxiety thinking about next year, when Evan would know he had a half sister. If all went well he'd likely have met her. Her mother would soon learn she had a grandchild older than Evan. Cora might easily accept Lark's decision to keep a secret, but Lark was certain her mother would be sad about being deprived of watching another granddaughter grow up.

Would her dad, and perhaps Dennis, too, be willing to jump back in time and remember the anger and chaos that had once defined their family? Or, would they judge Lark harshly? Paradoxically, it was both sad and advantageous they weren't a particularly close family. It made it easy to care very little about what her family thought of her decisions.

Pushing speculation about future Christmases to the back of her mind, Lark focused on the giggling twins opening boxes of crayons and begging Evan to color with them. Pretending to be put upon by their demands, he picked up one of their new coloring books and began to thumb through it while they sat on either side of him. Lark followed his actions with her phone and got another perfect holiday shot.

MILES DECIDED TO call late on Christmas night. Brooke was asleep and he was restless after the frenzy of his visit with his parents and his sister, April, and her family. He had a hunch Lark would understand the paradox of wanting to be with his family, but also feeling more than ready to leave when the visit wound down. She picked up his call on the second buzz.

"A call this time, not a text," she said with a laugh.

"Yes, it's time for a conversation. But I enjoyed your timeline—arriving at your brother's house, leaving and heading to your dad's place in Sturgeon Bay…then home."

"And I got a kick out of the rundown of your day, too," she said. "Truthfully, I'm awfully glad to be home."

"Why is that?"

"Uh, well, I don't know exactly. I haven't analyzed why it felt good to pull into my driveway with Evan. Maybe it was such a long day. Something like that."

"It wasn't a trick question," he said. "I asked only because I feel the same way." He paused to think of the right words. "For the first time since, uh, that first Christmas break, I was tense. Worried about what my sister and her family are going to think about all this. Let alone Brooke."

"Ah, Miles, that's inevitable. Even up at Dad's house I speculated how he'd react when he heard about Perrie Lynn. And I have much less at stake with him."

"Less at stake?"

"Like I told you, I'm not close to my dad. Never have been. And since he's not especially interested in Evan, I've drifted away. For all my mother's eccentricities we're close in our way."

Another unsupportive man in Lark's life— what was with these guys? No wonder she had such an air of independence about her.

Single or married, she'd been alone. "I'm glad you have your brother."

"Yes, Dennis is a good man. But enough about my family. Aside from being tense, did you have a good time?"

"Well, it's easy enough. April has always treated me like a much younger brother who doesn't have much sense, and as for my parents, they prefer the grandkids." In a voice he hoped was light and didn't reflect his irritation, he added, "My dad still wonders when I'll get a real job with retirement benefits and a paid vacation. You're probably used to that kind of talk."

"Oh, yeah, I sure am. Usually it's Lyle warning me about a bleak future as a bag lady sleeping on the park benches down by the lake." Deepening her voice to mimic his, she said, "'Lark, you will likely die poor, maybe even homeless.'"

"Nice guy," Miles blurted, making no attempt to cover his cynicism.

"What bothers me most," she said, "is the assumption that I couldn't *possibly* know anything about getting health insurance or setting up a retirement account."

"I hear you." Miles laughed at Lark's indignant tone.

"Hey," she said, "let's change the subject. I'm counting down the days to Boston. I've already composed a pitch for some articles, so I'm covered in terms of a reason for going away. I'll talk with Lyle this week. If for some reason he can't cover the extra couple of days, I'm sure my friend Dawn will be happy to have Evan overnight. Last summer, her son stayed here while she went on a camping trip."

"It's good to have friends like that."

"I'll probably miss one of Evan's basketball games. He's not a starter, and grumbles about why he bothers playing at all, but still… I always make the games."

Over the next few minutes, Lark's voice took on a happier tone when she described the way Evan treated his little cousins. "Knowing Dennis and Donna, the kids will have their miniature school and zoo set up in the living room all winter. My brother's home is everything our childhood home wasn't. I always feel good when I'm with them."

"And it sounds like Evan fits right in. It's obvious you've done a good job with him."

"Thanks for that," she said quietly.

The conversation hit a dead end, so he pivoted away from it. "Our trip is only a few weeks away." *Our trip.* That sounded so intimate. But he'd said it, and now it was out there.

"Right you are." She let out a snorting laugh. "I was about to thank you again, but I guess you're tired of hearing that."

"Absolutely. It's our new rule. No more excessive expressions of gratitude." He deliberately feigned a formal tone.

"Okay, I get it. So what's on your agenda the next couple of days?"

"I'm doing a presentation and a workshop at a family retreat a long-term client hosts every year over the New Year's holiday—in Florida. Theoretically everybody returns home revved up with new ideas for the coming year."

"Really? Sounds interesting."

"They invite me to speak every year and work with small groups to help strengthen collaboration skills." He wished he could invite her to come along. "What about you?" he asked.

"Evan will be just back from his ski trip up north. So he's with me that weekend. We'll order pizza and watch fireworks on TV. I suspect there won't be many more New

Year's Eves with Evan okay with being at home, so I'm going to enjoy it. As moody as he's been lately, he's pretty good company."

"Sounds nice, actually." Suddenly, Florida didn't seem so attractive. He'd never brought anyone with him to these gatherings, although he'd promised Brooke she could come next year, when she'd be old enough to participate without his supervision in the planned kids' activities and the day trip to Walt Disney World.

"Well, I better get to bed. It's been a long day," she said. "And happy New Year. It has some special meaning this year."

"Yes, it certainly does. Oh, and keep those texts coming."

She said good-night first and ended the call, leaving him at the kitchen table staring at his phone. He already missed the pleasant lilt of her voice.

CHAPTER ELEVEN

STILL OUTSIDE THE main entry to the airport, Miles spotted her through the glass wall. She sat on a bench near the check-in counter, e-reader in hand and deep in concentration. When he went inside and approached her, Lark looked up and her face beamed with happiness. That smile. It got to him every time.

"I'm not checking luggage. I have my laptop in here," she said, patting a leather shoulder bag, "and other than that, all I have is this rolling carry-on. I'm good at packing light. I won't need that much, actually. I…" She stopped talking abruptly and let her head drop back. "I promised myself I wouldn't be nervous. But here I am, chattering away."

"And here I thought we were past being awkward," he teased.

"Easy for you to say," she said, giving him a pointed look. "You always were better socially, if you know what I mean. It's your aura of confidence."

If she only knew how ridiculous I feel. A secret trip with the secret mother of my secret child. Maybe that was a little dramatic, but the clandestine nature of the trip was a first for him. Granted, Andi knew about it, but no one else.

"I'm kinda jumpy, too," he said with a shrug. "I can't explain it." Then he laughed and smacked the heel of his hand on his forehead. "I do know what it is. I always travel alone."

"Ha! I bet." She cast a flirtatious smile his way.

She didn't believe him? If Lark knew how seldom he dated these days, she wouldn't be so quick to mock him. Would she be genuinely surprised to hear she was the most interesting woman he'd met in years? *Many years.* But if he said as much, he might scare her off. His attraction made it even more important to be careful and keep his distance.

"I need coffee," she said, extending the handle on her rolling bag, "so let's get our boarding passes and head to the coffee shop."

Walking to a check-in screen, he asked, "Were you waiting long?"

"Yes, indeed." She grinned, clearly embarrassed. "But it's not your fault I always allow way too much time. I don't fly often these days, but when I do, I plan for every contingency. I've been here for almost an hour. If I weren't so jumpy I'd have been halfway through a novel by now."

"If I lived as far away from the airport as you do, I'd be way early, too." He changed the subject by pointing outside, where the sun glistened on snow that had fallen the day before. "Look at that—fresh snow is so bright and clean. Clear skies for flying today. Can't ask for more than that."

"Driving in, I thought the same thing. I dropped Evan off at Lyle's last night after pizza at Lou's. I'd already packed, but still, I barely slept." She grinned shyly. "Too excited to drift off for long."

"Me, too," he said.

A few minutes later, cappuccinos in hand, they snaked through a maze of tables until they found an empty spot in the corner.

"I've watched every online video of Perrie Lynn I could find, and I've played them multiple times," Lark said when they'd settled in. "I can't seem to get enough. Maybe because that's all I know of Perrie Lynn."

"I've been watching, too," he said. "I saw a couple of her interviews after she won the silver medal at Skate America. A big upset in the skating world. They were only sixty-second sound bites, but I was impressed by how poised she is."

Lark frowned. "I was going to add the cliché 'for her age,' but that doesn't apply. She handled the interviews well, period."

"I'm sure she's had some media coaching as part of her training," he added. "She's not just a skater, she has an image to create and maintain. In a way, it's like show business."

Her frown deepened.

"I know that sounds cold, but it's part of the sport these days."

"I suppose you're right. I've been focusing on the technical side."

"Oh, boy, I was in for an education," he said, laughing. "Brooke told me the names of all the jumps, and now you can probably explain what they are and the aerodynamics of how these athletes manage to lift off the ice and complete those turns—and land on their feet, at least most of the time."

"Ah, don't worry. I'll go easy on you." Suddenly, her expression changed and her forehead knotted up. "I'm expanding my article proposals to include more about head injuries. I've been digging, and the more I learn about concussions, the more worried I get."

"Seriously?"

"I don't know about speakers and consultants like you, but I'm never off duty," she said, grinning again. "I'm constantly observing and tucking away tidbits of information. That's where the ideas for articles come from."

He nodded. "I get it. Listening and observing are part of what we both do."

She smiled in response, perhaps enjoying that connection as much as he did.

With time to spare, they finished their cappuccinos and then meandered through the airport to the security gate. As they boarded the plane, a wave of contentment came over Miles. He smiled to himself when he noticed a couple of male passengers eyeing Lark. Yes, he was in the company of a pretty woman. *In your dreams, guys—she's with me.* He had to hold back a guffaw over that thought, but he couldn't help himself.

Later, at the hotel, they hit a stilted moment, when he got off the elevator at his floor. He'd booked separate rooms, but hadn't thought about the ride to the twenty-fourth floor for him, and the thirty-first for her.

"Half an hour or so?" he asked, confirming their plan to meet for lunch at the hotel pub.

She nodded eagerly. "You bet."

Walking down the hall to his room, he shook his head, amused by his own behavior. Why did he feel about fifteen years old?

THREE DARK-HAIRED SKATERS were among the group of six who came onto the ice together and spread out in all directions to warm up for their short program, the first of the two ladies' competitions. Feeling anxious, Lark was almost disoriented when she couldn't immediately identify Perrie Lynn.

"I think she's the girl in blue with the white flower in her hair," Miles whispered, as if reading her mind.

Although the nearest spectators were several seats away, Lark kept her voice low when she replied. "Thanks. I don't know why, but I was confused. She's smaller than the others." Her eyes filled with tears. "And a vision in that deep blue…midnight blue. But, oh, that flower, somehow it's just perfect."

"And now that we've seen the pairs skate,

we know what to expect," Miles said. "So much riding on this one performance."

"I know. I'm even trembling inside." Lark took in a breath and expelled it fast as she kept her gaze on Perrie Lynn. "I can only imagine how these girls feel. And I can't stop looking at her."

Miles nodded. "Just think. This morning we were in Green Bay. And this is already our second event."

"*The* event." Lark laughed and bumped her shoulder on Miles's arm. "Nervous as I am, this first day has been magical already."

Earlier, when the pair skaters began their short programs, Miles remarked that their view of the gleaming ice from the arena's lofty seats was like looking at a framed painting. "People say there are no bad seats here," Miles had said, "and maybe that's true, but ours are perfect."

"Ah, yes, they sure are." She'd spontaneously squeezed his hand. Embarrassed, she quickly pulled back and folded her hands in her lap. Only a friendly gesture, she'd told herself. But his skin had been warm, just like the warmth he exuded. She'd been pleasantly surprised that Miles had wanted to attend all the competitions, pairs and ice dancing included.

Lark had been riveted, completely enveloped in the romance of the pairs seeming to float above the ice and almost magically time their spectacular lifts and jumps to match their music. She could see Miles was less enthralled. Maybe for him, a little skating went a long way and he had no personal stake in the outcome of that competition. Yet, when the event was over, he'd suggested they wait for the crowd to thin before leaving.

He'd been eager to come back to the arena after a quick dinner, even admitting to pre-performance jitters, just like he had before his own presentations. They'd spoken little when the first group of skaters competed, followed by a second group that included two women considered among the top performers. One, Leeza Smith, was so outstanding she jumped ahead of all her competition, even a better-known skating star. Leeza had created a wide gap between first and second place.

"So, Leeza is someone else to watch," Miles said, groaning. "A bunch of them are clustered at the top and the scores are close. Now I know why they call it a competition."

As Perrie Lynn and the others warmed up, some sprinted ahead to gather speed, others skated at the pace of a relaxed stroll. Lark watched Perrie Lynn shake her arms and hands and roll her shoulders forward and back. Lark could almost feel her own muscles loosening, her body becoming limber. Pushing off the ice with one foot, Perrie Lynn extended the other leg behind her and bent in half to wrap her hands around her ankle before straightening up again. Such flexibility. *Like me as a child.*

"What a variety of skaters in this group," Miles said.

"I can't take my eyes off of them." One had vibrant red hair, not a color seen in nature, but she looked fantastic in her purple costume. Another contrasted her white blond hair with a shimmering black costume. One of the other dark-haired skaters had chosen a flowing skating dress in delicate pink that seemed to shimmer against her dark skin.

As she watched Perrie Lynn perform some practice jumps, Lark gulped back the painful realization that the young woman in blue truly was a stranger. She knew nothing more about the real Perrie Lynn than anyone else in the arena. The impact of that incongruity left her light-headed and shaky. Yet, she alone had held Perrie Lynn in her arms in the first hours after her birth.

From the moment she'd spoken with Maxine on the phone and heard the kindness in her voice, Lark had settled into an indescribable connection with both Perrie Lynn and the woman who'd raised her. *Maxine* had taken Perrie Lynn to the skating rink for the first time. *Maxine* had monitored the endless hours of practice and conferred with coaches. She even made a move to another state to serve Perrie Lynn's career.

Painful as it was to admit, Lark didn't know the name of even one of Perrie Lynn's childhood friends. Had she gone to school dances? Who was her date? What color was her dress? What had Maxine and Perrie Lynn bickered about? What rules had the teenager rebelled against?

As Perrie Lynn circled the ice with a steady pace, Lark flashed back to Evan's first day of kindergarten. She had delivered him into the new world of school, not Lyle. She'd been the one to let go of his hand so he could race into the room, where he'd spotted a friend from his half-day nursery school.

As Lark watched Perrie Lynn leave the

rink, she caught a glimpse of her gray-haired coach greeting her, and her responsive nod. A vast, strange world separated Lark from the tiny infant she'd held in her arms. On the other hand, knowing the truth had knit past and present in one long piece of many entwined lives. Perrie Lynn belonged to Maxine and Eric the way Evan belonged to her.

Miles squeezed her hand. "You were a million miles away."

Unable—maybe unwilling—to untangle her thoughts and attempt to explain them, she took an easier way out and told a small fib. "I was just thinking that even from way up here, I can see how much she resembles you."

Miles chuckled. "Every time I see a photo or video of Perrie Lynn my grandmother and my aunts come to mind."

"Such a contrast with the Olsons."

"Speaking of the Olsons," Miles said, "I wonder where they are."

"I've wondered if we'd spot them in the restaurant. Or coming in and out of the arena. We don't know where they're staying." Before Miles could say so, she added, "And that's as it should be."

He grinned down at her. "Who are you convincing?"

She sent him a wry smile.

When the competition began, Lark took in a deep breath and let it out slowly. "Four skaters before Perrie Lynn," she said, "and I promised myself I was going to enjoy every performance and embrace the whole experience."

"Here comes the first one," Miles said, pointing below to a skater in a white-and-silver costume entering the rink to the sound of the announcer's voice.

"The first of our girl's competitors," Lark whispered.

"Right," he replied. "I have to remind myself that they're not simply graceful dancers on ice, but athletes with grit and a will to win."

"I've been reading about the way they rack up points," Lark said. "Sure is a complicated scoring system."

The first skater finished her series of jumps and spins in a workmanlike way. Lark could almost hear the commentators say as much. A section of complex footwork seemed inspired, but the audience greeted her final spin with only polite applause.

"Brooke would have pointed out that as long as she hasn't fallen out of a jump, she did okay," Miles said, mildly amused. "I don't know how to judge other than hoping they don't take a spill."

And the second skater, the redhead in purple, did just that, falling but recovering quickly. The next competitor, Molly Walden, the current US champion, was greeted with loud clapping, and no wonder. A petite blonde in a sophisticated peach-colored skating dress, Molly took the ice like she owned it. And in a way she did. She held the title and would fight to keep it.

Miles leaned in close. "That's another skater Brooke mentions often. She took her US title to the world championships last year and walked away with the bronze."

"I saw that online. I got so interested in skating that I watched other skaters' online videos, and there was one of Molly's winning skate at the NorAms last year. She's tough."

Like the others before her, Molly confidently started her program with what Lark had learned was a triple-triple-jump combination, which brought on a round of applause rippling through the crowd. Lark understood that minute differences in scores often came from the degrees of difficulty of various spins and jumps. Molly's perfect landing and easy glide out of the jump set the tone for this twenty-four-year-old skater. No wonder that any medal for Perrie Lynn would be considered an enormous upset and a sweet victory.

After a final set of catch-foot spins, Molly's sudden stop brought roars from the audience as they got to their feet. She and Miles enthusiastically clapped right along with others. "I see why the audience loves her," Lark said.

"Well, according to a well-known authority, Ms. Brooke Jenkins, Molly is determined to keep her title and go on to the Internationals."

When the scores were announced, Molly jumped ahead of all the others, accumulating enough points to position her slightly ahead of Leeza.

The skater before Perrie Lynn was the beauty wearing the dramatic black costume. Although her skating was good, she lacked a certain artistic quality and that led to a tepid response from the audience. Starting at the pairs' competition, Lark began catching on to the varying reactions the audience had to the whole package, the term the commentators sprinkled liberally in their descriptions of the skaters. Technique wasn't enough, but artistry without landing the jumps and executing intricate step sequences and spins led to scores below what was needed to win. To Lark's unschooled eyes, the combination of technical perfection and the grace of dance seemed nothing less than magical.

Finally, the voice coming over the loudspeaker announced Perrie Lynn. Lark put her hand on her chest, which quickly grew tight and ached with nervous anticipation.

"I like the way she handles this part," Miles whispered as Perrie Lynn appeared and raised her arms to greet the audience, who welcomed her presence with loud applause. "The audience is fixated on her already."

As Perrie Lynn started her slow lap around the arena's ice, Lark drew in a calming breath. The air around her vibrated as she attempted to gulp back the rising sob caught in the back of her throat.

Miles captured her hand between both of his, whispering, "I understand."

Perrie Lynn skated to the center of the ice, and after one last quick pivot, she assumed her starting position in the center of the ice and the melody of *Moonlight Sonata* began.

Lark's tears flowed freely. Miraculously, though, after the first couple of jumps her tears stopped, as she lost herself in the wonder of Perrie Lynn's graceful journey across the ice and the triple jumps that brought outbreaks of applause. Maybe it was the lightness of her arm movements that enchanted Lark the most. No, it was the extension of her dramatic arabesques.

When Perrie Lynn finished her final spin, Lark let her head drop against Miles's shoulder. "Thank you for this."

He put his arm around her and kissed her forehead and then they stood with a few thousand other people and clapped long and loud. Lark closed her eyes to focus on the sound, but she quickly opened them again. She couldn't keep her eyes off Perrie Lynn, visible now on the big screens in the arena.

When they finally sat down Miles again took her hand. "Only a minute or two more for the score."

Lark knew that was the critical outcome, but somehow, the numbers didn't matter. Perrie Lynn had been magnificent.

When the score appeared and Perrie Lynn's reaction was shown on the screen, the arena filled with the roar of the crowd.

"Look," Miles said, pointing to the board,

"she's just behind Leeza Smith and Molly Walden. Third place—so far. Wow."

"You'd have to be a real expert to see a difference in the technique, huh?" Lark said. "I get the overall performance impression, but small differences in the technical execution are way beyond my untrained eye."

Miles nodded his agreement. "I only know a few of those details because of Brooke, who, by the way, must be so happy. I'll send her a text on Andi's phone later."

Lark glanced around, noting how few people were seated near them, giving them a degree of privacy. "I'd have thought every seat would be filled."

"Me, too, but I guess the revenue comes from TV sponsors. Maybe the live audience is almost like an afterthought."

"Well, we're incognito up here," Lark said. "No one is going to pan a camera up this far."

"We hope," Miles said, a frown forming.

The last group of skaters took to the ice, but although one knocked the previous fourth-place skater down to fifth, Perrie Lynn's third place short-program finish held.

When the event ended, they waited until most everyone else had filed out before they left.

"I'm keyed up," Miles said as they approached the exit door. "I'm still jumping and spinning in my head."

"You, too?" Lark pulled on her fleece-lined gloves and wrapped her scarf around her neck against the cold wind blowing off the Charles River and the bay. "I need to keep pinching myself to remember this whole experience is real."

"Shall we get a cab back to the hotel?" Miles asked.

"Are you up for a walk? It's not far. And maybe a glass of wine in the hotel bar?"

He grinned. "Great idea. Let's go."

When Miles held out his bent elbow in an invitation, it seemed only natural to accept it.

CHAPTER TWELVE

THE NEXT MORNING, Lark and Miles slid into a booth tucked behind an oversize banquette, where three couples sat with giant plates of pancakes and omelets in front of them. Even with the high leather seatback, she didn't need to purposely eavesdrop to catch their conversation. Lark expected talk about Leeza and Molly, but the name that came up again and again was Perrie Lynn. The group had been at the competition and were chewing it over like she and Miles had in the bar the previous night. Catching her eye, he nodded to the banquette, silently letting her know he'd also caught some of the conversation.

"Seems they like—and genuinely respect—all the skaters," Miles observed, keeping his voice barely above a whisper. "Just by observing and watching the reactions of the audience, I've already learned skating fans are a breed unto themselves. Not quite as partisan as the Green Bay Packer enthusiasts—or should I call us zealots?"

"If you're like Evan and Lyle the word *fanatic* fits." Feeling buoyant and carefree, she studied the busy restaurant filling up with a breakfast crowd. A skating crowd. "Isn't this wonderful?"

Miles flushed, as if embarrassed, but he nodded.

"A delicious secret." The remark just slipped out, along with the flirtatious tone. She cleared her throat. "I'll bet Brooke would love to be here."

Miles frowned. "I'd have imagined her wanting to be like these princess skaters one day, but she's happy being a spectator, playing soccer and waiting until she's twelve and gets a horse."

"I understand," Lark said. "For me, the thrill of skating didn't come in the form of costumes and glamour. It was about how fast I could pick up speed and race on the frozen river—the next best thing to flying. Maybe that's the way Brooke feels about riding a horse."

He rolled his eyes. "Thanks a lot. My daughter on a horse cantering across Wisconsin fields at breakneck speed. Great image. What could possibly go wrong?"

"Don't worry before the time comes," she said with a laugh.

As they fell silent and studied the menu, the mix of voices coming from behind distracted Lark again. Lowered voices. That made her more curious. She leaned to the side and tried to subtly turn her head to catch words and phrases.

"She looks better than she did at the beginning of the season," a woman said.

A male voice responded with something about *it*, whatever that was, being only a matter of time before something happened, but the sentence trailed off.

"Do you mean they expect it to come back?" a third voice whispered.

It? Come back? In Lark's experience, words like that usually meant an illness, often cancer. Miles opened his mouth to speak, but she raised her index finger in the air to stop him, so she could brazenly eavesdrop.

One more person spoke up in a louder voice. "Her mother wanted to do as much as she could for Perrie Lynn. Just in case she doesn't make it."

"It paid off, too. Look at the success she's had," a woman replied.

Suddenly, a man warned, "I hear they're being private about Maxine's situation. We shouldn't even be talking in public about the family."

But how do they know this information? And it involves Maxine.

With Miles already staring at her, puzzled, Lark forced herself to study the menu, then said, "The French toast with bacon looks good to me."

Miles nodded, but his frown deepened.

"I'll explain later," she whispered.

With a subtle nod, he confirmed he got the message.

When the waiter came, they were back to acting like people simply away on a trip. How odd to be with Miles and engaged in something so mundane as ordering breakfast. But considering what a good time they'd had on the flight to Boston, she wasn't surprised to feel so relaxed with him. They'd even managed to talk their way through the ninety-minute delay on the runway. Lyle would have groused and turned sullen, but Miles, a regular business traveler, took it all in stride.

Wait, wait. For all she knew Miles was an equally annoying grump when he'd been married and traveling with Andi. When Lyle was out on a date these days, he was no doubt his most charming self.

Had she just said the D word, *date*? Yes, that word had filtered through her mind at the Half Moon Café and again now in Boston. No matter what she called their time together, so far, Miles had been the best possible companion on this adventure.

The couples in the booth finished and filed out of the restaurant before she and Miles were finished eating. As soon as they were out of earshot, Miles spoke up. "So? Can you tell me what they said?"

"I'll tell you when we're alone, but I think Maxine is—or has been—ill." Her uneasiness grew about being privy to information she and Miles weren't meant to have.

"Then as soon as you're done, let's go. I'll make a pot of coffee in my room."

She nodded in response.

"And then," he said brightly, "we can be tourists until it's time to go back to the arena and see the men's event and an ice-dancing program."

"Then let today's show begin." Her cheeks

warmed with pleasure. But she couldn't deny being troubled by what she'd overheard.

As PROMISED, EARLY the next morning, Lark called Dawn, leading off the conversation with the thrill of seeing Perrie Lynn perform.

"I bet you were proud," Dawn said, "and I'm so glad you called."

Pride? Such a limited word, Lark thought, standing by the window and looking at the cityscape surrounding her, a mix of modern high-rises and the friendly older buildings with their carved stone facades still intact.

"I don't know how to describe what's going on inside of me. My body has been on full alert since we arrived," she explained, "and now her long program is *tonight*. On prime-time TV!"

Lark gave her friend a rundown on what she and Miles had been up to, but got off on a tangent about Perrie Lynn's performance. "She was magnificent, finishing third, which exceeded expectations. She's still so young."

"Were you nervous? Excited?" Dawn chuckled. "Dazed?"

"All of those things and more." She paused. "I need a minute here to pull myself together for this next part." Finally, she let out a big breath. "The thing is, and I mean this in a positive way, I saw for myself the life the Olsons have given her. That's why I've been on the verge of tears so often these last two days. I realized in such a profound way what Maxine is to Perrie Lynn. That's the way it will always be."

"Oh, Lark," Dawn whispered into the phone, "yes, you sound emotional, but I don't know, maybe not so terribly sad."

"That's it. I'm accepting the reality of Perrie Lynn and her family in my heart. It's not just an intellectual concept." She brushed away tears before they had a chance to trail down her cheeks. "But none of this is even about me. It's about Perrie Lynn and her parents. And I was struck by knowing that I have this blind love for someone I've only spoken to once in my life—way back when she was way too tiny to understand."

Lark could probably calculate the exact number of days and hours that had passed since she'd murmured reassuring words to the tiny bundle in her arms. *I'm so sorry, but it's for the best, little one.* She'd stared at the perfect little face one last time and drew her closer to her heart. *I promise you'll have a good life with people who will love you so, so much. They can give you what I could never hope to. A family.*

"At the time," she explained, "all I could think was that she'd have a family. My parents had managed to destroy ours."

"But that family has been put back together now, Lark," Dawn said softly. "When you meet Perrie Lynn, you can tell her about Evan. You have a wonderful brother and he and Donna have fun little kids. Even your quirky mom managed to pick up the pieces and assemble a new life."

"You're right. I should probably give Mom more credit, especially since I learned the hard way what it's like to marry a man who turned out to be so much less than I'd imagined."

"But the dreary past is gone, my friend," Dawn said. "Here you are seeing Perrie Lynn, and you're with her father, who happens to be single and not just able, but willing to share this with you. Now *that's* mind-boggling."

"So subtle, my friend. But since you bring him up, the trip is going very well. He's coming to all the events, like the pairs and the ice dancing. I'm certain he didn't become mesmerized the way I did by the sheer beauty of two people moving as one. But a romantic like you would have been over the moon to see them in person."

"You're right. But back to you. I suppose you've had dinners…"

"And a drink at the hotel after seeing Perrie Lynn." Lark paused, trying to find words for how special it all felt. "Ever since meeting at the airport, it's like we're under a spell or something. But it's, you know, not real life."

Dawn chuckled. "No, I suppose it isn't. I was about to come back with some smart remark about it being better than that, but I'll refrain. Just don't go assuming this experience doesn't *mean* anything."

"Thanks for that. I've laughed and cried, and had a lot of fun, too. We've played tourist and visited Faneuil Hall and Quincy Market. And tonight is Perrie Lynn's big night."

"I just hope you can stand having so much fun," Dawn teased, "especially with someone who, based on your own words, is pretty good company."

"I'll try to cope," Lark quipped. With that, she ended the call.

Grinning and buoyant, Lark turned her attention to answering a few emails and accepted an assignment for a piece about childhood headache syndromes. She finished up and still had time to kill before meeting Miles. Too restless to stay in the room, she took the elevator down to the gift shop in the hotel lobby to pick up a copy of the *Boston Globe* and browse the magazine racks.

Her mind kept returning to her conversation with Dawn, especially her reassuring words about family. As grateful as she was for her family, every time she thought about explaining her past to them, especially Evan, a wave of anxiety surged through her.

She distracted herself by glancing at the magazines, but saw nothing that piqued her interest and pivoted toward the checkout counter.

She froze in place. *Maxine.*

Lark was certain it was Maxine interacting with the cashier as she paid for her items. Lark had imprinted the woman's face in her mind when the camera in the arena had briefly focused on her and Eric as they waited for Perrie Lynn's scores. Maxine had waved for the camera and the audience had responded with cheers. Lark had noted her jaunty deep blue hat and dangly earrings. This morning, though, a bright fuchsia scarf was twisted elegantly around her head.

As tall and pretty as she was, Maxine's frailty confirmed the rumor. She'd most assuredly been ill. Maybe she still was. Perhaps sensing someone staring at her, Maxine glanced up and her face registered surprise.

Lark swallowed hard as Maxine quickly signed her receipt and approached with a cordial, social smile.

Taking in a breath to regroup, Lark moved forward and held out her hand.

"Hello," Maxine said in a cool voice, grasping Lark's hand. "No need for introductions, I suppose. You look exactly like the photo on your website."

Lark cleared her throat. "We… Miles and I have tried to stay out of the way."

She nodded, but didn't smile. "You've obviously kept your distance or we'd have seen you before now."

"Miles arranged for us to come here so we could see Perrie Lynn skate." Lark skimmed her fingers along her temple, where beads of sweat had appeared. "I'm sorry. I'm tongue-tied. I didn't imagine…you know, running into you like this. Miles chose this hotel because it's not too close to the arena."

Maxine scanned the area around her.

Turning toward the store entrance, she said, "Follow me."

On the way out of the store, Lark remembered to dig in her purse for change to put on the counter for the newspaper. She followed Maxine to an empty corner in the lobby, away from the elevators and the registration desk.

"Look, I don't have a problem with you being here," Maxine said, stopping abruptly and resting her back against the wall. "As long as you don't violate our agreement and you keep your distance. I realize you've kept up your end so far." She glanced down. "I know it's only natural that you'd want to see her. I get it."

"Thank you. For everything." Lark's voice choked with a rising jumble of emotions. "Especially for the family you've given Perrie Lynn."

Maxine waved her off. "I've been thanking you for eighteen years. Believe me, that's only natural, too." She held up the shopping bag she carried. "Muffins. This hotel has the best ones around. We're actually in an apartment in a high-rise down the street. Declan is staying in the same building. Fewer distractions in an apartment than in hotels."

Smiling as hot tears pooled in her eyes, Lark nodded. "Tonight is her big night, huh?"

"Yes," Maxine said, frowning slightly. "And it's not like any other day or any other competition. She'll spend much of the day with Declan and the pair team he coaches. She'll practice and get her head in the right place."

"Miles is as excited to see her as I am," Lark said. "This is all so unexpected. I can barely believe it."

Maxine's expression shifted when she said, "By the way, years ago we gave Perrie Lynn as much information as we had, short of identifying you." Maxine sounded slightly impatient as she glanced nervously around her. "We told her that you made a sacrifice to give her the best life possible."

Lark willed herself to hold back the flood of feelings ready to crash like a giant wave and demolish her composure. "And it's true, Maxine. You can't imagine what a relief it's been to know for sure that what I'd hoped for all these years matches the reality."

Maxine stared at the floor, placing her bone-thin index fingers in the corners of her eyes to staunch tears. "I fell in love with her, Lark.

And so did Eric. It's that simple." She looked up long enough to scan the lobby.

Always on guard, Lark thought. And there they were, in a public space with no privacy guaranteed.

Maxine began fidgeting with the long ends of the silky scarf extending over her shoulder. "When the subject of finding her birth parents first came up, Eric and I gently warned her that not all birth mothers, and fathers, want to be found. We were relieved to know you want to be in touch. And you and Miles seem to have made good lives." She tapped her temple with her fingertips. "Sorry, sorry. Such a cliché. I didn't mean it that way."

Extending her arm, Lark said, "Please, no apologies. What you said is true. I have a wonderful son. He's almost thirteen now. I have a business, and so does Miles. My marriage, well, that's a different story. Not important now." Lark spoke fast, as if desperately needing to convey this information. Or maybe she was defending herself, wanting to look worthy in Maxine's eyes.

"Well, let's just say that Eric and I couldn't believe our luck."

Lark exhaled the air she'd been holding in

her lungs, and her laughter wasn't filled with nervous energy this time. "I'm laughing because I'm so delighted just to be here, with you…to have a chance to talk."

"I feel that way, too, for all kinds of reasons I don't want to get into now. But I can't emphasize enough what kind of focus this level of competition requires. None of this *quarantine*, though, for lack of a better word, is meant to hurt you, or in the long run to prevent you from meeting Perrie Lynn."

"I do understand."

"But if we run into each other again, we're strangers," Maxine said. "Do you agree?"

"Absolutely." Every cell in Lark's body lit up with indescribable joy. "And as difficult as it is, I don't have expectations beyond meeting her one day."

Maxine nodded, a faint frown creasing her forehead as she straightened her scarf.

Lark weighed her next words. "Maxine, Perrie Lynn is your daughter. She always will be." Tears threatened to spill down her cheeks again, but not from sadness. She was filled with affection for the woman standing in front of her.

"You betcha." Maxine's voice carried a

pleasant inflection and her face beamed with a broad smile. "And one day you'll discover that she's far more than a figure skater. Her sparkle and brightness will take her far no matter what she chooses to pursue in the future."

Unable to add anything to that, Lark only nodded.

"I'm going to say goodbye now." She held out both her hands. Lark took them, knowing this wasn't about a handshake, but rather, a way of solidifying their connection through touch, hand to hand, woman to woman.

Maxine let go first. "Until the next time, then." She turned away, but quickly spun back to face Lark. "I've wanted to say something to you, but I don't want to upset you, either."

Lark reached out to touch Maxine's arm. "Please, say whatever it is you want. I'm overjoyed to have met you in person, and nothing you could say would upset me."

"Okay, then, here's the thing." Maxine touched her fingers to her lips before taking in a breath. "No matter what happens in the future, I will never, ever know how to thank you for giving me the gift of Perrie Lynn."

Before Lark could react, Maxine turned the corner and disappeared. Only then did Lark let a stream of tears cover her face.

CHAPTER THIRTEEN

MILES ANSWERED THE knock on the door and there was Lark, beaming with happiness. Immediately, he knew the day would exceed his already high expectations. Lark carried a bag of muffins and balanced two humungous coffees in a cardboard tray. She told him her story, as if reciting the details of a miracle. He asked for more details and she recounted everything she remembered about Maxine, including concerns that the rumors they'd heard matched Maxine's appearance. Still, by the time they took off for a walk Lark was still floating in the clouds somewhere.

What started out as light snow as they left the hotel grew heavier with every block.

"I suppose this is nuts," Lark said, her eyes sparkling. "I can barely see ten feet ahead."

"Doesn't matter." He brushed a few snowflakes off the strands of hair that escaped her hat. "We can always duck inside a café if we get cold."

"Hey, we're from Wisconsin. We can handle a little snow." She tucked her arm through his.

"True, but have you noticed we're almost alone out here?" he asked, conscious of the simple pleasure of walking arm in arm on the almost deserted street.

"Ah, yes, but other people aren't bubbling over with anticipation—or maybe I should call it a case of the jitters. I just need to burn some energy."

He grinned down at her, seeing in her face the radiance that had taken over her whole being when she'd told him about meeting Maxine. He was happy for her, but admittedly envious, too. He'd have liked to speak with Maxine—or especially Eric. He pushed aside his slightly bruised feelings and chose to revel in the joy the morning had brought to Lark.

"The only cloud on the horizon," Lark said as they walked through the accumulating snow, "is Maxine herself. She was thin and pale. It was kind of alarming. I wonder…"

She didn't finish the sentence, but Miles chose to be optimistic. "She's here, though. Maybe her treatment is over and she's recovering. Those people in the restaurant yesterday only knew that she'd been sick. For all they know, Maxine will be well again soon."

"I hope you're right," Lark said.

He heard skepticism in her tone, but remained silent.

"How's everything at home?" she asked suddenly. "Is Brooke excited about tonight's competition?"

Jarred by the instant change of subject, he nevertheless refocused and responded. "She never misses a chance to remind me about it." He paused. "I suppose one day, way off in the future, I'll tell her I was here."

"It gets complicated, doesn't it?" Lark said.

With his gloved fingers he squeezed her hand linked through his arm. "Let's get an early lunch before we're knee-deep in snow. A long, leisurely lunch. Then, it will be time to get to the arena for the afternoon events."

"I'm already jumping out of my skin."

"No kidding?" he teased.

By the time they found a pub a few blocks from their hotel, Miles realized that he enjoyed the simple act of walking down the street with Lark. He'd had so little of that kind of ordinary companionship in his life, especially after he and Andi split up. Thinking back, he and Andi had shared very few arm-in-arm walks or leisurely lunches.

Over their sandwich plates, he kept the conversation as far away as possible from Perrie Lynn's big night. The more they'd anticipated and speculated—and hoped— the more nervous they'd become. At Miles's prompting, Lark told him stories about Dublin and her side trips to the Irish countryside with new friends. He offered his impressions about a three-week trip he and Andi had taken after they'd married. How easy it was to picture driving through England and Scotland with Lark, and then flying first-class to Paris as he and Andi had done.

"Sounds wonderful," Lark said with a sigh. "The most Lyle and I ever did was fly to London—a package deal."

Miles noted that her expression darkened, but only for a second or two before she burst out laughing.

"Last winter, Dawn and I pooled our money and took our boys to Key West for their long Presidents' Day weekend. Our package included a couple of snorkeling excursions. We were in the water so much, our skin shriveled up. Dawn and I still joke about our two boys trying to avoid our attempts to slather them with sunscreen. It was great fun to escape the winter for three days and give the kids an adventure." Grinning, she added, "Now *this* is an adventure. Every minute of it."

He glanced at his watch and signaled for the check. "And it's almost showtime for the pairs' and dance finals," he said. "I know you don't want to miss those. We can head right to the arena."

The snow had lightened up a little so it took only a few minutes to get to the building and settle into their seats. The rest of the afternoon flew by. Miles could probably have skipped the event, but Lark sat riveted, transfixed by the combination of speed and grace and impossible-looking throws, not to mention lifts that made him hold his breath.

As much as his mind wandered away from the performances, Miles was as stunned as everyone in the audience when one of the pairs' lifts went awry and sent both skaters tumbling to the ice for a hard landing. But even with blood running down her shin from her knee and splotches of blood on her chin, the woman picked herself up and she and her partner completed their program—including two more lifts. They finished to a standing ovation and thunderous applause that acknowledged their grit.

"It's easy to forget those incredible lifts and throws are riskier than they look," Miles said when they took their seats again.

In a serious voice, Lark described a pair of ice dancers forced to take a whole season off because one of them suffered a concussion and the other broke an ankle.

He grabbed her hand. "Don't go worrying about Perrie Lynn. I can see the wheels turning in your head and hear the concern in your voice."

"I can't help but fret a little. I think seeing actual blood was a bit of a wake-up call. I've been enchanted by the grace and romance of the sport, and tend to forget the dangers."

Was she still holding his hand for emotional support, or was she attracted to him the way he was to her? At some point, he'd have to find out, but not during that critical weekend when so much was on the line for their daughter. *Their daughter*. What a strange, but wonderful, sound.

LARK WRAPPED UP the leftover cheese and put it in the refrigerator in her room. "Ready to go? We can finish up the cheese and crackers when we get back—when we break open the champagne."

"Oh, no. No talk of champagne yet," Miles said. "We don't want to jinx her."

"We couldn't do that, not with all the hope we're bringing to that arena." She took a deep breath and pulled her coat off the hanger in the closet. "Besides, no matter what happens, we'll celebrate with champagne."

Miles tilted his head and grinned. *He's flirting again*, she thought. And she enjoyed every minute of it.

"You look nice," he said. "Like you've got someplace special to go."

She glanced down at her long black skirt, flared at the bottom and perfect with her high boots. She'd cinched a woven belt around her blue sweater and added a necklace of silver beads. "Thanks. The occasion calls for festive clothes." She waved a paisley shawl before wrapping it around her shoulder. "I'm prepared if it's cold inside the arena."

As she buttoned her coat, she sighed. "It's like I'm inside a dream, watching myself move around. I look normal on the outside, but really, I'm occupying another world."

"You do have a way of putting things," Miles said softly as they left the room.

Once again, Lark accepted Miles's silent offer of his arm as they took off down the street in the dark of early evening. They said little, but their silence was companionable in a way that touched Lark. Instantly, she warded off a wave of sadness about these good times coming to an end when they returned home.

Finding their seats, Lark was surprised she could relax into the atmosphere and observe others as they arrived and settled in around them. Based on the noise level it was clear many more spectators attended the skaters' final programs when the stakes were higher. The ladies' final was the biggest draw of all the events.

As if echoing her thoughts, Miles said, "This feels like old hat now, as if we're die-hard fans."

She nodded. "I'm so exhilarated, I find myself rooting for all the girls. Oh, I want Perrie Lynn to win a medal, but deep inside I want them all to have their best performances."

As if signaled by her words, the competition started with the first group of skaters taking their allotted warm-up minutes on the ice. Lark pressed her palms together and rested them against her chest. "At last."

As the music for the initial competitor started, Lark sat forward in her seat to watch the scene unfold. She winced with every fall, and cheered the steady landings and dance-like moves from one end of the rink to the other, but left the complex point system to the experts. In the end, a couple of the skaters moved up in the standings, and a couple of them brought the audience to their feet with personal best performances. Two skaters in a row took hard falls, one even sliding on her hip several feet across the ice before she managed to stand and carry on with her program.

She and Miles spoke little until the third group of skaters took the ice and they spotted Perrie Lynn, this time sparkling in dark red. She put her hand over Miles's arm. "Look at her. So beautiful."

"For us," he whispered, letting his cheek touch her hair, "it's obvious she's a combination of you and me." He swallowed hard. "But she's also her own unique person."

"With passions and accomplishments we're about to witness—again."

As the skaters created their magic on the

ice, Lark could see that a couple of the top contenders were coming in at least slightly under expectation, including Leeza Smith, who bobbled more than one jump, not falling, but not producing the smooth transitions that had made her such an extraordinary performer. The audience responded to each completed jump with encouraging applause, but it was clear to Lark that Leeza would pose no threat to the defending champion.

"I'll bet Brooke is disappointed," Miles said as Leeza, head lowered, left the ice to wait for her scores. The camera focused on Molly Walden, who was due to skate next. "Leeza was one of the first skaters that Mamie and Brooke followed. But Brooke also understands that even top contenders can have a bad night."

"Oh, boy, a life lesson at age eight," Lark said. "But that leaves Brooke free to root for Perrie Lynn without feeling torn."

They looked on as Molly performed every jump and spin to perfection, easily shooting into first place, leaving the fourth-place Julia James to start her warm-up pace and glide to the center of the ice. Julia had worn blush pink for her short program and was equally stunning in deep aqua. Seconds later, the music started and the skater lived up to her reputation. Even a novice like Lark knew that Julia was even better than she'd been in her short program. One jump flowed into the next in perfect harmony with the music. Lark glanced at Miles, who had leaned forward, too, riveted by what was unfolding. The program ended with a series of spins and the crowd got to their feet even before the dramatic finish. The skater's arm extended overhead, before she punched the air with a triumphant fist pump.

The crowd stayed on its feet as Julia wiped away tears and bowed and waved. As she skated to the rim, she scooped up flowers and stuffed animals the fans had tossed onto the ice. With the camera on her and projecting to the large arena screens, spectators could watch as she embraced her coach and slipped on her blade guards before sitting on the kiss-'n'-cry bench to await her scores. Only when she waved to the crowd to acknowledge her second-place standing did the applause start to subside.

"I can't believe Perrie Lynn has to follow her," Lark said as the moment passed.

"From what I've heard from the commentators, some skaters feed off the energy of the crowd, but others are intimidated by it." He paused. "Especially the young skaters."

"Wow. I can't believe how nervous I'm getting."

"That's why they call it a competition," Miles said with a quick laugh. "But right now that doesn't make me feel any better."

"On the other hand, I've reminded myself hundreds of times that she was never expected to get this far." Lowering her voice, Lark added, "She's achieved a triumph already."

Miles grinned. "I needed that reminder."

When Perrie Lynn's name filled the arena Lark tried to quiet her internal trembling, but she couldn't manage it. "Just look at her greet the crowd with her arms high in the air."

"She knows she has to refocus the audience's attention on her now," Miles said, "so they'll forget about Julia's performance."

"That's no trick for me," Lark whispered.

Perrie Lynn finished her circle around the ice, with a smile that said "Welcome to my performance."

A hush came over the crowd when Perrie Lynn took center ice. The seconds ticked by and the first notes of *Scheherazade* signaled the start of a pivot into footwork and a dramatic kick that launched the buildup to the first jump.

Lark wrapped her fingers around Miles's hand and leaned sideways so their shoulders touched when Perrie Lynn completed her first soaring triple jump. They emptied their lungs simultaneously and each took another sharp inhale as they watched the setup for another jump. Two triples followed to the sound of loud clapping.

As wonderful as the jumps were, it was Perrie Lynn's balletic extensions that filled Lark with awe. Her daughter was an *artist* with polish and poise. With a gentle lull in the music, Perrie Lynn went from one end of the ice to the other with her hands wrapped on one ankle, her other leg in a perfect six-o'clock extension. An arabesque followed that curved into a long glide that took her to center ice again. She extended her arms to the side as if embracing the crowd.

Intricate dance steps led to the final extensions and spins that displayed her agility and ability to use all her body's strength. Lark's tears started in earnest when applause accompanied the final spin.

Miles wrapped his arm around her shoulders. Unable to speak, Lark relaxed into the curve of his body and circled her arm around his waist. She was aware only of the comfort of Miles's embrace and the magic of Perrie Lynn's bows and waves. Smiling widely, the young skater filled her arms with flowers and teddy bears and left the ice. After a hug from Declan, the camera followed her to the kiss-'n'-cry bench, where she waved again.

Miles reached into the pocket of his jacket and handed her a handkerchief. "I picked it up just for this occasion."

Laughing through tears, she said, "You really did think of everything."

He didn't respond, but pointed to the screen where the camera caught Maxine's radiant face and Eric's elation. "No matter where she comes in, everyone in the arena knows she not only did her best, but she also gave the others a run for their money. She may not win, but I bet she medals."

"If I'm so touched, imagine how Maxine and Eric must feel," Lark said, suddenly aware she and Miles had witnessed the culmination of years of sacrifice. "It's really their moment as much as Perrie Lynn's."

As if she'd ordered it, the screen again showed a close-up of Eric's and Maxine's faces. Ah, Lark thought, a deep red hat this time, with a band replete with sequins. Through the happy tears and joy on Maxine's face, Lark also detected underlying fatigue and strain. As if on cue, Eric leaned in and whispered something in Maxine's ear. She nodded and gave him what looked like a reassuring pat on his hand. Intuitively, Lark was certain Maxine had assured Eric she was okay.

As anticipated, Perrie Lynn had repeated her pattern and accumulated enough points to bypass Julia and move into second place. And that's where she stayed through four more skaters. In the end, Molly held on to her title and Leeza finished a disappointing fifth.

"These medalists must be thrilled beyond words," Lark said when they took their places on the podium.

"Perrie Lynn's silver is considered a true upset, you know."

Lark nodded, letting her mind jump ahead to February. "She'll likely be headed to Norway for the Internationals."

"That's right. The silver gets her on the team."

As if in a dream, Lark watched Perrie Lynn raise her arm and wave the bouquet of flowers to the appreciative crowd.

"Just think," Lark said, her legs weak, "we get to come back tomorrow for the men's final and then for the exhibition program. She'll skate one more time before we have to leave this fairy tale."

They sat down to wait for the arena to empty, but really, Lark needed the time to come back down to earth. Eventually, though, they went out to the street and headed in the direction of the hotel.

"Let's duck in here," Miles said, pointing to an elegant-looking restaurant and bar. "I'll bet we can get ourselves a glass or two of champagne. We can drink the room champagne tomorrow night."

"Another good idea," she said. "And I'm hungry. Those cheese and crackers didn't cut it."

Miles laughed. "I might have guessed." After asking the host for a table in the back, he turned to Lark and said, "In an abundance of caution."

She nodded in understanding. It wouldn't do to run into the Olsons, not on this important night. Still light-headed, almost dizzy, she slid into her side of the booth. "I can't help but wonder what the Olsons are doing right now. I imagine there was a press room for interviews and photo ops, which would take time for Perrie Lynn and Declan. But after that, is it possible they'd just go back to their apartment and call it a night?"

"I would imagine they're too excited to sleep, like us." Miles grabbed hold of the menu with an air of authority. "So, what would the bottomless pit like to order to go with the champagne?"

She glanced at the appetizer list on the menu. This excursion was going to be her treat. Miles had insisted on paying for almost everything so far, but not this time. "How about an order of bruschetta and then a couple of other appetizers. And I leave it to you to pick the champagne."

They passed the next hour or so sipping champagne and going over every minute of the competition.

"I think I'm coming back into my body." Lark sat back in the booth and laughed. "I was walking on air before. That was always just a phrase, but it took food and champagne to get my feet on the ground again."

"The memories will never leave me." Miles shook his head. "I'm afraid the image of Maxine will stick with me, too."

Lark closed her eyes and sighed. "I wasn't

going to say anything, but since you brought it up…well, I don't know what to say. She didn't look as well as she did just this morning. Maybe she's worn-out."

"I suppose." He squared his shoulders and lifted his glass. "Here's to her health. And that's a heartfelt toast, not just an expression."

Their glasses met midway in the space between them. "This is one thing we have no control over. Only time will tell."

In an attempt to lighten the mood, Lark picked up the table knife and made an elaborate show of cutting the last piece of bruschetta in half. "Fair is fair." She slid one piece on Miles's plate and the other on her own.

Suddenly, Miles let out a loud guffaw.

"What? What's so funny?"

"I was thinking that this is a far cry from that off-campus dive we used to go to for burgers or nachos."

Lark scanned the dim restaurant with its dark wood and stained glass, white tablecloths and candles. With a sidelong glance, she said, "I feel so grown up."

Miles appreciated her obvious attempt at humor. "I wouldn't have thought to put it that way, but you're right. We've graduated from the campus dives and here we are sipping champagne."

"So we have," she said, lifting her shoulders in contentment. What it all meant was another story.

CHAPTER FOURTEEN

MILES INSISTED ON going to the airport with her to catch her flight home, allowing time to spare for breakfast before she went through security and said goodbye, not just to him, but to the nearly indescribable weekend. Lark wished they were going home together, as if closing a circle. Home meant routine, writing, interviews, the regularity of Evan's practices, coffee with Dawn. And now, the added element of waiting for the Internationals.

"I have a confession to make," Lark said as they stood near the security lines.

Miles raised his eyebrows expectantly. "Oh? Well, let's hear it."

"I thought the trip might be awkward, you know, between us. Like we wouldn't know how to relax with each other or we'd have to think up stuff to talk about. How wonderful to be dead wrong. I had so much fun."

"Me, too," Miles said.

"Such a nice morning at Quincy Market

and even that walk in the nearly blinding snow was lovely," she mused, reminiscing about their good time. "We were carefree tourists."

"It's like *we* took home a silver medal." Miles chuckled. "And now we'll have a vicarious trip to the Internationals—on TV, anyway."

Lark lowered her gaze to stare at her boots. "The only shadow is Maxine's illness." Lark had heard more buzz about Maxine's health in the crowd. The *Boston Globe* had even mentioned it in their coverage. It seemed that Maxine's ovarian cancer was no longer a private matter, but had suddenly become a sidebar to the story about a breakthrough skater. Lark couldn't imagine the Olsons liking that much.

Inevitably, the time came for her to get into line. How would they say goodbye without tripping over words and becoming stilted again?

Lark took the initiative. "Like it or not, I'm going to do this one more time. I'm going to thank you."

Miles let his head fall back in an exaggerated response. "Oh, no, not again." Then he laughed. "It's weeks to the Internationals.

Let's have dinner one night this week after I get back. I mean, if you have time, what with Evan…"

No need to consider her answer. "Sure. Friday is free. Evan is going to a parents-and-kids bowling-club night with Lyle."

The rest was easy. They set up the time and place and that was that.

She grabbed the handle of her suitcase and slipped into the end of a short line. "See you soon."

"So, goodbye then." He lifted his hand for a last wave.

Her cheeks heated up as she turned away. And why did she feel the pressure of tears forming behind her eyes?

AMUSED BY HOW proud he was that he'd asked Lark out on a real date, Miles's heart raced. Even his hands were clammy, like a teenager who knew that his date wasn't just any girl. She was special. At some point, maybe after watching Perrie Lynn skate live for the first time, Miles was hit by how fast the weekend had passed. He'd wished he could have slowed it down, made it last.

Nineteen years ago, he'd found Lark interesting and fun—and pretty. He still did.

What would have happened if there had been no pregnancy? Could he and Lark have developed their relationship into something more lasting? They were alike in some important ways, namely that she loved her work as much as he loved his. He hadn't met many people who enjoyed such professional satisfaction. He smiled to himself. Lark was a walking encyclopedia about the latest health studies, even poking fun at herself when she tossed out some random tidbit about everything from mononucleosis to malaria.

Half a dozen times in the last four days Miles had wanted to kiss her. But he'd held back, fearing he'd deliver a message she wasn't prepared to receive.

Wishing he'd been with Lark on the flight back home, Miles took the shuttle back to the hotel. He had a meeting later that afternoon, which he was ready for, and a lunch presentation the next day that still needed work. He shut the door to his hotel room and opened his computer. A few seconds later, he got a videoconference signal and opened the program. It was Andi. And she wasn't smiling.

He'd barely said hello before she started in.

"Did it not occur to you that the camera might show the audience at that event? You were a second or two away from blowing your supposedly well-planned cover." Andi crossed her arms and pursed her lips.

"What do you mean? We sat up in the highest seats."

"And the camera panned that area to show the banners that some fans brought to support their favorite skaters."

His stomach flipped "Are you saying Brooke saw me. Us?"

"No, but only because she happened to be looking away at that moment. Then I hustled her into the kitchen to help me with a snack. It's a good thing I knew where you were."

Surprised by the anger in her voice, he said, "You *always* know where I am. We don't keep secrets, Andi."

"That's not the point. When there was a lull in the action, the cameras focused on the crowd—to offer proof of the record-breaking number of spectators. They showed the filled upper levels of the arena more than once."

"Really? We were surprised by the empty seats around us, since most of the arena was packed. We never saw our section on the big screen." He paused. "Well, it's over now. Brooke must have been happy about Perrie Lynn."

Andi laughed. "What an understatement. She was thrilled. And you're both right—the girl is a beautiful skater. But you don't sound all that happy. Did you think she should win the gold?"

"No, no, nothing like that," he said. "It's just that it was all so exciting, and now it feels like a letdown that regular life goes on. I have a meeting at Stiles to evaluate their communication skills training program later this afternoon and a keynote at a state nurses' conference tomorrow. It seems pretty mundane after the last few days."

"You're right." She grinned, leaning in to enlarge her image on the screen. "It sounds dull as dishwater. On the other hand, from the flash I saw, you and Lark seemed like quite a couple, huddled together, all smiles. Is there something you're not telling me? Are you and Lark planning to go to the Internationals?"

He wished. "We're definitely *not* going to the Internationals. We'll be watching at home with everybody else. My calendar is filled. I even have talks out of town during those weeks in February." He told Andi about Lark running into Maxine in the hotel shop. "That was a chance encounter and it worked out fine, but it's just as well we aren't heading for Norway. Wouldn't be like slipping in and out of Boston."

"Right. It's subterfuge, though, no matter how you look at it, Miles."

"Are you saying we should tell Brooke about her half sister now?"

She shook her head. "No, but the time can't be too far off. And what about Perrie Lynn's mother? I heard she's sick."

"You heard that on TV? The commentators talked about it?"

"Uh-huh. You didn't hear the stories? More like sound bites. Seems like these top athletes almost always have some kind of family situation going on."

"But none of this is really any of our business," Miles argued, trying to convince himself more than Andi.

"I didn't get the impression that Maxine's illness is in the past."

His mood darkened, just thinking how Lark would feel about that. Mentally, anyway, he'd become oddly protective of the Olsons and their privacy. "That may be, but it doesn't change what Lark and I are doing. Which, our trip to Boston aside, is pretty much nothing at this point. The ball isn't in our court. We have no choice but to wait."

"I suppose. But what about you and Lark? It's obvious you're getting closer."

Was she reading his mind? He struggled to respond.

"Your silence speaks volumes," Andi said drily.

"Okay, okay. Yes, we're becoming closer." He tried to make sense of his thoughts. "I can't go back to regular life, which was too much like self-imposed isolation. Yes, I see lots of people through work, but other than my time with Brooke I've been by myself. And the thing is, I enjoy Lark's company."

"Well, I'm glad you're finally admitting it."

Andi's knowing smile set him on edge, although he couldn't fault her positive attitude. Besides, what she'd implied about his feelings for Lark was true.

"Brooke is all I really care about," Andi said, switching her tone from teasing to serious, "and how we handle the explanations and the timing."

"There's no need to break the silence now, not with all that's going on with Perrie Lynn." He lowered his voice to say something that had been on his mind for weeks. "I can't believe how lucky I was to learn about her at all. If it hadn't been for Brooke—and Mamie—becoming skating fans, I would still be in the dark. And I'd never have reached out to Lark. Even from here in the background, it's a privilege to know the truth and be a witness to what's happening in Perrie Lynn's life."

"Okay, then, it's probably not a good idea to introduce Brooke to Lark, either."

"Wait, wait… I haven't even thought that far," he said emphatically. "I mean, we're having dinner on Friday. Not a serious step."

Andi groaned. "Right. It's written all over you—I can see it through the computer screen. I think you've fallen in love with her."

That hit him in the gut. In a good way, he thought, laughing inside at his own reluctance to face what was happening. "So, tell me how *you* are. How's the job—or the job search?"

Casting a pointed look his way, she said, "Ah, you're a quick change-of-subject artist. That's okay, but I have to admit nothing in my professional life has changed yet. Apparently, the merger is taking longer than expected. Let's just leave it at that."

"I'm here if you need anything." The last thing he wanted was for Andi to be under stress. As badly matched as they'd been as partners, they shared Brooke, and Andi was a great mom. Always had been. Somehow they'd ended up friends, remaining on each other's side.

When they ended their call, it wasn't Andi's job conundrum that stayed on his mind, it was her observation about him—and Lark. Truthfully, he'd have been happy if the weekend had gone on and on. And now he'd asked her out. Confusing or not, he was looking forward to Friday.

LARK STIRRED THE eggs while Evan watched the toaster and kept up his analysis of the pros and cons of his most recent idea for a science-fair project. Lark let her mind drift back to projects from the past. One year, she'd helped him layer oatmeal, rice, corn-flakes and kidney beans to represent layers of the earth in a terrarium, finally ending with trees in the topsoil, constructed with cardboard and foil wrapping paper. Evan had added twigs from birds' nests to the trees, giving the project extra flair. She smiled at the memory of the mess they'd made in the kitchen of their house, a big sprawling place in an upscale development across town. A terrific house, she admitted, but only for the right family. Lyle still lived there, but Lark had never felt at home in its many rooms. Or maybe she'd never felt at home with Lyle.

"A girl in my class wants to team up. Parker's really smart, but kinda quiet," Evan said with a shrug. He dropped the hot toast on the plate and added a dollop of strawberry jam on top. "She thinks we should do a graphic display showing where some of the new planets are. Like how far away they are from the earth. Parker will write the descriptions, but she wants me to do the talking when we have to explain what the distances mean."

"Sounds like a fair trade-off," Lark mused. "I'm always in awe when scientists tell us how many years it would take us to get to some of those new planets. New to us, that is. They've been out there all along."

"Yeah, we were thinking about how old we'd be if we did a round-trip to some of them, maybe showing on the computer how the space travelers would age, compared to the people back here on Earth," Evan explained.

"Okay, you've officially sent me deep into the weeds. Good thing I can scramble eggs the way you like them." She grinned. "I might write about science and health, but physics and relative time stump me every time."

Evan shook his head, grinning. "I'll make sure Parker writes the script using words *everyone* can understand."

Lark put the finished eggs on his plate. "You do that, my friend. Accessibility. I earn my living making complex medical information easy to understand."

"I told Parker about your articles. She thinks it's cool you're a writer. And you can work without leaving the house."

"That *is* cool." Working at home was definitely one of the big perks of her business.

Evan ate quickly and got ready to catch the bus with little time to spare. As usual, they reviewed their plans, which included the bowling event that night, with an early return home on Saturday morning.

Lark spent the morning and into the afternoon organizing her notes and previous interviews for an article on what her editor at the online magazine called emerging viruses—the scary ones. At least the target audience for this particular feature was older adults, not parents. Otherwise, she feared she'd needlessly alarm parents, and she included herself in that group.

Her to-do list pared down, Lark happily left the computer at home and went off to meet Dawn for coffee. This was the first chance they'd had to talk since she'd gotten back from Boston.

After choosing a table tucked away in a corner of the Bean Grinder, Lark scanned the restaurant for familiar faces.

"I think the coast is clear," Dawn said. "I've been so eager to talk with you. Like I said in my text, I watched Perrie Lynn on Saturday night. I made up a story and told Chip I needed to see it because a couple of women are thinking of opening up a skating school in Sturgeon Bay and they might need some PR. Not a serious lie, all things considered."

Lark grinned. "She was really something, wasn't she?"

Dawn nodded. "And I could see *you* in her happy smile. And now she's going off to Norway. Wow. But then the announcers on TV talked about her mother being sick."

Lark quickly related her conversation with

Maxine, not leaving anything out. "I assume Maxine will be well enough to go to the Internationals with Perrie Lynn and the rest of the US team."

"What about you and Miles?"

Lark shrugged, wanting to avoid too much talk about a subject she had yet to figure out. "Well, we're having dinner at Hinterland in Green Bay tonight."

Dawn flopped back in the chair. "Ah, then you *did* have a good time in Boston. And it wasn't all about Perrie Lynn, was it?"

The skin on her face and neck heated up yet again. "I suppose I'm blushing."

"Of course. It's marvelously charming. And revealing. So, did something happen? Something special?"

"Special? I guess so." She leaned forward so she could lower her voice. "We had such fun. All the awkwardness between us vanished. We took long walks and shared all our meals and on Saturday night after the skating we went out for champagne."

"Sounds like a long date."

"Yes, I'm finally willing to say that. That's what the weekend was like."

"This is good," Dawn said, nodding.

Yes...it was good.

Lark arrived at Hinterland a few hours later, buoyant with happy energy. She spotted Miles inside and he smiled broadly when he saw her. They spent the first few minutes grinning, almost giddy as they caught up on what they'd been up to since Monday, when they'd parted. It was easy to be together, Lark thought, when they let themselves show their feelings. But a stab of caution distracted her. She was feeling excited and happy, true. But did Miles feel the same way, or was his conversation just casual banter?

"We have a long wait ahead of us before we see her skate again, so we might as well settle in," Miles said after the waiter brought a basket of hot bread to the table.

She nodded. "We've got weeks to go."

"So, here's what I'm thinking," Miles said. "Perhaps we could see each other more often now. I'd like to meet for coffee, share some meals, maybe go to the movies." He grinned. "Act like adults."

"Of course," she said, her heartbeat picking up speed. But the cautious side of her waved a red flag. "But it's probably not a good idea to talk about it. You know, to tell other people we're *seeing* each other, or anything like that. I mean, I can't introduce you to Evan. And you can't introduce me to Brooke."

"I know what you're saying, Lark. I do." His expression had turned serious. "Yes, we need to be careful. But I don't want to pretend I don't feel what I feel. It's not all about Perrie Lynn anymore."

She glanced at her hands folded in her lap, aware she was blushing. "I don't know exactly what this reaction is all about, but somehow, I understand what you mean."

Miles nodded. "Like something that we thought couldn't happen between us is now happening? Even if it shouldn't be happening?"

She raised her hands in a gesture of confusion. "I don't know. Maybe it's all a little too magical. I'm happy when I'm with you. I was thrilled in Boston. It's confusing, though. I drift into the past and wonder."

"Wonder why we so easily went our separate ways years ago?"

She jerked her head back in surprise. She had been looking for words that would soften the harsh reality of what Miles had just said.

"We were *kids*, Lark. I was particularly immature. But I'm not that guy anymore. And yes, my feelings for you have come as a great surprise." He gestured around the restaurant. "That's why I want more evenings like this."

She squared her shoulders and looked him in the eye. "You're right. When we met at Hugo's so many weeks ago, I never imagined I'd look forward to spending time together."

"So, no matter what ultimately happens between us," he said, "we're united when it comes to Perrie Lynn."

"It's a deal." She picked up the menu. "Let's order or I'll fade away."

Miles shook his head and laughed.

Lark turned her attention to the page with that evening's specials. If she didn't divert her thoughts to more mundane things, she'd be overwhelmed with the possibilities opening up in her life. Situations, emotions, a bond with Miles blooming like a rosebud, opening and revealing its petals. Casting a furtive glance his way, she watched him studying the menu with a faint smile softening his features.

CHAPTER FIFTEEN

"THIS SURE IS an odd way to watch TV together, isn't it?" Miles observed. He was in the overstuffed chair in a hotel room in New Orleans, while she sat on her couch in her TV room. Yet even with the distance, she was good company.

"Odd, but fun," she said. "So far, it's been quite the spectacle."

"Between the depiction of Norwegian fjords and Norse folktales," Miles remarked, "I'm beginning to wish we had gone to Norway and could see this opening ceremony live."

"I only wish you were here," she said, "although Evan is due back from Parker's house soon. He's spending a lot of time over there working on his science-fair project. Apparently, it's not easy to make travel arrangements between planets."

"Yeah, those light-years are tricky," Miles quipped.

"Exactly. But getting back down to earth, is Brooke excited about the Internationals?"

"It's all so new to her, and get this," Miles said with a snorting laugh. "Mamie is teaching her the finer points of ski jumping. I hope she doesn't decide to try that sport on for size."

"Here they come," Lark said. "Now why didn't I buy a TV that spans the whole wall?"

They were quiet while the US athletes filed in, looking sharp in their white uniforms. The oldest athlete, a thirty-nine-year-old silver-medal-winning skier, wasn't ready to pack away the skis and was back to compete again and enjoy the honor of carrying the flag.

"No sign of Perrie Lynn yet." Miles spoke as the camera zoomed in and scanned the last of the cluster of Americans waving at the cameras.

Miles was about to speculate why they couldn't see her when Charlie, the network announcer, said, "We know all the athletes are wishing the best for their missing teammate, Perrie Lynn Olson. It remains to be seen if she will be here in time to compete."

As he heard Lark's gasp, Miles sat up straight and planted his feet on the floor.

"In case some of our viewers haven't heard

the sad news," Charlie continued, "a few days ago, US silver medalist Perrie Lynn Olson quietly delayed her travels to Norway when her mother's health took a sudden turn for the worse. Unfortunately, after a long battle with cancer, Maxine Olson died early this morning."

"Oh, no, Miles. This is terrible… I don't know what to say."

Her voice was hoarse, and he was hit with a longing to gather her in his arms. It was just as well that the commentators continued talking about the situation, because he, too, had no words.

"It's still unclear if she'll arrive in time for the competition," Allen, one of the two skating commentators, remarked. His on-camera partner, Katie, pointed out the problem of being ready to compete with little time to prepare.

"It sounds like she might miss out altogether," Lark said. "And that's not the half of it. What a devastating loss for her. I can't imagine."

Miles was still figuring out how to respond when Charlie began to speak again. "Her arrival date and time remains uncertain, but Declan Rivers, Perrie Lynn's coach and now the spokesperson for the family, issued a statement, confirming that the young skater and her father will arrive soon. Rivers reiterated that she *will* compete—as her mother would have wanted."

"Sadly, we've seen this kind of tragedy happen before in the International family," Katie added in a subdued voice, "but the athletes usually call on every ounce of courage and determination they can muster and perform through their grief."

"It's a point of pride," Allen added.

Charlie closed the segment by saying they'd provide updates over the following days.

"I guess we have to just wait and see," Lark said. "Several days ago I noticed a Facebook message more or less saying that the page would be quiet until after the Internationals. I assumed Maxine had posted it for Perrie Lynn. It was a bit vague, now that I think about it."

"It's difficult to believe this happened, but it's almost eerie how significant your encounter with Maxine turned out to be," Miles said. "I can only imagine what Eric and Perrie Lynn are going through."

"I know." Lark's voice wavered. "I'm

going to have to get myself together here, though. Evan will soon be coming through the door."

"I understand."

"One more thing before we go. I think it's time I went to Lyle and filled him in."

"Now?" Miles asked, surprised.

"Well, yes. He's not going to be nice about it, so I figure he needs time to get used to the news. I know for certain, he'll be shocked."

She fell silent, but Miles sensed she was trying to find her way to an explanation.

"I was a safe choice for Lyle," Lark said. "A hometown girl and all that. Looking back, he saw me as respectable and smart enough to fit into his business crowd."

"It's hard for me to hear you describe yourself in those terms, as if marrying you was a calculation of some kind." As if he had any insight into the reasons anyone married the wrong person. "I know it's complicated, though."

Once they ended the call, Miles couldn't get himself to turn off the TV, even when he went online and saw the news about the Olson family added to the network's website. Without Lark on the phone with him, he was restless, even anxious. He surfed through the channels, finally settling on a late-night rerun of an old crime show. The specter of Lark going to talk to her ex-husband loomed and stole his attention. He was so preoccupied with the thought that the simple show challenged his ability to concentrate, not even the grisly thriller he'd brought with him seemed an adequate distraction.

He smiled to himself. Another day dominated by thoughts of Lark.

"LYLE IS EXPECTING YOU." Jen's tone was typically friendly. "He's on the phone, so it will just be a few minutes."

Despite the satisfaction of knowing she still got along well with her husband's longtime assistant, Lark began to regret arranging this meeting with Lyle at his office and giving him home-field advantage. But since she had no idea how he'd react to what she had to say, she hadn't wanted to meet in the house they'd once shared, or in a public place like a coffee shop.

"No problem," Lark said, taking one of the empty chairs in the reception area of the office. "I'll check my phone while I wait."

She pretended to focus on a couple of messages, but the butterflies beating their wings in her stomach were too distracting. To bolster her confidence she'd called Miles from the car before venturing inside. Despite all his encouraging words, his pep talk was clearly forced. Her ex-husband was nothing like his ex-wife, who'd already known about Perrie Lynn, anyway. *Face it*, she thought, *Andi is a far nicer person than Lyle.*

A few minutes later, Lyle appeared in the doorway, his mouth a grim slash. He remained silent but waved her inside.

"Are you sure this is a good time?" she asked. "Is something wrong?"

"It's as good a time as any. You're the one who sounded serious on the phone. You had to see me." Smirking, he added, "What? Do you need money or something?"

Stunned, the muscles in her neck and shoulders tightened. "I most certainly do not. When have I ever asked you for money?"

He flicked his hand dismissively, then pointed to the chair across from his desk in a half-hearted invitation for her to sit. He sat in his own chair. "Okay, okay. Just checking. You're looking well, by the way. Evan keeps me posted about your latest articles. Are you worried about him?"

"No. This isn't about Evan, although it will affect him." Admittedly, an understatement.

For the first time, Lyle knit his forehead in curiosity. Taking advantage of the opening, she jumped into the conversation. "I need to tell you about something that happened to me long before I met you." She stared past him out the window to focus on the darkening sky. More snow was on the way. She'd hurry through this and go home, where she'd be safe before the roads became blanketed in snow. With her gaze on the thickening bank of pewter-tinged clouds, she said, "When I was nineteen, I had a child, a little girl."

Lyle's eyes widened at first, and then his mouth fell open as she spilled all the important details about that pivotal year, right up to fleeing to Dublin. "I never told my family about the baby—they still don't know. It was my secret and I've kept it all this time."

"And why are you telling me now?" he asked, his blue-gray eyes as icy as his tone. "Did she contact you?"

"No. I ended up finding her, completely by accident." She wiped away the dampness forming on the back her neck. "As it happens, she's a figure skater, a silver medalist at the North American Figure Skating Competition in Boston. Now, she's supposed to compete in the Internationals, but that's a bit up in the air."

Lyle tilted his head back as he said, "Oh, I get it. That's why you went to Boston. To see the girl?"

"Well, yes, but I haven't met her." She was puzzled. "Of all the things you could have asked me, you started with my trip to Boston?"

"Oh, I've got questions, all right." Lyle used his tightly folded arms as a shield over his broad chest. "Not that they matter all that much anymore. But I wanted to clarify that you lied about the reason you went to Boston. Have it on the record, I mean."

His voice couldn't have been any flatter, but Lark knew that was Lyle's way of controlling smoldering anger. "If you want to call it a lie, then by all means do so, but I have article assignments based on some research I did in Boston about young athletes." She couldn't resist, and asked, "Besides, what difference does it make to you?"

"Your sarcasm is charming. Of course you lied." His accusations brought back painful memories for Lark. It was obvious Lyle still enjoyed any chance to criticize her. "Turns out you've been lying for years."

Lark nodded. "I realize I should have told you a long time ago. But I was afraid."

"Of what?"

Lark extended an open palm toward him. "You. You aren't tolerant of weakness or mistakes. I assumed you'd find ways to throw this in my face. But long ago I stopped caring what you think of me." How freeing. His good opinion of her mattered not a whit. Good thing, too, because at the moment, she couldn't remember what she'd ever found appealing about him. He was classically handsome, and he'd worked hard to make his food-distribution business successful. She'd admired that. Still did.

"Hmm...as I see it, our son will be badly hurt by your mistakes. How do you think he's going to feel when he finds out his mother was a careless teenager, who got herself pregnant and then gave away the kid? His secret half sister. And when were you planning to break the news?"

Lark forced herself to look directly at him. "I don't know yet. It depends on many issues, and I plan to wait until it's closer to the time I can meet her." She told Lyle about Perrie

Lynn's training and Maxine's illness and recent death. "Perrie Lynn and her dad are in charge of what happens and when. Miles and I are happy to go along with their decisions."

"Miles? That's the guy? Did he go to Boston, too?"

Lark's voice shook when she answered. "Well, yes, he arranged it. He's the one who first made the connection between the young skater and—and us."

"Oh, really? So, you flew off to Boston with the guy who got you pregnant. Nice image. Evan will be impressed."

"For heaven's sake, Lyle, this all happened half a lifetime ago." Did she really need to spell it out? "We both went on with our lives. He has a daughter of his own now. Miles and I both grew up, and so did our child. She's a lovely and accomplished young woman."

He jabbed his index finger at her. "You don't have any wiggle room here, so don't go using that exasperated tone with me." Lowering his hand, but not his voice, he kept going. "And what does any of this have to do with me? Nothing. Other than protecting Evan as much as possible from your secret past." Lyle sneered as only Lyle could. "And you can bet I'll do what's necessary to make sure he's not hurt."

"I'm expecting you to help him understand," she said, raising her voice to match his. "I hope I can trust you to support me when I explain the situation, and I assume you'll keep your nasty judgment to yourself. Evan will likely meet his half sister one day."

"Ha! You really expect all that of me?" He stood up behind his desk.

Flinching at his booming voice, Lark sat alert on the edge of the chair and watched his every move. He turned his back to her and stared out the window.

"I should make this easier for you, huh? You're a *liar*. Talk about false pretenses." He whirled around to face her. "You had a huge secret and married me, anyway. You gave away a kid, Lark. It's a big deal."

Realizing the only important part of the conversation was over, she stood. "I don't expect you to make any of this easy on me. I don't care what you think of me, but to save you some trouble, I've been hard enough on myself that nothing you can say or do can touch me." She picked up her bag and headed to the door. "I expect you to cut me some slack because you want what's best for Evan. Your contempt for me won't help him."

"You can't dictate how I feel, Lark."

"You and I aren't kids," she said, her hand on the doorknob. "We share custody of a boy on the brink of becoming a teenager. We've managed to stay civil through our divorce, because we both wanted what's best for him. I trust you want to keep it that way."

Lyle stepped toward her. For the first time since she'd arrived, his features were relaxed, his expression more curious than disgusted. "How do you know this girl wants to meet you? After all, you abandoned her."

She winced at his words. "After this conversation, it's become even clearer to me why I didn't confide in you. I've been second-guessing myself for years, but no more."

"What? You expect me to feel sorry for you?"

She let out a cynical laugh. "Not at all. Maybe I hoped you'd try to understand what it was like to be a scared young woman, maybe try walking in my shoes. But I can see now that you haven't mellowed over the years." She paused and sighed heavily, disappointed that the sliver of hope she'd had for this conversation had vanished. "I'm not asking anything of you. I just thought you should know the story."

Lyle narrowed his eyes. "Evan will need someone to talk to when he finally learns this distasteful story about his mother. You bet I'll be there for him. And don't be shocked if he's not overjoyed when he hears your news."

Enough. She could go a few more rounds with him, but what good would that do?

She opened the door. "Thanks for seeing me."

After managing a smile for Jen on her way out, she hurried back to her car. At least it was over. That's the best she could say about her meeting with the man she'd once shared her life with. Impossible as that seemed.

Filled with the same old pain for past mistakes and bad judgment, Lark turned the key in the ignition and started the drive home under heavy cloud cover.

CHAPTER SIXTEEN

SITTING NEXT TO Miles on her couch, Lark was hyperalert in the most positive way possible. With every sense awake and alive, she reveled in nearly perfect contentment. She and Miles had tried to relax as they watched a couple of groups of skaters perform their short programs, and now they were waiting for Perrie Lynn's turn. Only the pain she felt for Perrie Lynn and Eric over Maxine's death drew her attention away from the moment.

Earlier, the network had shown footage of Perrie Lynn arriving, her father on one side and Ophelia Bensen, her choreographer, on the other. The reporter had explained that Ophelia, better known as Leffie, was a legendary skater in the 1970s. For two years, Leffie had worked closely with Perrie Lynn to create complex but artistically sophisticated programs, which had been one element of Perrie Lynn's great leap forward. Leffie would be by her side and, along with Eric and Declan, see her through the competitions.

"It seems Perrie Lynn is all Charlie and the commentators can talk about," Miles remarked.

"But think of it. It was her first time at the NorAms and now the Internationals. Even without the tragedy of losing Maxine, they'd be talking about her as the surprising newcomer on the scene." She paused. "But it wouldn't be anything like the frenzy of coverage over these last couple of days."

Lark was aware of the way she referred to "losing Maxine," rather than simply saying that Perrie Lynn's mother died. Still, deep in her heart she knew the teenager had lost the most important person in her world—and a woman who had loved her with her whole heart. Someday, maybe, she'd tell Perrie Lynn what Maxine had said to her: *I will never, ever, know how to thank you for giving me the gift of Perrie Lynn.*

Even with her maturity, Perrie Lynn was still young and likely had no idea of the depth of Maxine's love for her.

Miles nudged her. "Hey, you went quiet on me. Were you thinking about Maxine?"

"Uh-huh. She's on my mind a lot."

"I find myself thinking about Eric. He's also had a tough time these last couple of years. Now he has to hold it together for Perrie Lynn. Seems like so much pressure."

"Odd how concerned we are about people we don't know, including Perrie Lynn." She pointed toward the TV. "And she has no idea we're here, heartbroken for her. Showing up is a victory in itself for her."

"Funny how familiar all this feels now," Miles said, amused. "Even that the final group will include our old friends Molly and Julia."

"Brooke must be excited. Is she with Mamie?"

"Not officially." Miles grinned. "But Andi invited Mamie to come over to the house to watch with them. Mamie has a waitress job and college classes, but she juggled things around and accepted. Brooke is thrilled."

"Your Brooke sounds like such a terrific little girl," Lark said. "We're lucky, you and I, to have such great kids. I just hope..." She stopped herself from going on because she'd drift into Lyle territory and the road ahead when the time came to tell their kids about their half siblings. Lyle's words still haunted her.

"You hope Lyle doesn't try to turn Evan

against you," Miles said. "That's what you were about to say, isn't it?"

She nodded, but then rubbed her palms together with enthusiasm. "But that's a worry for another day. Right now, I want to revel in this moment."

"Good. They're almost ready to start."

Lark quickly got up and fetched the snack tray from the kitchen. Cheese and crackers, grapes, and pieces of rich dark chocolate. She topped off their glasses of merlot and flopped down on the couch.

"A feast," Miles said.

In tandem, they leaned forward as they watched the screen intently, and there she was, standing outside the rink with the others, waiting to glide onto the ice in the now familiar blue costume and the white flower in her hair. Lark flashed back to the image of Maxine in her blue hat.

"She's so, so beautiful," Lark said with a deep, long sigh.

"Like you, Lark."

She turned her head at his words spoken only a note above a whisper. "What a sweet thing to say."

He pressed his warm lips on her forehead. "It's true."

She knew she was flushing, something she couldn't control. But so what? Miles always left her feeling warm all over.

They stayed perched on the edge of the couch as the skaters went through their practice spins and jumps and only settled back once the short programs began. Miles joked that the skating world and its conventions and lingo had become familiar, as if he'd been a fan all his life. Lark felt the same way as one skater after another took to the ice. Unlike being in the arena in Boston, they heard the running TV commentary about the skaters, including the high hopes for Lilibeth Alain, a French skater who had won a bronze medal four years earlier. She was going for the gold this time.

When Lilibeth lost her footing coming out of a jump and tumbled to the ice, the commentators immediately began to calculate the deductions for lost points.

"So far, one of the top Russian skaters underperformed, and now the only French skater here had a glitch," Lark said when Lilibeth finished her program and slowly made her way off the ice to loud applause from her loyal home-country supporters. "It's scary that the commentators are so sure that one mistake is devastating—wonderful skaters all but booted out of the competition."

"They also keep track of who does better than expected, like Maya Watanabe, one of the Canadians," Miles pointed out. "I wonder what they'll say about Perrie Lynn."

At that moment, Katie's voice broke in. "Well, so far, there's room at the top," she said, adding that the short program scores were topsy-turvy.

"As soon as we come back, it will be Perrie Lynn Olson's turn to skate," Charlie said. "No matter what happens, the young woman's presence here is a miracle in itself and a testament to her courage."

Lark muted the TV and picked up a piece of chocolate. "I'm ready to jump out of my skin. I was calmer while we waited in Boston."

"Me, too." Miles's eyes softened as he stared at her. "It may be a miracle that she's there, but it seems equally miraculous that we're here together watching her."

Surprised that she found herself unable to speak, she nodded her agreement.

They moved closer together and Lark reached for Miles's hand at the same moment he reached for hers. Seconds later, Perrie Lynn made her graceful entrance, quickly establishing her presence.

As the music began, Lark found herself experiencing the skate as if she were on the ice with Perrie Lynn. With each jump, she held her breath, and almost felt the muscles in her own legs stretching into long extensions. The commentators telegraphed each move, including the jump near the end of the program. A double axel, Allen said, remarking that it often proved the bane of a skater's existence.

Perrie Lynn set up for the jump, but even Lark instantly noted the uncharacteristic tentative lift off the ice, resulting in an awkward landing. Perrie Lynn tipped to the side on one wobbly skate.

Lark squeezed Miles's hand as Perrie Lynn touched the ice with her fingertips to right herself—successfully.

Miles exhaled. "She stayed on her feet."

Katie and Allen remarked that although she hadn't exactly saved the jump she hadn't lost all the points, either. "Unfortunately, the bobbled landing will prove expensive," Katie added.

Perrie Lynn finished her final spin and held her last position for a mesmerizing few seconds before breaking the pose. She lowered her head and for just a second or two she ran the backs of her hands across her eyes. When she raised her head, she was the proud skater once again, bowing, waving and smiling in response to the outburst of applause. Then it was Lark's turn to release the air she'd held in her chest. Letting her shoulders slump, she felt her body collapse.

As if on cue, Katie spoke about an otherwise flawless program. "Vintage Perrie Lynn, and it leaves her within striking distance. And considering what she's gone through it was an incredible night for her."

By the time the rest of the skaters finished and the rankings were listed, Perrie Lynn ended up in fifth place. By all accounts, not a bad place to be.

"I better check my phone," Miles said. "Andi agreed to let Brooke text me after Perrie Lynn skated." He read the message aloud. "'Don't worry, D. Mamie and I still think she'll medal.'"

Lark watched him text back. He spoke the words as his fingers worked the pad. "'Not worried. PL was great. One mistake not too bad. See you tomorrow night.'"

Lark sighed to herself. What a dad, especially for a little girl. She wished she felt as good about Lyle's influence on Evan. Suppressing those negative thoughts, she watched the studio commentators discuss Perrie Lynn…one more time. She let her head rest on Miles's shoulder as the sports journalists filled in some details of Maxine's long illness.

"Four years," Miles said, echoing the commentator's words. "Perrie Lynn was only fourteen when her mom got sick the first time."

"I know life isn't always fair," Lark said, "but that must have been a terrible struggle. And Maxine found the strength to take Perrie Lynn to Michigan to work with Declan."

Miles shook his head. "This whole child-athlete undertaking seems like a family affair for all the skaters."

When the commentators moved on to another topic, Miles got to his feet to go home.

"This was so much fun," Lark said, "but I'm really sorry we can't watch the long program together."

As they moved slowly out of the TV room and toward the front door, Miles put his arm around her, drawing her closer to him. "I wish I didn't have to be out of town, but I've had this booking for over a year. No way to change it."

Instead of dropping his arm when they reached the door, Miles put his other arm around her. "When I'm away I think about you all the time."

She rested her head against his chest. "It's the same for me."

"I'm glad," he whispered, running his hand lightly across her hair.

Before she had a chance to consider if being this close was a good idea, his fingers lifted her chin and he lightly brushed his lips across hers. He raised his mouth, but she stood on tiptoes and found his lips again. As he deepened the kiss, his arms tightened around her.

When they separated, he ran his thumb across her cheek and whispered, "Good night, Lark." He hurried out the door.

She touched her fingertips to her lips as she stood in the doorway and watched him drive away. They'd also come a long way from their stilted goodbye the morning they met at Hugo's.

But…the questions. They were always there, the questions that disturbed her ability to enjoy the moment. Why couldn't she relax? Why was she sad when Miles left, but sometimes fearful of her own longings? Shutting the door behind her and leaning against it, she closed her eyes. Images of Perrie Lynn lifted her up into the joy of recalling her glide across the ice. When Lark opened her eyes again, she went to the window and gazed at the dark night sky. The moon was hidden behind heavy clouds. She smiled, resigned to her confusing emotions. Unable to sort through them, she simply let them be.

THE KISS. IT WAS all she'd thought about the last two days. She sat on her couch in the TV room with her feet tucked under her, warm in heavy wool socks. Her open tablet sat balanced on her lap. *How delicious to be held in his arms.* She shook her head—again— to concentrate on the article displayed on the screen. Normally, a piece on rare and virulent viruses captured her attention. Dawn even teased her about her fascination with medical research. But not that evening. She checked her watch. Lyle should be bringing Evan home right about now. Evan himself had said he preferred to come home after dinner and work on his science-fair project rather than spend the night at Lyle's house.

When she heard the door open, she called out, "Hi, honey, I'm back here."

A weak hello followed, but then another voice came from the living room. She put the laptop on the coffee table and went to the living room where Lyle stood next to Evan. "Oh, hi, Lyle. I didn't expect you to come in." When was the last time he'd followed Evan into the house when he dropped him off? She couldn't recall.

"No, I suspect you didn't." His sneer sent a shiver down her back.

"What's up?" Was that a quaver in her voice?

Lyle straightened. "I guess you'll have to tell Evan what's up. I decided he deserved to know the truth about his mother and her little surprise."

Lark glanced at Evan, who kicked off his second boot and stared at the floor. No doubt wishing he could drop through it. She closed her eyes to block out the sight of her ex. A low moan escaped, along with the words "How could you?"

"How could *I*?" That nasty sneer remained, as if it had become a permanent feature.

Why was he enjoying this so much? She

pushed away her emotions. Evan was the priority now. "I'll talk with you about this when we're alone, Evan."

Evan nodded, cutting his eyes to her for the first time.

"You can leave now, Lyle. I think you've done enough damage for one night." She moved alongside Evan in the small space by the front door. Showing her alignment with her son was the only way to contain her rage at her ex-husband.

"Yeah, well, like I said in my office the other day, you don't have much room for judgment. You want to talk about damaging our son, look in the mirror."

"Get. Out." She didn't need to shout, nor did she need to hide her anger. And dismay.

Lyle turned to Evan. "You call if you need anything, son. You can stay with me anytime. You know that."

Evan continued looking down, not reacting to Lyle's words.

Lyle let himself out the door and shut it behind him. Lark followed and snapped the lock with conviction, hoping her ex heard the sound of being shut out.

"Let's go to the kitchen and talk," she said.

"What's to talk about?" Unfamiliar belligerence had seeped into Evan's voice.

"For starters, I want to know exactly what your father told you."

He brushed his bangs out of his eyes as he looked up at her. "That you got pregnant and gave away...you know, the baby."

Reeling at the stark words, Lark led the way to the kitchen and pulled out the chair. "There's a little more to it than that. And your father never should have told you without my knowledge. I trusted him to let me work this out with you in my own way."

"It's true, though, huh?" He dropped into the chair, plunked his elbows on the table and rested his chin in one palm.

"Sweetie, yes, I had a baby girl and her father and I put her up for adoption for what we believed were all the right reasons." She told the truth, but her heart pounded so hard her ears pulsated. "We were young and couldn't give her the life she deserved. We weren't ready to be parents, not at all like your dad and I were when you were born."

"But you lied to Dad." He lowered his eyes and his voice. "That's what he said."

Lark flipped the switch on the electric kettle. She needed a cup of whatever tea would calm her down. But no balm was strong enough to heal her heartbreak. "This isn't the way I planned to tell you about this part of my past. I told your dad about it for the first time a few days ago, because I learned who she is—who that baby grew up to be."

"Dad said she's sort of famous. But you were, like, careless and irresponsible. You never told him because you were, you know, ashamed of yourself."

No surprise Lyle had made her look as bad as possible. He was finally getting his revenge for her demand for a divorce. He'd never gotten over that. Hurt pride. An affront. Whatever. He'd never understood that his constant disrespect, especially with respect to her writing career, had poisoned everything in their marriage and had spilled over to Evan. Protecting their son from the constant negativity had been her primary motivation to leave him.

"I made lots of mistakes, Evan. But I did the best I knew how at the time. The day she was born, I longed to keep her. But for so many reasons I knew I couldn't do right by her."

"So her father didn't want her, either," Evan said.

"Did your dad tell you that?"

"Nope. But I can figure it out."

She turned away to steep chamomile tea and pour a glass of juice for Evan. When she sat at the table, she took a few seconds to gather her thoughts. "I'm going to start from the beginning. I really want you to understand this."

It didn't take long to fill in the basics, especially admitting her mistake in withholding from Lyle this important fact of her life. She took a deep breath. "That was my biggest mistake, and one that affects you now. But your dad should not have told you—he had no right."

"So, she's really a figure skater?"

The question didn't surprise her. "I was getting to that."

In almost one long sentence without pauses, she explained Miles's December call. Evan's blue-gray eyes opened wide when Lark began talking about the North American Figure Skating Competition and the Internationals. "So, to bring you up to the present, Perrie Lynn is due to skate again on Saturday." She considered her next words. "I'm going to be here at home watching her, and I hope you'll be here, too. No matter what happened in the past, she's your half sister. When the time is right, you'll be able to meet her." She stopped to let that sink in. "But only if you want to."

"Dad said you *really* went to Boston to see Perrie Lynn."

"Yes, that's why I went." She took a sip of her tea. "And by chance I met her mother, Maxine. She was sick, and now she's gone. She died only a few days ago."

Evan's penetrating stare startled her. "You lied about that trip. And you missed one of my games."

"Your dad was there, right?"

He nodded.

Evan's expression, his accusatory words and tone—they reminded her of Lyle. That started the smoldering in the pit of her stomach. She protectively wrapped one arm tightly around her waist as if that could settle her. "I don't intend to get picky about this, but Miles was able to get tickets, and I said yes. No, I didn't tell you or your father the whole story of why I was going. True enough."

"If dad hadn't told me, when were you going to?"

"Fair question, Evan." She paused, nervously running her fingers across her mouth as she searched for the right words. "I was going to wait to tell you everything, start to finish, when I was free to make contact with Perrie Lynn. We think that will be later in the spring. But maybe it's better this way. It's all out in the open now."

"What about that guy…Miles?"

Lark's heart jumped at the unexpected question. "Um, what about him?"

"Do you like him? Are you going out with him or something?"

To lie, or not to lie. Not a difficult decision at that point. "Miles and I have become closer. We aren't kids anymore. And we do like each other. A great deal. No matter what happens we'll be friends."

"You talk to him a lot. And text with him, don't you?"

"Why, yes." Puzzled, she asked, "Did your dad tell you that?"

"No, you never liked texting, but now you do it all the time. And you go into your room and close your door after you think I'm asleep."

"Does that bother you?"

"Nope." He made circles on the table with his juice glass. "But here's what I want to know. Why didn't you tell Dad, back then, I mean, before you married him?"

She took a sip of the still hot tea and felt its sting on her tongue. "That's a hard one. But my silence was a mistake. I admit that. No argument." Regardless of what Lyle had done, she didn't want to violate the unspoken rule about not talking down the other parent. "Let's just say that back then I was a little intimidated by your dad's anger. You see, Miles and I weren't careless, but I knew it would seem that way."

She laid her hand on his arm, as if signaling an important point. "Sometimes things happen even when you're careful. But no one is perfect, and I didn't think your dad would understand that I'd made a bad choice to get involved with Miles. Not because of who Miles was, but we were much too young. And we didn't know each other very well."

Evan raised his eyebrows and nodded. Lark suspected her son understood more about his father's judgment than he was letting on. He also might have more than inklings about the relative freedom of college life and the carefree mind-set that went with it—or could go with it. That had been true for her.

Lark squeezed his arm. "I'll answer any questions you want. And I'll keep you posted about the way things unfold. But, facts are facts. You do have a half sister."

Evan quickly rose from the chair and said a perfunctory good-night before disappearing down the small hallway to his room. Lark let out a long low grunt, emblematic of her unhappiness about what Lyle had unleashed. As if the news itself wasn't serious enough, she'd been forced to deal with it after Lyle put her in the worst possible light.

She allowed herself a minute for a cynical huff. She'd seen her parents at their worst. Their clay feet had been all too evident. Now it was her turn to suffer the bad opinion of the person she loved most in the world.

CHAPTER SEVENTEEN

LATE ON SATURDAY AFTERNOON, Miles sat at his desk making last-minute decisions about what to keep and what to cut out of the speech he was due to deliver in only a few hours. Unfortunately, fine-tuning his presentation was taking much longer than he'd anticipated. *Maybe because I can't concentrate?* His own question made him laugh out loud. He wouldn't get his focus back until Perrie Lynn's performance was over, and that was still hours away. The way his evening schedule had worked out, he'd likely get back to his room that evening with plenty of time to spare to watch it.

Lark's call was a welcome distraction, not to mention his eagerness to hear her voice. She'd had a couple of difficult days, too. "The countdown begins," he said.

"Doesn't it just." She paused. "I wanted to check in. By the way, have you heard anything from Declan or Lisa Mandel?"

"No, not a word from either one, but I didn't expect they be in touch." He had left a message with Declan's assistant, simply asking the coach to pass on condolences from Miles and Lark.

"Reaching out to Eric through Declan was the best way to acknowledge the loss, but without violating our agreement," Lark said. "I couldn't imagine not doing something, even in the most roundabout way."

"You're right. Uh, how's Evan?"

"In a word, *quiet*. And now he's at Parker's house for the afternoon. They've been building quite the wire model of the location of planets, along with brightly colored arrows and mile markers. But…"

"Has he said anything about Perrie Lynn?" Miles asked, wishing he were with Lark and could wrap his arms around her. For the longest time they'd pretended these feelings weren't growing between them. The kiss had changed that. They needed to talk soon, and not about Perrie Lynn.

"Evan has been silent, so far, but he'll be here tonight. I intend to make sure he knows when she's skating, but I can't demand that he watch her with me."

"True, but you're taking every step you

can…" Miles wanted to say something, but searched for the right words.

"What? You didn't finish the sentence."

With a snicker, he said, "Ah, you caught that."

"And?"

"I was only going to say that we can't go back and fix what happened in the past. How many times can you apologize?" He'd let a note of rational logic into his tone. "And don't you think that Lyle is going to dig his own ditch? From everything you've said about Evan, I doubt he's easily turned against people, especially you."

"He is mature in some ways, and he's not mean," she said. "Believe me, I watched for that. Lyle has a cruel streak I'd just as soon not see passed on."

"For obvious reasons, you can't have any faith in Lyle, but I'd have some faith in that boy you had a major role in shaping." *I hope I'm right.*

"Thanks, Miles. I needed to hear that."

After they ended the call Miles acknowledged that Andi had been right. He'd fallen in love with Lark.

He saved the file of his speech and closed the computer. If he weren't careful, he'd soon be overcome with regrets about the past he'd been trying to put behind him. Better to go find distractions and stop the self-recriminations.

LARK PULLED THE two baked potatoes out of the oven and put one on each plate, along with slices of hot meat loaf—a couple of extra pieces for Evan. As she tried to focus on the vegetables in the steamer, she almost laughed out loud. Broccoli had never commandeered so much of her attention.

"Evan? Dinner's ready," she called in a voice louder than intended. Nerves, she thought, a bad case of nerves. Odd, her muscles tensed up talking to Evan and then were equally tense anticipating Perrie Lynn's performance. She took a deep breath and spooned broccoli onto Evan's plate.

"You don't have to yell," Evan said, appearing in the kitchen. "I was only in my room."

Lark couldn't miss the sullen expression, and before she could stop herself she made some trite remark about meat loaf being his favorite. She groaned inside listening to her lame attempt to sound normal in a situation that was anything but.

Pulling out a chair at her place at the table, Lark asked about the science-fair project.

"It's okay—we're keeping the model at her house. There's more room there."

Was that an embarrassed smile she saw? He was fighting hard enough to keep his feelings under wraps. "I'll bet there is," she said. That begged the question about why the kids hadn't set up at Lyle's house. Not that it mattered. "In any case, I'm glad you're enjoying the project."

He smirked. "It ranks up there with skiing and chess." He took another bite of meat loaf. "This is good."

She nodded her thanks, but then put down her own fork. "Look, I need to talk to you about tonight. You know it's the time for the women's long program. It determines who medals and could determine who goes on to the world championships."

He kept his eyes focused on his plate. "I know. I looked it up."

"Do you mean you looked up Perrie Lynn online?"

He shrugged. "What was I supposed to do?"

"Of course. I'm glad you did that on your own. I hope you'll watch her skate. With me."

She paused and consciously removed the desperation from her voice when she asked, "Will you do that?"

Another shrug, quick and noncommittal.

When they'd finished eating, she left the table to transfer pieces of chocolate cake to two plates. Evan muttered a quick thank-you when she put the plate in front of him. They ate their dessert in uneasy silence. Then, without needing to be reminded, Evan rinsed their plates and put them in the dishwasher, one of his regular chores. Obviously, he was carefully avoiding conversation of any kind.

"I won't push you, Evan. It's your choice, but I'll be watching and you can join me anytime."

Then she was alone with her thoughts. Evan had gone off to his room, saying that he and Eduardo, a friend from his chess club, were going to play chess on the computer.

A cup of strong coffee in hand, Lark turned on the TV and settled into the evening's International program, all the while wishing Miles was with her. Given his need to be in a tux at an awards banquet, they couldn't talk on the phone and watch together. He'd assured Lark he'd check his phone now and again for the scores she'd promised to text.

With any luck, he'd be able to slip away and get to his room in time to watch Perrie Lynn.

Her thoughts drifted back to Evan. Would he insist on isolating himself in his room? Apparently, he didn't lack curiosity about his half sister, but was he embarrassed to sit with his mother and watch? Would that be like confronting his mother's bad judgment and secrets?

She listened to the announcers with half her attention and her thoughts switched back and forth between Miles and Evan. But the magic of the night finally enveloped her like a cloak. First, the roaring crowds, and even Katie and Allen, all dressed up as if going off to a prom, showed their excitement and recounted their experiences of preparing for one of the biggest nights in any skater's career. Earning a ticket onto International ice was a sign of achievement, no matter the final standings.

Over the next couple of hours, the groups of women skated and Lark felt it all—the heartbreak of missed jumps and lost points, as well as the big smiles when they saw their posted scores and celebrated a personal best with excited hugs. Maybe for the first time, Lark understood the triumph of finishing in the top ten of the final standings in an International competition. That placement could determine if a skating career could continue to go forward.

Finally, the last group of skaters took the ice, and there she was, Perrie Lynn in her sparkling burgundy-red costume, perfect for the music from *Scheherazade*. Lark laced her fingers under her chin and hunched her shoulders in happiness, maybe mixed with a minor case of nerves. She laughed inside when she spotted Molly Walden and Julia James and realized she hoped they did well, too. Because of their dedication and determination, those two young women claimed a little corner in her heart.

The internal debate began, and when commercials for jam and jewelry droned on, Lark got up off the couch and went to Evan's door. She knocked with conviction, before opening it to see him at his computer. He looked up with surprise in his eyes. "Perrie Lynn's group is skating, and this is it for the Internationals." She paused and took a deep breath. "No matter what happens in the competition, I don't want you to miss her performance. Yes, the situation is unusual, but sooner or later, Evan, you'll meet her in person."

She'd never know for sure if she'd coaxed him out of his room or he'd have come out on his own. But without argument, he stood and followed her in time for the first skater, Maya, who was representing Canada. She'd just finished her warm-up and was in her starting pose at center ice. She had decided against classical music for this season's long program and chosen a medley of Beatles songs. She completed every jump and executed every spin, and got the audience clapping to the beat of the music. The commentator agreed she had the most complex program of all the skaters and had executed it perfectly. She immediately sat in first place.

"I read about the jumps," Evan said. "They have names like axel and lutz and salchow. I guess they were named after skaters."

"But not the loops and flips," she said, chuckling. "The jumps are spectacular and all that, but my favorite are the long extensions—the arabesques." So, Evan had been learning a little about skating. She kept her surprise to herself, hoping he'd reveal more without the need to prompt him.

Molly's program was breathtaking, perfection itself. Katie and Allen couldn't stop talking about it, remarking that Molly took the confidence gained from her NorAms title and let it fuel her International performance. Molly overtook Maya, and then Julia skated and turned one triple into a double, which caused her to drop into third place behind Maya. Once again, Allen and Katie talked about room at the top.

"I've learned the lingo now," she remarked. Lark explained to Evan that one small bobble had put Perrie Lynn in fourth place, but she still had a good chance to move up. "If she skates her best."

"But her, um, her mom died." Evan shook his head. "Must be tough."

"I know. They talk about it on TV a lot."

"Do you think she can skate her best?"

An important question. "I think the drive to finish what her mother helped her start is the motivator. They've worked for years to reach this level, even moving to Michigan to train with a famous coach. For most of these International-level athletes, the quest is all there is, and they don't do it alone."

Evan had stumbled a little over talking about Perrie Lynn's mom, but Lark believed that was to be expected. She herself was finding it easier to refer to Maxine as

Perrie Lynn's mother. It was the reality, and her language had to match it.

"She's such a beautiful skater," she said as Perrie Lynn made her way around the circumference of the ice, arms extended. "Miles says she gets everyone on her side before she even starts to skate, kind of the way the top speakers do before they utter the first word."

Evan frowned as if thinking about what she said, but he didn't take his eyes off the screen.

A pleasant buzz traveled through Lark when it struck her that Evan would like Miles. As much as Miles was athletic and fit, he was also an ideas person, curious and smart. Given the chance, he'd ask all the right questions about the science-fair project and show a natural affinity for a kid who studied chess moves.

Perrie Lynn took center ice and from there the first jump setup unfolded. A triple, perfectly executed from the lift and the turns high in the air, to the solid landing and easy transition to the next move. Allen commented that Perrie Lynn came into the building on fire, ready to skate. Knowing that was true, Lark cupped her hands over her mouth, breathing deeply to stay calm as Perrie Lynn continued to mesmerize the audience. Lark stole a sidelong glance at Evan and he was watching intently. Enjoying it? She couldn't say, but he was paying attention.

The four minutes passed in a flash of dizzying spins and dazzling arabesques. After a final one-foot glide the length of the ice and an impossible looking spread-eagle jump, Perrie Lynn completed the final spins— the exclamation point on the program. The standing ovation began before she came out of the spin into the dramatic ending pose.

"I haven't seen her skate very much, but this was truly remarkable," Lark said, just as Perrie Lynn broke the pose and covered her face with her hands. "Oh, Evan, it's hitting her now. The loss. All that love and commitment her mother poured into her came to fruition in those four minutes on the ice."

Evan nodded, and Lark staunched hot tears.

"Such a bittersweet moment," Allen said, expressing what every viewer was feeling.

"She rose to the occasion. Making her mother proud. She left everything out there on the ice," Katie added.

"Do you think she won, like the gold?" Evan asked.

Lark considered her answer, but pulled herself into an objective place. "The skaters before her were at their best, too, but there is room for her to jump ahead. I don't know enough to predict the technical score, but this was an incredible skate, adversity or not."

An image flashed on the screen and grabbed her attention. She pointed to Eric Olson, who was on his feet and smiling through his tears. "That's Perrie Lynn's dad."

Evan nodded. "It must be kind of tough for him, huh?"

"I'm sure it is."

"Seems like this stuff happens at the Internationals all the time," Evan said. "I remember there was a gymnast whose dad died on the way to arena and one of the swimmers lost a brother."

"Charlie, that network commentator, talked about that the other night."

The camera went back to Perrie Lynn, who sat between Leffie and Declan, their shoulders touching her. Protection, Lark thought. Perrie Lynn waved, for the moment, anyway, smiling in triumph.

When the scores were announced, Perrie Lynn jumped from her seat and thrust her arms over her head. She had moved up to second place, which meant Maya dropped to third. Two skaters were left—one a top contender from Japan, the other a little less reliable skater from Russia.

"She could win a medal, couldn't she?" Evan asked. "Or at the worst, come in fourth."

"That's right."

Captured by the tension of competition, she and Evan sat silent as Emi Hanyu mesmerized the audience with a gripping, dramatic performance to the music of *Phantom of the Opera*. "Emi is one of the most beautiful skaters of the group," Lark said, when the joyous artistic expressions led to a score that put her in first place, causing Perrie Lynn to drop to third.

"Uh-oh," Evan said. "If the last one, the girl from Russia, does really well, does that mean Perrie Lynn will drop?"

Lark, realizing she'd dug her fingernails into her palm, consciously opened her hands and stretched and spread her fingers. "Yes, that's exactly what it could mean. I've heard Katie and Allen say that particular skater is not as artistic as many others, including Perrie Lynn. That could make just enough of a difference. But I don't like rooting for a girl to skate poorly."

"Kinda makes you nervous, doesn't it?" Evan said.

Smiling to herself, Lark knew that no matter what happened, Evan would always be a little curious about Perrie Lynn.

In the end, the Russian skater took a bad fall, and the scores held. Perrie Lynn won the bronze.

"Cool," Evan said.

Squeezing his arm, Lark said, "Very cool."

Later that night, Lark told Miles about her evening with Evan. "So, I guess all in all, I'd have to say it was a pretty *cool* night," she said.

"And I can't wait to get home to celebrate with you."

Her stomach doing a little flip, she asked, "How soon can you get here?"

His delighted chuckle topped off a perfect day.

CHAPTER EIGHTEEN

THE RIVER WAS shallow and narrow along the stretch closest to town. Stepping away from the bumpy sloping bank, Lark took off down a long, smooth expanse of ice that ran through the middle of dense woods in the state park. The biting wind brushed her face, prompting her to reposition her scarf over her mouth and nose. That same strong wind would be at her back when she returned to the public dock and boat launch.

Not surprisingly, she wasn't alone on the river. Other skaters, both young and not so young, zipped past her. Unlike Lark, her companions were sure-footed. It would take more than a few minutes on the ice to feel secure on her feet like she had as a teenager. No matter. Simply skating after so many years was enough for Lark.

Until that morning, she'd all but forgotten she still had skates stashed in the basement, left over from her high-school years. She'd brought them out only a couple of times when she tried to interest Evan in skating years ago.

She passed a series of docks that jutted into the water in front of clusters of houses and cottages. Many were occupied year-round, but some were vacation getaways used for weekends of kayaking and canoeing on the river. As she skated, memories of childhood moments flowed through her. It was so easy to imagine herself as a young girl moving on to figure skating, spinning in place or lifting her body off the ice and turning two or three times in the air. Not that she'd ever done that. It had never even occurred to her. As a child, she'd been motivated by the thrill of speed.

Despite being awkward and slow, and feeling the hot strain in her thigh muscles, Lark realized the skating was calming her, preparing her for what was to come. Yesterday afternoon, she had texted her mom and asked her to watch the ladies' final International skating event—explanation to follow. Then she'd invited her to an early dinner on Sunday at the Half Moon Café, adding that she had something important to talk about. Good intentions to get together aside, Lark hadn't seen her mom since Christmas. With

Evan now aware of Perrie Lynn, the time had come to tell her mother everything.

Turning to head back, Lark pulled her knit hat tighter over her hair. Her early-morning skate had taken her away from the house when Evan was still sleeping, but she'd left a note for him, which also promised pancakes and bacon for breakfast. What would they talk about while she cooked and he ate his fill of his favorite pancakes? Maybe, now that Perrie Lynn had become more real to him, he'd ask some questions. Talking Evan was preferable to Silent Evan, even if she didn't like what he had to say.

Her fingers stiff from the temperature hovering around zero, Lark managed to replace her skates with her boots and drive the few blocks home. But she vowed to go back, maybe even the next day. The river wouldn't stay safely frozen for long.

She let herself into the house, calling out Evan's name. When he didn't answer, she went to his room, but heard the sound of the shower from his bathroom. She headed to the kitchen to start breakfast, and by the time he joined her, the smell of bacon was wafting through the house.

"Hey, pancakes coming up."

He nodded, a lopsided grin showing his pleasure. "So, how was your skate?"

"Slow and wobbly, but exhilarating. I don't know why I haven't found time to go out on the river before. It was my favorite thing when I was about your age."

"Maybe Perrie Lynn gets it from you…the interest in it and all," Evan said with a quick one-shoulder shrug. "She looks like you, sort of." He pointed to his forehead and the more subtle version of Lark's widow's peak that he'd inherited.

"You could be right about her affinity for skating. Maybe I would have liked spinning and jumping as much as I liked building speed and flying down the river." She swept one palm across the other to emphasize the notion of speed.

"Uh, Dad called. He's really mad."

She dropped silver-dollar-size dollops of batter on the heated griddle before turning around to look at Evan. "At me. He's mad at me. Nothing will change between you and your dad."

His eyebrows lifted. Lark read doubt in his reaction, and Evan hadn't looked her in the eye, either. "You don't believe me. I can see it in your face. Let me be clear. Your dad is entitled to be angry with me. But it has nothing to do with you."

Lark turned back to the stove to flip the pancakes and turn off the burner under the bacon. She'd expected questions, was happy to answer them. Secrecy had its limits and it also had the potential to harm. She understood that now.

"If Dad wants me to stay with him all the time that sure affects me."

Her gut rolled. She took in a breath before pivoting to face him. "Did he say that he'd like to change our arrangement?"

Evan nodded. "I guess. He asked if I'd like to move most of my stuff into my room at his house and be there more…uh, most of the time. He made a big deal about how much bigger the room is. As if I didn't know. I'm not dumb, Mom, I know what he was asking me."

"I see." She quietly seethed as she drained the bacon and put the first round of pancakes on a plate for Evan. So far, Lyle was two for two. First jumping the gun about Perrie Lynn and now proposing a change in custody without consulting her. The answer would be no. She put the plate in front of Evan. "So, what did you tell your dad?"

He glanced up. "I said I like things the way they are."

She nodded and smiled. "I do, too." One day Evan would understand the power of those words. Was it possible their strong feelings would be enough to put an end to Lyle's vindictive fantasy? She turned her attention back to the batter. She'd been ravenous when she'd started cooking, but her appetite was gone, replaced by the anxious fist tightening in her gut.

"But he said we'd talk about it again," Evan added, his voice low.

"That means he and I will talk about it," Lark said, letting her anger seep through. "I don't want you worrying about it, Evan." She sat down in the chair next to him and lightly touched his arm. "There's no reason that anything in your life needs to change. One day, you'll meet Perrie Lynn, but that's separate from anything going on between your dad and me."

Evan nodded and popped a piece of bacon into his mouth.

In the calming silence, the tension inside her began to disappear. She went back to the stove and ladled more pancake batter into the skillet. She was no longer a young woman easily intimidated, not as she'd been when she married Lyle. Back then she'd been fooled by his take-charge attitude and mistaken it for maturity. No more. She'd protect Evan from his dad's desire to punish her because she'd discovered her own voice and power.

After breakfast, Lark burned her nervous energy dusting and vacuuming the living room and scrubbing the kitchen counters and cabinets from top to bottom. The house was nearly spotless by midafternoon, when she left Evan working at his computer and headed to the Half Moon Café. In the parking lot, she answered another text from Miles, glad to hear his day with Brooke was going well. She texted how much she was looking forward to seeing Perrie Lynn perform at the exhibition skate later that evening, when she'd get to watch all the medalists one more time.

Once inside the restaurant, she spotted her mother in a booth near the front. At least she thought it was her mother. Where had all her hair gone?

"Well, well, look at you," Lark said as she took off her coat and slid into the booth. "I almost didn't recognize you."

Her mom fluffed the sides of her new short haircut. "I've decided to surrender and live in the twenty-first century."

Lark suppressed an urge to blurt, "It's about time." Instead, she said, "It's gorgeous." The dyed, bottle-yellow was replaced with a soft darker blond. "And that sweater looks great."

"I should have treated myself to a makeover years ago," her mom said, running her hand down the sleeve of her light pink cable-knit pullover. "It actually took a couple of younger coworkers showing up in vintage sequined clothes to wake me up. Their appliquéd puppy dogs looked a little silly at thirty-five. I saw myself and didn't like the image."

"But you can still have your cats, Mom." Lark pointed to the giant silver-and-garnet cat pin on the edge of the sweater's neckline. "And you can still be fun Grandma Cora."

Cora grinned and fidgeted with the pin. But the small talk had nowhere else to go. Knowing she'd keep it simple and have the grilled salmon plate, Lark suggested they order, and get the food out of the way. Cora ordered a martini, but Lark stuck to sparkling water.

"I have something important to tell you," Lark said.

"I figured as much. You were uncharacteristically insistent about meeting today."

Shaking her head, Lark said, "I know, it's been a long time. Too long. But I've been dealing with something that required my focus...and silence, at least temporarily."

"Now you have me worried. I was hoping you were going to announce an engagement or something fun." Cora's forehead wrinkled. "I watched the skating, by the way. Pretty spectacular, but why did you text me about it?"

Lark sighed over the engagement remark, although Miles's smiling face popped into her mind unbidden. "I'm getting to that, but be patient. You see, what I'm about to tell you is huge. It's about the past, but now it's about the future, too." Lark rubbed her temples. She'd dreaded this moment for so long.

"Now you've really got me worried, so go ahead, tell me."

Lark clammed up when the waiter brought their drinks and took their order, the salmon plate for her and a giant bacon cheeseburger with sweet potato fries for Cora. Under other circumstances, Lark would have teased her mom about the burger with the works, but not that afternoon.

When the waiter walked away, Lark observed the alarm in her mother's eyes and plunged in. "It's about the skater I told you to watch last night. The bronze medalist, Perrie Lynn Olson. Do you remember her?"

"I do. Those commentators were talking about her a lot, because she's just lost her mother. I guess it was only a few days ago."

"Perrie Lynn turned eighteen the second week of December." Lark drew air deep into her lungs. "And she's my daughter."

Lark ignored her mom's stunned expression and rushed through the basics of the story right up to the present. She watched her mother's face register shock and wonder as Lark ended with Maxine's death and Perrie Lynn's last-minute arrival in Norway.

"*I* can barely believe that this happened so quickly," Lark said. "I expected a long drawn-out process to find her, taking years, not days."

Cora flopped back in the booth. "I'm speechless."

Lark pulled her tablet out of her handbag and brought up a close-up of Perrie Lynn in her blue costume and the white flower in her hair. Her happy wide smile dominated the photo. She turned the pad around so her mother could have a look. "This picture does her justice. For Miles, the widow's peak was the biggest clue, other than her hair color and skin tone, which she got from him. She's breathtaking, isn't she?"

Her mom glanced at the photo and nodded. But she wasn't smiling.

"With any luck, I'll see her soon. World championships are next month. Then, we—Miles and I—think her father will invite us to Minnesota to meet her. That depends on Perrie Lynn, of course. She has to be ready."

Glancing at the photo again, Cora finally spoke. "I can see her distinctive smile is all you." She took two quick gulps of her martini. "I don't know where to start with my questions. You've caught me completely off guard." Her eyes clouded. "But it's devastating to realize something like this happened and you didn't tell me. I'm heartbroken. You truly didn't think you could bring her home?"

"What? Into our family craziness?" Lark couldn't squelch her angry reaction, but she forced herself to lower her voice to a whisper. "You and Dad were completely immersed in your fight over Dennis. Let's leave it at that.

I'm not *blaming* you for anything that happened. But the situation was behind my decision to flee to Dublin."

Covering her mouth with her hand, Cora shook her head. "But in all these years. I'm surprised you—or Lyle—didn't let something slip out."

Lark lifted her shoulders in a show of diffidence. "That's easy to explain. Lyle didn't know. Not until recently, when I told him. In his typical contemptuous, double-crossing fashion, he gave Evan his version of my deception before I had a chance to break the news myself. It's complicating things now."

"Wait, wait," Cora said, her palm almost in Lark's face. "Are you saying you never confided in Lyle before you married him?"

"Exactly." In a dispassionate tone, Lark ran down the list of reasons she'd kept her secret. "I suppose if I had told him, he'd have broken our engagement. As positive as that seems in hindsight, I wouldn't have Evan. And that's unthinkable."

As if still trying to grasp the reality, Cora said, "All this time I had a granddaughter growing up without me...or any of us. She even has cousins."

Lark remained silent when the waiter appeared with the tray of food.

"I never liked the secrecy, not to mention the uncertainty," she said, once the waiter walked away. "Not ever knowing for sure she was okay. And all these years she's had a loving family that was *hers*—parents and grandparents, and probably cousins."

"How is Evan taking all this?" Cora asked.

Lark considered her words, concerned that she had no real answer. "The best I can say is that it's too early to know. Lyle isn't helping. He's hinting at changing our custody agreement, but fortunately, Evan doesn't like that idea."

"That's good, isn't it? Your ex can't fight you over custody of a nearly thirteen-year-old boy with a mind of his own."

Oh, sure. Right. Why would her mother, of all people, say such a thing? That's precisely what had happened with Dennis, and to end the custody fight, the compromise had been two years of boarding school. Lark had no intention of letting family history repeat itself.

Lark cleared her throat. "I don't know what Lyle is capable of. He's openly calling me a liar and doing whatever he can to discredit me."

Her mom winced at her words, then reached into her purse and brought out a tissue to dab her eyes. "I'm sorry. You know, crying like this."

"That's okay," Lark said. "I don't know when I've cried more, years ago when I was consumed with grief and regret about giving her up or in these weeks since we found her."

"We, as in you and Miles?"

She nodded. "Like I said, he got in touch with me, and we've become…well, close. It was a lot to work through." She scoffed. "We had to forgive ourselves for being young. He's had the added burden of knowing he didn't jump in to help me figure out a way to keep her. I've had to forgive myself for not fighting harder for her."

"Perrie Lynn was lucky, though, in terms of the people adopting her," Cora said, her face set in thought. "You must be relieved knowing that."

"That's the biggest outcome for me so far. The relief." Lark pushed her plate of half-eaten food aside and leaned across the table. "When Maxine called me and confirmed that this accomplished young woman was truly the baby we relinquished, I knew, really knew in my heart, she'd had the life she deserved."

"And you decided to just run off to Boston with Miles to see her skate?"

"I did. Well, once Miles pulled the tickets out of his pocket on Christmas Eve." The memory of that moment made her laugh.

With her face still pinched in pain, Cora said, "I'm glad you finally revealed this secret, but it's a lot to take in. I realize we've never been particularly close, especially after my hideous divorce from your father. Still, you kept a huge secret." She raised both hands in the air, a gesture of helplessness. "I'm hurt. I can't help it. I wish you'd made a different choice." She quickly added, "About telling me, that is."

Lark nodded, hoping her mother would eventually understand. "I learned to live with my decision. By the time I had Evan, I didn't want you thinking about a baby girl every time you looked at me—or your grandson."

Her mom averted her eyes. But to Lark, wounded feelings seemed inevitable. Given the circumstances of the past, would she have made a different decision about confiding her secret? Probably not.

LATE THAT NIGHT, she relayed to Miles an abbreviated version of what had happened at lunch with her mother. Miles asked a few questions, but otherwise kept his observations to himself. "I'm glad you're not telling me how I should or shouldn't feel," she said. "I had to take the same attitude toward my mother. I'm still convinced I was right to keep my secret."

"Well, this is about feelings, anyway," Miles pointed out. "No one is right and no one is wrong."

Lark laughed softly. "That sounds like reasonable Miles. But my mother and I will be okay. Besides, no matter what she does, she gets points for not trying to claim perfection. She's made her own mistakes and paid a heavy price for every one of them."

"Did Evan watch the exhibition with you tonight?"

"Yes, he sure did." She paused, trying to find the words to explain her response to watching Perrie Lynn skate to the evocative song "Moon River." "Even at such a young age, he caught on that the choice of music, the performance itself, was about her mother and their closeness."

"Even little eight-year-old Brooke sensed

that," Miles said. "There is something about that pair of drifters in the lyrics. The song has a direct path into my heart. Our friends Katie and Allen said there wasn't a dry eye in the house."

"I'll always picture her soaring and gliding and bringing the entire arena to tears." She swallowed back a wave of emotion. "What a memory. I only wish we could have been together and shared the excitement over these last few days." She was almost afraid to say the next words, but went ahead, anyway. "I'm glad Evan had the chance to see Perrie Lynn, even from a distance. But I missed you."

"I know, Lark. I feel the same way, maybe more than you know." He chuckled. "And let's make a plan. I'm not waiting all the way to the world championships to see you."

"Get out your calendar, my friend. Let's see when we can get together."

Within minutes they'd arranged to meet for breakfast at Hugo's on Wednesday, once again before Miles had to fly out of town. "It will be much more fun this time," she said, "and I'll polish off one of their giant platters, too."

"I'm counting on it."

Still laughing, they ended the call.

CHAPTER NINETEEN

MILES ANSWERED THE call in the lobby of the hotel in Seattle, conscious of the sudden wave of nervous anticipation coming over him. "How good to see your name on my phone, Eric."

"Well, I knew it was time to get in touch," Eric said. "And, uh, thanks for your condolences. Declan's assistant passed on your kind words. Yours and Lark's."

"We haven't stopped thinking about you and Perrie Lynn. Not for a minute." Miles moved out of the way of a bellhop pushing a luggage cart and dodged a couple with a stroller on his other side. "It's got to be a tough time."

"I won't lie to you. We've had some bad days. By the way, Maxine told me about meeting Lark that morning at the hotel." A quick chuckle followed. "She went to that hotel store for what she considered the best poppy-seed muffins in New England. But she took me aside and told me about their encounter—one of those chance things. She was really happy about it."

Lark would be pleased to hear that, he thought. "Lark felt the same way."

"At the time, I wasn't so sure it was a good thing, but given what's happened, I changed my mind." A couple of silent seconds passed. "You know we never had negative feelings about Lark—or about you. But to be honest, if Maxine hadn't been sick, she wouldn't have reached out as she did, or, rather, *when* she did."

Miles gathered his thoughts to make sure the words he spoke expressed what he truly meant. "Acknowledging our presence in the background helped us a great deal. It allowed us to become attuned to Perrie Lynn's career and the life she's had."

Eric cleared his throat and let out a couple of low groans. "I hope what I'm about to say doesn't change how you feel, but…"

But? A tingling sensation traveled down Miles's arms and into his hands. *I'm not going to like this.*

"It's hard to explain, I guess, but Perrie Lynn is only beginning to deal with losing her mom."

Of course—the shock, the numbness, is wearing off. Wishing he was in his room and not leaning against a pillar in the hotel lobby, Miles braced himself for what he was certain was coming.

"I've spoken with others on her, well…let's call it a team. Specifically, Declan and Leffie. We're in agreement about this," Eric said without a hint of hesitation. "We need to give it more time before we tell Perrie Lynn about you and Lark. A few months, I'm thinking, depending on how she's doing. She already has so much to deal with."

Miles could have recited all the reasons Eric and the others were making wise choices. In that moment, he forced a response he knew reflected his ability to be a reasonable person. A quality that served him well—at least most of the time. "I understand, Eric, dad to dad, to quote your own words. You need to do whatever you believe is right for Perrie Lynn."

"I'm sorry, though," Eric said, sadness bleeding into his voice. "Maxine spoke well of Lark, and—"

"Please, don't apologize," Miles said. "Lark and I have been concerned for Perrie Lynn, too." As sincerely as he meant those words, his dread about repeating this conversation to Lark sat like a rock in his gut. Her eagerness to meet Perrie Lynn had blinded her in some ways. For her, the world championships loomed like a magical deadline.

"It's a matter of making an adjustment." Eric was back to a businesslike tone. "Right after the worlds, Perrie Lynn joins a three-week tour. By skating-show standards, that's a short trek through a dozen or so cities. After that, she'll finally have a break, and we'll go to Santa Fe to see my dad. Then the new training schedule starts." Eric's guffaw broke through and lightened the mood. "Another season means new music, new programs, new costumes."

As a dad, Miles didn't doubt Eric's wise decision. "You know, Lark and I have also been thinking of *you*, Eric. This is a profound loss for you."

With dismissive gruffness, Eric said, "I'm doing okay."

A promise from Eric to keep Miles posted followed, along with a positive exchange of words about meeting in the summer that brought the call to its logical close. By the time Miles was inside the elevator on the way to the tenth-floor conference room, he'd practiced what he'd say to Lark later. Even if he'd had the time to make the call then and there, he wouldn't have done it. He needed time to adjust himself.

LARK STUDIED HER screen as she scrolled through the flowchart of the PR plan Dawn designed for Party Perfect. They'd been together for over an hour in a study room at the library going over the elements of Dawn's plans for a business she hoped would turn into a long-term client. After going over the first draft of the party-planning handbook, Lark was satisfied she could meet Dawn's deadlines. She glanced at her friend, who was reviewing the same document on her own screen. "I can get started on all these pieces right away, and I'll try to work a little ahead. You've done an amazing job launching this campaign."

"Thanks, I'm excited about the challenge." Casting a pointed look Lark's way, Dawn added, "But I hope you don't find the work too awfully boring."

"Are you kidding?" Lark teased. "I just finished producing three pieces for adults about superbugs, so you bet I'm happy to write about baby showers and Halloween."

Dawn sighed in a show of mock relief. "I'm so glad you feel that way. These two women are committed to becoming the biggest party-planning business in the region."

"And with your help, they'll accomplish their goal."

"In terms of scheduling, though," Dawn said, "I don't want to pry, but aren't you expecting to take a trip to Minnesota soon?"

Lark smiled. "My pulse races at the thought. But life goes on. Every week I take on new assignments and agree to deadlines. Meeting Perrie Lynn isn't going to change that."

Dawn snickered. "I know. I'm just getting excited for you—*and Miles.*"

Warmth rippled through Lark at the mention of Miles. "I have to admit I miss him when he's gone. We've spent more time together these last weeks." *And shared a few more kisses, too.* "When he's away, we text and talk a lot."

"I'm happy it's going well for the two of you." Dawn closed the computer and grabbed her jacket off the chair. "Mostly, I'm proud of you for opening your heart—with my encouragement, if you recall." She playfully patted herself on the back. "Where is Miles, anyway?"

"Seattle. He was admiring Mount Rainier while we chatted. He'll be back in a couple of days." She stood and began gathering her things, but she needed a minute to calm herself. She couldn't think about the world championships and the end of the skating season without being flooded by a mix of emotions. Excitement, certainly, but anxiety, too, as if fear were attempting to sneak in through the back door. She couldn't rationalize the vague apprehension she walked around with every day. About Perrie Lynn, but mostly about Evan.

Dawn peered into her face, pretending to examine her features. "Hmm… I have a new word for you. *Radiant*."

Distracted from her concerns, Lark touched her cheeks. "Cut it out. You're making me blush. I admit, though, sometimes I need to pinch myself."

Pulling her hat over her hair, Dawn said, "Okay, Ms. Radiant, meet you at the Bean Grinder—five minutes."

In the few minutes it took to drive from the library to the coffee shop, snowflakes began to fall and swirl in the air on the windy day. Alone in her car, Lark let her underlying worries about Evan break through the facade of busyness. Until the email from the chess-club teacher-volunteer, Mr. Howard, Lark had convinced herself that Evan was adjusting, doing okay. Yes, he was the master of one-word answers, and sometimes his mood was best described as flat. But wasn't that typical for an almost thirteen-year-old? The email, labeled as a friendly "heads-up," made it clear Evan's sulkiness had bled over into school.

According to Mr. Howard, Evan had begun isolating himself from the others in the club. But what grabbed the teacher's attention was acting like a sore loser after his good friend, Eduardo, beat him fair and square. *Out of character*, the note said.

When Lark pulled into the Bean Grinder's parking lot she spotted Dawn standing next to her car with her palms open to catch snowflakes on her gloves.

"Hey, what can we expect? It's only March," Lark quipped when she got out of her car and approached Dawn.

"I know. I won't despair over this long winter, as long as they have my favorite Bean Grinder chocolate-chip cookies today..."

Dawn stopped talking and pointed beyond Lark. "There's someone heading toward you—he's jogging pretty fast."

Lark turned just as a man with short-cropped gray hair closed the distance. "Lark McGee?"

"Yes, what can I do…"

The man thrust an envelope toward her. "For you." He hurried away and crossed the street.

"Oh, no," Dawn said. "Lyle?"

Nodding, Lark stared at the envelope. "It's from Lyle's lawyer. You don't think he's…" She didn't know how to phrase it.

Dawn grabbed her forearm and held on tight. "Yes, my friend, I do. Open the envelope, Lark."

Doing as she was told, Lark tore the seal, pulled out the papers and scanned the first page. "You're right. He's suing me for full custody of Evan!"

Dawn cupped her elbow and steered her off the walkway to the coffee-shop door. Lark's grip tightened on the sheaf of papers as she fought the urge to tear them into little pieces and let them swirl in the air with the snow. "Unbelievable. He declared me *un...fit.*"

"Get out your phone, Lark. Now. Call your lawyer." Dawn circled her fingers around Lark's wrist. "Lyle won't get away with this."

"I'm going to call Lyle first." Lark stood a little taller. "That's what I'm going to do."

"No you're not." Dawn spoke quickly and with authority. "That's exactly what he wants you to do—get emotional and show your rage. But don't give in to him. Keep your distance and let the lawyers do the talking."

Before she could stop them, tears flowed down her cheeks. "Evan doesn't want this. We talked about it after Lyle went behind my back and told him about Perrie Lynn. Lyle told Evan he could stay with him anytime he wanted."

The note from Mr. Howard flashed in her mind, darkening her mood even more. What else was Lyle communicating to Evan behind her back? Was her son too nervous to talk to her?

Dawn dug around inside her shoulder bag and pulled out a tissue and handed it to her. "Look, this is Lyle's bluster—he's willing to part with his money just to get back at you. Fortunately, Evan is old enough to express exactly what he wants."

"And he has done that. But, what if—if he's afraid to fight with his dad?"

"Doesn't matter. *You* aren't afraid."

Lark waved her off. "At this moment, every cell in my body is in a state of terror." She turned to look Dawn in the eye. "You're right, though. First step, call the lawyer. Something like this sure puts things in perspective. What happens with Miles, and even seeing Perrie Lynn, has to take a backseat. Everything is about protecting Evan now."

A FEW HOURS had passed since he'd left Lark a message and he hadn't received so much as a text to tell him when she'd be free to talk. He was back in his room for the evening and wanted—needed—to unload the news. But not in a text, or even in a voice-mail message. Odd not to hear from her. They'd developed a habit of getting back to each other quickly, even if only to confirm a later time to talk.

Miles stood at the window and absently tapped his hand against the frame, every muscle tense from the knowledge that he had critical information to pass on to Lark. It was too much like keeping a secret from her, even if not intentionally.

He got out his phone and sent another text: When can u talk?

Although not especially hungry, he ordered a burger from room service to get dinner out of the way. Then he called Brooke to hear about her day before he stretched out on the king-size bed and turned on a basketball game for distraction.

When the call came, he sat up fast. "I'm so glad to finally hear your voice."

"Something's happened." Lark was almost shouting, and before he could respond, her story poured out.

Eric's call suddenly shriveled in importance, where only minutes earlier it had been the most critical development of the day. Lyle's mean stunt was a thousand times worse. "I'm so sorry, Lark. What can I do?"

"Nothing."

The ferocity of the word stung and left him without a ready response.

"I've called my lawyer, Ned Williams. It's all I can do."

"But please, Lark, slow down. Talk to me. What is Lyle arguing in order to convince a judge to give him full custody? What grounds?"

"He's calling me unfit. That my past—

my *secret* past—and deliberately withholding information about my *other* child makes me unfit." She talked so fast the words ran together. "Obviously, I have to stop seeing you immediately. We'll work something out when it comes time to meet Perrie Lynn."

"Whoa! What do you mean?" He didn't even try to keep the incredulity out of his voice.

"Come on, Miles," she said, her voice cracking. "If I'm going to establish my fitness, then I can't have a man lurking around in my life, let alone the father of my so-called secret child."

"You're crying, Lark, I can tell. I'm so sorry, but please try to calm down so we can think about what's best to do." How was he going to tell her the other news? "Where is Evan now?"

"He's spending the night with Lyle, as scheduled. Much as I hate to admit it, that's just as well. I'm a mess. Fortunately, the custody papers don't allow him to change anything now, so Evan will be here after school tomorrow."

Relieved to hear that, Miles prepared to speak in the most determined tone he could manage. "We'll figure this out, Lark. Together. And by the way, I'm not *lurking*. I'm in your life."

"Oh, Miles, stop. When it comes to Evan, there is no *we*. There is no *together*."

His gut burned with rising confusion. Or maybe it was panic. "Wait, wait. I know you're upset, but a lot has happened since our first meeting at Hugo's. *We* happened."

Lark groaned. "Right. Silly me. I was living in some kind of fantasy world where we had a future, but I can't risk losing Evan. I have to face a simple fact. Our past will always come up. It isn't going away."

"Maybe so, but I'm not going away, either," Miles said, quickly adding, "I'll recede into the background for now—if that's what you really want. You need to marshal all your energy to fight Lyle. I get that. But I'm not turning my back and walking away from you. You don't have to figure this out on your own."

Silence.

"Lark?"

"I'm here, Miles. I just don't know what to say." She sighed into the phone, leaving behind the sound of defeat. "This is all coming at such a bad time. With the skating season almost over, we're expecting to hear from

Eric. I never thought this would be easy, but still."

I have to tell her. Now. "I'm so sorry about dumping more bad news on you, but I don't have a choice. I heard from Eric."

"You did? Why didn't you say so?"

He closed his eyes, a lame attempt to block growing frustration. "I left a message and wanted to talk. It's why I left another text. Eric is having second thoughts about the timing of our visit to meet Perrie Lynn."

Miles winced against the low moan coming from Lark.

"Wait, Lark, it's not all bad news." He plunged in and repeated what Eric had said about Perrie Lynn. "He's going to delay telling her about us, because the loss of her mother is just hitting home now. He—and Declan and Leffie—think she needs more time to make peace with Maxine's death. It's understandable, really."

"Maybe so," she whispered, "but I still don't know what to say. The disappointment is crushing. And now it's piled on top of my fear for Evan that has left me weak and shaky."

"You don't have to talk. I'll stay on the phone with you. You aren't alone." Miles closed his eyes and dug his thumb and index finger into his forehead, as if he could force the tension away. If only he could hold Lark in his arms and stroke her hair. He'd whisper that everything would be okay. He'd give anything to be by her side when she confronted that miserable man she'd married.

Seconds passed.

Finally, he broke the silence. "I need to ask you something about Evan."

"Uh, okay."

Keeping his tone measured, he said, "Haven't you already talked to Evan about the custody arrangement?"

Without hesitation she said, "Evan was worried. And I asked him outright if he wanted to keep our arrangements the same, and he said yes. That's why I'm determined to fight Lyle. It's why I need to be careful about the image I project. He's already made my past look tawdry—he spits out the word *distasteful*."

Miles tightened his jaw in response to the ugly term being associated with her.

"Evan knows I'm in touch with you," she said, "which adds fuel to Lyle's efforts to turn my life into a scandal. When I was in his office he made a big deal about deceiving him about the Boston trip."

"You can't let him control you like this, Lark. There was nothing wrong with that trip."

"Except that I did lie about the reason I went. It won't sound so innocent in court." Another deep sigh. "I need to go. I can't talk about this anymore. We were going to have dinner when you get back, but obviously, I'm calling that off."

Resigned for now, but not for the long haul, Miles said, "I hear you, Lark. Right now, you do what you need to do. I'll keep you posted about Eric."

He decided not to argue. *For now.* He knew one thing for sure. He was not going to let Lark permanently walk out of his life. "Keep this one thing in mind, Lark. At the moment, it feels like you're fighting against Lyle."

"With every nerve ending," Lark interjected.

"But based on what you know about Evan's feelings, you aren't so much fighting your ex, but standing up for your son."

Seconds ticked by.

"Thanks for that," she whispered.

The call ended. The woman he loved was in pain, and he had no way to help her. Miles tossed the phone on the bed in frustration. Once again, he'd complicated Lark's life.

CHAPTER TWENTY

"WHAT HAPPENS NOW?" Evan asked.

A direct question, but he'd averted his eyes, apparently preferring to study the gray tweed living-room rug.

"You know me pretty well, Evan, and I don't make promises I can't keep." She swallowed back the urge to demand her son look her in the eye. "Agreed?"

The weak nod would have to do. Lark had lived with the papers from Lyle sitting in a drawer in her dresser for just over twenty-four hours, and in that time, she'd abruptly broken things off with Miles, chastising herself for what had clearly been a pie-in-the-sky fantasy. Who had she been kidding? While she was spinning daydreams about her future with Miles, Lyle had been busy spinning a custody suit.

"I wish it weren't true, but you have an important role in what happens next."

Evan looked up at her with troubled eyes.

"What do you mean? Dad said it doesn't matter what I want."

"He's wrong." She reminded herself to keep her tone strong and confident, but not hostile. "Weeks ago, I asked you if you wanted to spend more time at your dad's house. Remember that?"

Evan nodded. "I said I like things the way they are."

She rested one hip on the corner of her desk. "Has anything changed since that night?"

"No." Instead of meeting her eye, he stared intently at the tall bookshelves to her left. "Dad told me I'd be better off with him, because…" His voice trailed off.

"Go ahead. Finish the sentence. Because…"

"You had a baby and didn't tell him." He lowered his gaze to again focus on the rug. "That makes you a liar, he says."

She folded her arms across her chest, a strategy to contain her anger. She hated grilling Evan, but in order to fight *for* him, as both Miles and Dawn phrased it, she had to know the truth. "And because of my mistakes, he claims I don't deserve to share you."

Evan jutted his chin defiantly. "I told him

I didn't mind about Perrie Lynn. It's not her fault she was born."

Such insightful logic. It was obvious Evan had given this some thought. "You said that to your dad?"

"Uh-huh. I told him about the bronze medal she won. Was that okay?"

The worry in his eyes stabbed her heart. "Evan, whatever you think—or say—about this situation is okay." Leaving the perch on her desk, she led Evan to the couch, where she pointed for him to sit. She took the chair across from him. "So, by now you know that your dad is taking me to court. Basically, suing me for custody of you."

Evan nodded and nervously ran his hand over his mouth.

"I intend to stand up to him, Evan, but in order to do that I need to know for sure what you want." Miles's and Dawn's words echoed through her head. "I like the arrangement the way it is, too, but that's not good enough, not in court. Do you understand?"

"I already told Dad I didn't want anything to change."

"I believe this suit could be dismissed in a hurry, if it's clear that you didn't ask for this change. You'll be thirteen soon, and that counts for something." She leaned forward in her chair and touched his knee. "In any case, nothing will change right away. Unless I agree to your dad's terms. But I won't do that."

For the first time, a faint smile appeared on Evan's face. "You said we'd get a chance to meet Perrie Lynn, like maybe after the world championships."

That sent a ripple of anxiety through Lark. "Uh, that's still true, but when that will happen is unclear." In as few words as possible, she recounted Miles's conversation with Eric. "I think the reality is probably hitting her now. It must have taken so much strength to honor her mother by skating at the Internationals, but I'm sure a letdown was inevitable."

The change in Evan from the beginning of the conversation to this more relaxed moment confirmed her decision to bring up one more issue.

"Would you tell me what happened between you and Eduardo?"

Evan's eyes widened in surprise.

"Mr. Howard sent me an email. He's concerned about you. I think you've been stressed out about your dad and me."

"I told Eduardo I was sorry about being a jerk." Evan lowered his head. "He beat me, and I got mad."

"Does Mr. Howard know you apologized?"

"No," he said with a groan.

He probably knows exactly what's coming next. "Then will you tell him?"

"I guess." A quick shrug followed.

"Mr. Howard thinks a lot of you—that's why he was concerned. He won't think less of you if you admit you were wrong."

Lark smiled to herself, satisfied that she'd said everything possible to convince Evan that she'd stand up for him. She was out of words, and only her actions would do going forward. She fixed tacos for dinner and by the time she went to bed, she was almost numb with fatigue. Evan had done his part, but she had to do hers.

Should she call Ned Williams, check with him about the plan she'd conceived? Probably. But her instincts told her she trusted herself more. She was resolved to fight Lyle for as long as it took. She'd cash out her retirement account, run through every saved dollar she had and swallow her pride and borrow money from her dad. She'd fight for years and run out the clock, but she would not allow Lyle to bully their son.

After a night of fitful sleep, she watched Evan leave to catch the bus to school, and with the determination worthy of a trained athlete like Perrie Lynn, Lark put her plan in motion. No responding to messages from Miles and Dawn, or calling Ned Williams. It felt odd—wrong—to avoid Miles, but it had to be that way. She got into her car and drove to Lyle's office and waited in the parking lot.

When she saw his car pull in, raw adrenaline pushed her to follow him when he got out of the driver's side and headed to the entrance. She moved to step in front of him before he had a chance to reach the door. In the split second before his expression turned hostile, she caught the flash of surprise in his face.

In a tone as cold as the March air, he said, "I suggest we communicate through our lawyers."

"No way. I suggest we settle this ourselves, especially if we both want what's best for Evan."

Lyle narrowed his eyes. "You settled this long ago with your lies."

Ha! Just as she'd expected, he used her secret as his opening salvo. "Let's talk about long ago, Lyle, and agree you and I were a big mistake. We never should have married." She let those words sink in, then added, "What a disaster, huh?"

"What does that have to do with the situation now?"

"Evan is the only good thing about our marriage." His face again registered surprise. She'd caught him off guard—as planned. "Our son is the most important person in my life, and I'm sure that's true for you."

"Of course it is." He pointed his index finger at her. "And that's why I'm going to make sure you have as little time with him as possible."

She shook her head. "You're not helping Evan. You've chosen this foolish route to get back at me. Despite our son telling you he likes things the way they are. You go ahead with your vindictive custody suit and you risk losing Evan. Or at least you'll lose his respect."

Lyle's eyes flashed with anger, making it difficult for him to talk. She could see he wanted to shout, call her names, order her off his property. Lark could almost smell his rage.

"If you try to change our arrangement, Lyle, not only will I fight you, so will Evan. *No matter how long it takes.*"

Lyle shifted his weight from one foot to the other. She read his face, seeing in it his struggle to find the right words. She had the advantage there, but she willed herself not to speak...yet.

"There's the little matter of your baby," Lyle finally said. "Imagine how that's going to sound in court."

"Not good. Your justification for telling Evan about Perrie Lynn against my wishes won't sound so good to a judge's ears, either." She thrust her arms out, palms up. "How are you going to explain that talking about me behind my back protected our son?"

"You *lied* to me."

"I did. And you would have broken off our engagement if I'd told you about giving up my baby."

"I'd have dropped you so fast..."

She scoffed. "Don't bother finishing the sentence. We were a big mistake. But Evan isn't. We've both experienced the joy of raising him. That's where I get stuck in my regrets, Lyle. Without you, I don't have him."

They were in a standoff. Lyle was used to

getting the last word, but she wouldn't let that happen this time. Despite the cold weather, beads of sweat trickled down her back. A response to her pounding heart, no doubt.

Fixing his face in his characteristic sneer, Lyle said, "What do you really want from me, Lark?"

"I want us to raise our son well. So far, I've done nothing to cast you in a negative light. I've not talked to Evan about the way you mocked my writing career." She paused to catch her breath and consider her next words. "I've never described your disrespect, your name-calling. Even now, I've refrained from calling your custody suit vindictive."

"Oh, yeah, poor you," Lyle said, thrusting his hands in his jacket pockets.

Swallowing back her disgust, she stuck to her plan. "Obviously, if you create a custody fight, that will need to change. You've gone after my vulnerabilities, behaving as if you have none of your own. You've been a good dad, Lyle, but the way you've been talking about me is not lost on our son."

She let her words hang in the air.

"He's stressed, and it's not only because he knows about Perrie Lynn—Evan has looked her up on the internet. He's seen her skate.

He's aware that when the time is right, he'll meet his half sister in person."

Lyle rolled his eyes. "Oh, really? How wonderful."

Ignoring his sarcasm, she said, "Yes, it will be. But right now, he's upset because he's seeing your nastier side on full display."

Conscious of her knees shaking, Lark took a few steps back, as if in retreat. But if sarcasm and sneering was all he had left, she could bring this episode to an end.

"Drop the custody suit, Lyle. Stop the damage before Evan is hurt any more than he already is."

She turned on her heel and hurried back to her car. She pulled out of the parking lot and headed down the street, leaving him standing outside his office door.

MILES PACED THE grassy edges of the lakeside park, watching late afternoon turn to evening on the first warm night of April. It was exactly the kind of night he'd been looking forward to since December when he and Lark first hatched their plan to try to identify Perrie Lynn. In the weeks that followed his life had taken on an unexpected shine. He'd even known the exhilaration of falling in love—for real—and it had changed everything.

He'd gone along with Lark's wishes and retreated. They hadn't seen each other for a few weeks, but he'd never considered the idea of letting her go permanently. Not again. If he walked away, he'd never have another chance. The time was right, too. The world championships were behind them now, with Perrie Lynn coming in fourth, not a bad finish considering the season of triumph and sorrow she'd been through.

Based on her abbreviated text, Lark had successfully fought for Evan. Apparently stunned by her unwillingness to give in to his threats, Lyle had quietly withdrawn his quest for full custody. Miles took that as his signal to come back and fight for her. That's why he was standing in the park with his heart racing and his eyes fixated on the cars turning onto Night Beach Road. "Come home, Lark," he murmured. "Please. Whatever you're doing, come home."

He laughed out loud at his own impatience, glad no one was around to hear him talking to himself. He spotted headlights in the distance, but they turned onto another street. He anxiously studied the sky, knowing the full moon would rise soon. When he'd thought this through, the moon was icing on the cake. Now it mocked his hopes.

Another set of headlights approached, then another. *So, are you prepared to stay here all night? Maybe sleep in your car?* The answer was yes.

He almost laughed out loud when at last a set of headlights came close to the park and turned right onto Night Beach Road. When the car turned into her driveway he was sure it was Lark. He waited a few minutes so she could get inside before he pulled out his phone.

Minutes later, he made the call and got her voice mail. "I'm in the park next to your house, Lark. Will you join me?"

Pacing the edge of the park again, he waited, agonizing over the minutes ticking by. Five minutes, then ten. He called again. No answer. Only voice mail. "Lark, I'm in the park—I'm not leaving. I'm not walking away. It's a beautiful night out here."

He stuck his phone in the pocket of his windbreaker and let out an impatient sigh. But no matter what happened, he refused to see this as a mistake. It was only one try— if it didn't work he'd come up with plan B.

"Miles?"

He turned to the familiar voice.

"What are you doing?" She pulled her coat tighter around her.

"Exactly what it looks like. I'm waiting for you."

"But why?" she asked in a plaintive voice.

He stretched his arm toward her. "Why do you think? I'm here because we belong together." He paused. "The sooner the better."

"I can't be with you," she said, enunciating each word. "Or anyone. Too much is on the line. Besides, we were living some kind of fairy tale, Miles." She circled her hand above her head with a fanciful flourish.

"I don't buy that. I love you, and it's grown-up love, Lark. And I think you have the same feelings for me."

She threw her head back and groaned.

He'd struck a nerve. Of course he had, he'd told the truth. "How hard are you going to make me fight for you?"

"Miles, c'mon."

He widened his stance and threw his shoulders back. "Did you seriously think I'd accept the notion that Lyle won't let us be together? You fought for Evan and you won.

Lyle knows he has no power over you. Not anymore. It's done…gone forever."

"But you have Brooke to consider. As it is, she's going to have to adjust to having a sister." She shook her head, dropping her gaze to the patchy grass. "This isn't *only* about Evan."

Good, she was arguing with him. That was progress. "I'll worry about Brooke. In fact, I'm way ahead of you. I have a plan."

Even with only the dim streetlight illuminating Lark's features, he could see her frown. At least he'd aroused her curiosity, so it was a good time to dive right in. "I happen to know about visitors night at a certain science fair. Whaddya know, the fair happens to be right here in Two Moon Bay. In two days."

That brought a laugh. "Okay, tell me how that's relevant to what actually unites us— namely, Perrie Lynn."

"It isn't related to Perrie Lynn," he stated bluntly. "Not everything between us is. The science fair is about Brooke and Evan. It's about you and me. It's about the family we're going to have one day."

She swiped her eyes. "Thanks a lot. I thought I was done crying for a while."

He took one step closer, but she took a step back. "No. Don't."

"Evan knew you were in touch with me. You told him we'd become close, that we'd always be friends," he argued.

"What's your point, Miles?"

"That Evan won't be the least bit surprised when you introduce me to him at the science fair. And I'll introduce you and Evan to Brooke. I guarantee she'll find Evan and his interplanetary travel project very cool." He took another step closer and waited for her reaction, but she stayed planted where she was. "This is not a fairy tale, Lark. Boston wasn't a passing fancy. I miss our texts, our calls, our dates. I miss holding you in my arms."

She cocked her head. "The science fair, huh?"

He suppressed a laugh. He was almost there. Well, maybe.

"That's right. A small start. Let the kids get used to each other—and to us. Because that's the end point. I love you, Lark. And I'm not afraid to say it."

Silence. She cocked her head the other way and shifted her weight.

"So? What do you say? It's just a science fair?"

"Can we take the kids to Lou's for pizza afterward?" She put her hand over her mouth to hold back laughter.

"Absolutely." He closed the distance between them and wrapped his arms around her. "I can hardly wait. I know this won't be easy, Lark. We don't even know when Eric will contact us." He cupped her cheeks in his palms and lowered his mouth to cover hers, deepening the kiss when she responded.

"I'm confident Eric will call when Perrie Lynn is ready," he said. "But let's not delay *our* lives together. This conversation is about us, no matter what happens." He kissed her again.

Moving out of his embrace, she turned toward the lake and tucked her arm through his. "You do make it sound easy." She pointed to the moon rising high enough to leave its shimmering reflection on the calm water. "As easy as the mirror moon on the water."

Shaking his head, he said, "No, don't misunderstand. I'm not naive. You know that, Lark. But I'm not afraid of doing whatever it takes to make *us* work—kids and careers and all." He smoothed his hand over her hair.

"If I'm afraid of anything, it's what my life would be without you. That's why I showed up here, ready to fight you every step of the way."

She let out a long wistful sigh. "I've missed you so much, Miles. I thought I had to sacrifice us for Evan—and maybe even for Perrie Lynn."

This time he pressed his lips to her forehead and pulled her closer. "We're standing here in one of your favorite spots in the world, gazing at the moon shining on the magical lake in the town you love best. So, what better place to make it official. Marry me, Lark. Say yes."

She tightened her arms around him and rested her head against his chest.

He waited, determined not to interrupt her thoughts. Time, he reasoned, was on his side.

She lifted her head off his chest and tilted it back, so she could look him in the eye. "How about this for an answer, yes…and no."

His loud scoff escaped before he had a chance to think. "Hmm…not exactly the response I was hoping for, but I'll hear you out."

"The answer really is *eventually*. But we have kids and another child who might want to meet us only once or twice to satisfy her curiosity. Then she could say goodbye and go back to her regular life and never care to see us again. Surely you know that. We fell in love because this special young woman brought us together again. But what if she goes away?"

Miles stepped back and held both her hands in his. "That's the chance we have to take. But if we're together, we'll adjust to whatever happens."

Turning away from the lake, she took his arm again and started walking across the park toward the cottage. In a voice full of fun, she said, "So if our life is going to start now, we might as well celebrate with a glass of wine."

"Ah, I like the way you think," he said. "Brooke will be so excited about gaining a brother in this family we're putting together. She's still young enough not to ask too many questions."

"You're right," Lark said. "I'm glad Evan knows the story and is interested in meeting his older sister. He'll enjoy meeting Brooke, too."

Miles stopped and drew Lark into a tight embrace. "Whatever happens, you and I have a daughter. She's why we found each other again, Lark. That's the magic between us."

Lark nodded and he tightened his embrace, ready for whatever happened next.

CHAPTER TWENTY-ONE

THE WHITE FRAME house with its yellow trim and wraparound porch was exactly as it appeared in the photographs Perrie Lynn had sent. Their phone conversations had dispensed with what Lark called the preliminaries, including family photos. She'd had the joy of congratulating Perrie Lynn on her successes, but equally valued the chance to express her sorrow over Maxine's death. Although her talks with Perrie Lynn were awkward at first, once Miles told her they'd recently become engaged and were in the midst of planning a small autumn wedding, Perrie Lynn's interest rose.

Still sitting in the passenger seat of Miles's car, Lark closed her eyes for just a second, in a vain attempt to quiet the thumping in her chest.

"There she is," Brooke said, pointing to the porch. "Just like Mr. Olson said, huh, Daddy?"

True. In an earlier text, Eric wrote they'd be waiting outside for them on the porch, and there they were.

"Let's go, let's go." Brooke's excited voice drew a laugh from Evan.

"Just a second, Brooke." Miles squeezed Lark's hand and whispered, "You go ahead. We'll follow close behind."

Grinning at the two kids in the backseat, Lark opened the passenger door and stepped out of the car and onto the grass in the front yard. She kept her eyes on Perrie Lynn, who moved to the top of the stairs as Lark began walking toward the house. Perrie Lynn's long dark hair hung loose down her back, and the skirt of her gauzy white sundress billowed in the breeze.

Lark smiled at the sight as she held down the deep purple skirt of her own dress in the gusty air. Perrie Lynn seemed to giggle in response as she started down the stairs.

Lark raised a hand to wave to Eric, who'd stood but stayed behind on the porch. Looking behind her, she saw that Miles and the kids were lined up by the car. Miles had one hand on Brooke's shoulder, holding her back. Evan's face was a study in curiosity.

Fixing her gaze on Perrie Lynn, Lark

sensed the next moments could either be stilted or as natural as the August breeze that had ruffled their skirts.

As Perrie Lynn approached, her grin widened, and Lark recognized herself in the young woman's face. Exactly what Miles had said all along. Choosing to take a chance on the simple grace of the moment, Lark stood still and slowly opened her arms.

The hesitation lasted only a second, maybe even less, before Perrie Lynn stepped into her arms. They drew each other close until they were cheek to cheek. The hug lasted only seconds, but Lark understood. She let one hand slide slowly down Perrie Lynn's arm as she stepped back.

Lark spoke in a whisper. "You're as lovely as your pictures."

Perrie Lynn smiled shyly. "I'm glad you came."

"I promise I'll answer every question you ask," she said. "We'll have all the time we need, Perrie Lynn."

Perrie Lynn nodded but lowered her gaze to Lark's hand. "Is that your ring from Miles?" She grinned at Lark, but then glanced quickly at Miles in the distance. Amused that the ring would become a focal point, Lark held out her hand so Perrie Lynn could examine the opal and tourmaline stones set in silver. "They're my October birthstones. Miles had it specially made." She leaned a little closer. "Once I said yes."

Perrie Lynn laughed, but then her gaze shifted to Brooke and Evan.

Lark turned to face Miles and the kids. "There's a little girl who is jumping out of her skin waiting to meet you. Your biggest fan. And Evan, also a huge fan, is brimming with curiosity. You'll see for yourself."

Lark led the way toward Miles and the two kids, who began walking toward them. Finally, Miles let go of Brooke's shoulder and whispered something to Evan, who looked every day of his thirteen years. Miles let Brooke jump and skip the rest of the way to Perrie Lynn. Lark pivoted to face the house and greet Eric as he came down the stairs to join the group.

Watching Miles lean forward to hug Perrie Lynn, Lark felt her heart overflow with the happiness she'd lost faith in only a few months before.

Miles stepped back and let Brooke stand completely enchanted in front of Perrie Lynn.

Brooke grabbed Evan's hand and said, "Evan is going to be our brother, Perrie Lynn."

"So I've heard," Perrie Lynn said. She glanced at Lark, her eyes sparkling in amusement. "I never knew I'd have a brother *and* a sister one day."

Lark glanced at Miles, who caught her eye and mouthed, *Love you.*

She mouthed the same words back. Along with Eric, Lark closed their circle of six, three adults and three young people, linked for the moment by all their complicated connections. And one day, Lark knew, they'd be united by love.

* * * * *

*If you enjoyed this debut romance from
Virginia McCullough,
watch for her upcoming books and
check out these titles by fellow
Harlequin Heartwarming authors:
RESCUED BY MR. WRONG
by Cynthia Thomason and
THE WEDDING MARCH
by Tara Randel.
Available at www.Harlequin.com*

Get 2 Free Books,
Plus 2 Free Gifts—
just for trying the Reader Service!

Love Inspired®

Get 2 Free Books,
Plus 2 Free Gifts—
just for trying the Reader Service!

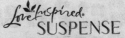

HOMETOWN HEARTS ♥

YES! Please send me **The Hometown Hearts Collection** in Larger Print. This collection begins with 3 FREE books and 2 FREE gifts in the first shipment. Along with my 3 free books, I'll also get the next 4 books from the Hometown Hearts Collection, in LARGER PRINT, which I may either return and owe nothing, or keep for the low price of $4.99 U.S./ $5.89 CDN each plus $2.99 for shipping and handling per shipment*. If I decide to continue, about once a month for 8 months I will get 6 or 7 more books, but will only need to pay for 4. That means 2 or 3 books in every shipment will be FREE! If I decide to keep the entire collection, I'll have paid for only 32 books because 19 books are FREE! I understand that accepting the 3 free books and gifts places me under no obligation to buy anything. I can always return a shipment and cancel at any time. My free books and gifts are mine to keep no matter what I decide.

262 HCN 3432 462 HCN 3432

Name	(PLEASE PRINT)	
Address		Apt. #
City	State/Prov.	Zip/Postal Code

Signature (if under 18, a parent or guardian must sign)

Mail to the **Reader Service:**

IN U.S.A.: P.O. Box 1867, Buffalo, NY. 14240-1867
IN CANADA: P.O. Box 609, Fort Erie, Ontario L2A 5X3

* Terms and prices subject to change without notice. Prices do not include applicable taxes. Sales tax applicable in NY. Canadian residents will be charged applicable taxes. This offer is limited to one order per household. All orders subject to approval. Credit or debit balances in a customer's account(s) may be offset by any other outstanding balance owed by or to the customer. Please allow 4 to 6 weeks for delivery. Offer available while quantities last. Offer not available to Quebec residents.

Your Privacy—The Reader Service is committed to protecting your privacy. Our Privacy Policy is available online at www.ReaderService.com or upon request from the Reader Service.

We make a portion of our mailing list available to reputable third parties that offer products we believe may interest you. If you prefer that we not exchange your name with third parties, or if you wish to clarify or modify your communication preferences, please visit us at www.ReaderService.com/consumerschoice or write to us at Reader Service Preference Service, P.O. Box 9062, Buffalo, NY. 14240-9062. Include your complete name and address.

HHBPA17

Get 2 Free Books,
Plus 2 Free Gifts—
just for trying the
Reader Service!

HSRLP17

Get 2 Free Books,
Plus 2 Free Gifts—
just for trying the
Reader Service!

Love Inspired HISTORICAL

LIH17R

Get 2 Free Books,

Plus 2 Free Gifts—

just for trying the Reader Service!

HARLEQUIN

HEARTWARMING™

Get 2 Free Books,
<u>Plus</u> 2 Free Gifts—
just for trying the Reader Service!